VENGEANCE IN VALESCURE

BY

BILL FLOCKHART

Edinburgh :: 2021

VENGEANCE IN VALESCURE

Chapter 1.

'Morning Sir' said Freddie Sharpe, the personal assistant to Richard Hartley, Assistant Controller of MI6, 'Here is your mail, most of it routine reports from around the world and one handwritten letter from HMP Askham Hall marked 'Private and Confidential – Addressee only.'

'Thank you Freddie. I will look at it all, once I have finished doing this report to our man in Cuba.'

Two hours later Hartley cleared his desk and picked up his mail. He immediately opened the handwritten envelope which he knew was probably from Mhairi McClure, one of the inmates at HMP Askham Hall. He began reading:

HMP ASKHAM HALL GRANGE

15.8.2011

Dear Mr Hartley,

It is now five months since I returned to Askham Hall after completing an assignment for your department.

One of my 'Conditions of Employment' was that I had to agree to have two microchips inserted into my body which have never been removed. One was a tracker to keep you informed of my movements and the other, of which you may recall I was initially oblivious, if exercised by MI6 could kill me instantly. They are not causing me any discomfort physically but mentally my condition is weakening at the thought you could activate them at anytime and terminate my life! I have adhered to the Official Secrets Act although I know the media would thrive on my story. I have placed a copy of this letter with my legal counsel and the contents will be made public if I am assassinated.

All I would ask from you is to arrange to have both microchips deactivated and removed.

Yours truly

Mhairi McClure

Richard Hartley, Assistant Controller of MI6, put down the hand-written letter on his green leather surfaced desk and swivelled his chair round so he could look down on the River Thames from his London headquarters. He clasped his hands together as though in prayer and contemplated his reply to Mhairi McClure's request.

McClure, a convicted IRA terrorist, was serving a twenty-year prison sentence for atrocities she had committed. He had arranged to have her released from HMP Askham Hall Grange to assist him in his revenge against three Estonians who had brutally murdered Elke Kohl, one of his most promising agents. In return Hartley had been able to get the Home Office to give Mhairi McClure a substantial reduction in her prison sentence. Richard Hartley had a reputation for using 'out of the box' tactics when dealing with any threats to the U.K.'s security and took pleasure in his successes against enemies of the State. Picking up his phone he instructed Freddie Sharpe 'Get me Armitage Brown on the phone.'

A few minutes later the telephone rang and the deep polished tone of Armitage Brown filled his ears, 'Richard! Good to hear from you old boy! How are things at MI6? Still keeping the country safe from our enemies? What can I do for you on this fine English summer day?'

'Well you seem full of the joys AB', as Armitage Brown was known in the security services, 'I haven't seen you since you retired from MI5 and thought we should get together for a spot of lunch.'

'Sounds good, Richard. Where and when would you like to meet?'

'I looked at my diary before phoning you and I am free this Friday, how about the Savile Club at say 12.30?'

'That's perfect Richard. Look forward to seeing you then. Bye for now.'

Armitage Brown put down the phone and stroked his chin. He thought to himself, 'What is Hartley up to? It's not like him to invite a retired spy-catcher to lunch unless he has a problem. Well, it will be good to catch up and find out how well both MI5 and MI6 are performing.'

Chapter 2

The Savile Club was formed in 1868 and moved in 1927 from its original home in Savile Row, famous for gent's tailoring to 69 Brook Street. Originally the membership came from the literary community and included in their fold Robert Louis Stevenson, H.G. Wells and Rudyard Kipling. More recently, members of the intelligence services frequented The Savile so it was no surprise when David Cornwell alias John le Carre joined the Club, himself having worked for MI6.

Richard Hartley made a point of arriving at The Savile early as he knew from experience Armitage Brown was a stickler for timekeeping. One time he had arrived late for a section meeting with AB and to break the ice, flippantly announced 'Better late than never!' to be met by a cold stare from his boss followed by, 'No Mr Hartley the phrase is 'Better never late!'

Armitage Brown entered the building looking like a man who had settled into retirement. Gone was the pinstripe shirt and suit with the black brogues, to be replaced by a bold blue and white checked shirt, yellow tie, under a brown check sports jacket. His lower half supported light beige slacks and brown suede shoes while in his hand he carried a Panama Jack straw hat. The change in sartorial elegance made Hartley stand back and admire the old sleuth's new image.

'Well AB, I have to say retirement seems to be suiting you. I can't wait to hear what you are up to these days.'

'Not bloody much Richard' rebuked AB 'or I wouldn't be here!'

Hartley smiled and thought 'He hasn't lost any of his cantankerous nature', followed by saying 'I've booked a private room for lunch but let's go into the bar first for an aperitif.'

The two intelligence grandees made their way into a lounge reeking of a colonial past. Settling down in a couple of Chesterfield leather armchairs they arranged for a waiter to bring them a couple of large pink gins. For the next ten minutes they made small talk about their children's progress in life. The Maitre d' who had previously taken their selections for lunch arrived to tell them their meal was ready to be served in their private room.

Once they sat down Richard Hartley opened the conversation, 'Armitage thanks for coming in from Buckinghamshire. I wanted to get your thoughts on a couple of potential problems we are faced with at present.'

AB fidgeted in his seat, anxious to hear what he was being asked to consider giving an opinion on, 'Carry on Richard.'

'Armitage, we are very concerned about the speed of change taking place in North Africa which looks like making the area very precarious and saddled with an unstable future. The politicians are happily putting out glowing reports about how the fall of Muammar al Gadaffi will bring an end to terrorist attacks being funded by Libya. What a load of tosh! MI6 is not altogether sorry to see the back of Gadaffi although the one thing you had to admire about him was his fearsome control over Libya. My fear is it leaves these countries - Egypt, Tunisia, Libya and Morocco wide open to exploitation by Muslim extremists who will also be active in the Yemen. In these situations, one has always to look twenty years ahead and we could be living in a Europe facing nuclear weapons lined up only a short distance from major cities in France, Spain and Italy. Another long term consideration is the flow of immigrants from the sub-Sahara nations who will seize their opportunity to try and get political asylum on the European mainland. Early signs are they shall sail across the Mediterranean in rubber dinghies heading for the south coast of Italy. The refugees will probably consist mostly of men and children to get the sympathy vote but once they are granted asylum they will send for their wives and family dependants. That's when the multiplier effect will kick in.'

Hartley took a rest to have a gulp of red wine giving Armitage a chance to speak, 'Richard, I can sense this is a very touchy subject for you. How do you think we can halt this invasion you are describing and do you not think in doing so we are being a bit callous.'

'Callous AB!' exclaimed Hartley, 'This is the modern version of the Trojan Horse. These kids who we expect to be arriving in their droves will be radicalised in mosques throughout Europe. In ten to fifteen years' time they will make life hell for Europeans and destroy the opulent lifestyle we enjoy in comparison with the poverty in some African and Middle-East countries.'

AB pushed Hartley further, 'So how do you propose to stop this insurgence?'

Hartley responded 'My fears will require funding and we know the African countries do not possess the level of expenditure to set up what I have just described unless Saudi Arabia comes to their rescue, but I don't see that happening as they depend on Europe for their oil revenues. It is more than likely to come from further afield, Russia or even China.'

Armitage Brown was about to continue the conversation when the waiter appeared with their starters – oxtail soup for AB and a prawn cocktail for Hartley. Both men remained silent until the young waiter exited the room.

'How do our friends in Washington feel about what you have just described?'

Hartley replied, 'I don't know. I haven't asked them. I am a bit concerned, as you have just identified AB, that I may be getting a little paranoid about the Arab Spring.'

'Perhaps so Richard, but history has told us not to be complacent. It is only sixty odd years ago when the Service was leaking like a sieve and suffered from characters like Burgess, Blunt, McLean and Kim Philby who were making the enemy aware of every movement in our foreign policy. It took us a while to recover from that and even then the horrible George Blake betrayed many of our colleagues who were assassinated around the world.'

'What would be your strategy Armitage?' asked Hartley.

The retired spy-catcher was starting to enjoy his lunch but delayed his reply long enough for the staff to clear the table and deposit the main course of guinea fowl with all the trimmings in front of them.

'Richard in these circumstances you have to, as they say, 'Follow the money' and find out who has stepped up their armament spend. Not an easy task as most of these gun runners, to give them a crude name, tend to operate from neutral venues you would not normally associate with these sordid practices. Switzerland and European tax havens like Luxembourg or Monaco are attractive venues for armament operatives. Have you a strategy for minimising the problem?'

Hartley took another slug of Malbec before responding to the question, 'My preference is to destroy the threat at source. If we narrow down the search via our spies regarding both the potential problems, our agents will provide the intelligence to our military leaders. Illegal immigrants will most likely arrive in rubber dinghies and we have to uncover who is manufacturing them with a view to destroying the factories producing the marine crafts. As regards where the money is coming from, I would like to put officers into the field operating between the tax havens you mentioned.

This brings me nicely to my second item for discussion Armitage. You will remember Mhairi McClure!'

AB nearly choked on his guinea fowl at the mention of her name 'How could I ever forget that bloody woman who gave me quite a few sleepless nights? What has she to do with what we are discussing?'

'Nine months ago we lost one of our brightest young agents, Elke Kohl, who was brutally murdered by Estonian drug dealers. I sent Hugh McFaul to investigate along with Police Scotland. To cut a long story short I decided to use McClure's expertise to get into the confidences of a major drug dealer based in Edinburgh who led us to Elke's killers. '

'I don't know about this Richard. Are they awaiting trial?'

'No AB, they made the mistake of picking up a gun we had carelessly laid down and my men defended themselves by shooting all three of them dead where they stood!'

Brown gave Hartley a quizzical look 'Self-defence?'

Hartley smirked back, 'Of Course! The bonus for us was that this enquiry also allowed us to apprehend an Afghan terrorist, Mohammed al-Basiri, as he was about to launch an attack on Edinburgh. Mohammed al Basiri will be sentenced to a long imprisonment.

Campbell Anderson, one of my best operators worked closely with Ms McClure and gave her a glowing report which made me think I could use her in some other operation.'

Brown felt his hackles coming up and he could not contain himself 'Richard that is madness! The woman is a proven killer who has been responsible for terminating the lives of several of her enemies, including if I can remind you, one of my senior officers Colin Inglis. I take it she is not in any intimate relationship with this fellow Anderson?'

'No, Campbell has kept his distance despite McClure propositioning him. Armitage, how can you possibly use Inglis as an objective reason for me not pursuing this strategy? He was a horrible character who gunned down his own soldiers in cold blood to save his military career. If evidence had come forward earlier about his misdemeanour he would probably have been facing a court martial. It was because of his actions that Mhairi McClure's future husband was killed which kicked off her career as an IRA activist.'

'But Richard how are you going to control a fiendish rebel like McClure? If you let her out of prison, before you know it she will be across the Irish Sea to join forces that are not conducive to British Government policy. What will the media make of this if they find out? I can just see the headlines now 'Dangerous Irish Mata Hari released back into Civvy Street by MI6.'

'Calm down AB' instructed Hartley raising his hand up and down in a peaceful gesture, 'I have taken steps to ensure Mhairi McClure can't abscond the way you have described. I had her fitted up with two microchips which have been inserted into her shoulders, one on each side.'

'To do what?' demanded AB.

'One acts as a homing device so we know where she is at all times. The other one is secreted with deadly poison which will kill her in a few minutes should she make a wrong move.'

'Good God Hartley! Who acts as executioner in that instance?'

'I do, but in my absence there are controls in place to activate the microchip.'

'Knowing you as I do Richard, you will not hesitate to act in the Service's best interest.'

'You have my word on that AB'

Chapter 3

Mhairi McClure was preparing a budget analysis for the Governor of Askham Hall when the phone rang asking her to come up to the Governor's Office at 2.00 p.m. Mhairi looked at her watch, 11.30, and thought to herself, 'I'll not have the budget analysis ready by then.'

The last five months had been difficult for Mhairi who had been plucked from prison to assist MI6 and Police Scotland in bringing the Scottish drug Tzar Geordie McNab to justice. She had enjoyed the experience which meant living in five star hotels, wearing expensive clothes and enjoying the company of men for a change. Coming down from the buzz of working as an intelligence officer to the dreary routine of Askham Hall, was having an effect on her mental state.

Askham Hall is a womens prison for inmates no longer considered to be a threat to the public. Most of the prisoners were women who had made errors of judgement of one sort or another usually of a financial nature in their effort to achieve a higher standard of living for their families.

At 2.00 p.m. precisely Mhairi knocked on the Governor's door which was answered by Anita Taylor, the Governor's personal assistant who showed her through to the inner office. The Governor, Angela Smith, a sturdy lady in her late forties, dressed in a blue pinstripe business suit, the jacket of which partially concealed a white cotton blouse open at the collar.

'Afternoon prisoner 13462, I trust you are well and getting on with the prison budgets that I am anxious to see as soon as possible.'

'Yes Governor I should have them finished by tomorrow lunchtime.'

'You had better!' replied The Governor sternly before breaking into a smile and adding, 'I have received a request from Assistant Controller Richard Hartley at MI6 for you to attend an appointment at 11.00 a.m. on August 25 at MI6 headquarters. You will leave here a day earlier under guard and go to a prison nearer London. Following the interview you will be returned to Askham Hall. Mr Hartley has said he wants to speak to you to tie up some loose ends from when you last visited. Do you know what that is all about Mhairi?'

'No.' said Mhairi, trying to look surprised and not wanting to inform the Governor of the letter she had secretly sent to Richard Hartley.

'Very well, enjoy getting out of Askham Hall for a few days and I will hear all about it when you get back.'

Mhairi left the office leaving Governor Smith pondering why one of her prisoners was important enough to qualify for a meeting with the hierarchy at MI6. Angela Smith was a control freak who wanted to know everything about those in her care at all times.

Chapter 4

August 25th was a beautiful summer day and London was heaving with tourists all anxious to take in the major attractions the Capital could offer. The dark blue Vauxhall Insignia swept into the MI6 car park once the security bollards had been removed and parked under a 'visitor' sign. Mhairi, handcuffed to one of the female prison guards, was wearing a loose high-necked white summer dress bedecked in a floral pattern which was cool enough to protect her from the sun's rays. On her head she sported a straw bonnet. The visiting party made their way through the strict entrance security checks. Once the entrance security checks were completed Mhairi found herself being transferred into the care of MI6 security, who guided her to Richard Hartley's office.

Due to the high temperatures Richard had decided to conduct his meeting on the lawn situated outside the French windows behind his desk where the staff had set out garden furniture complete with a green umbrella. Hartley was sitting on a basket chair discussing some papers with two men Mhairi knew well, Commander Hugh McFaul and his assistant Campbell Anderson. Surprisingly for such a hot day they were all wearing jackets, collar and ties.

As pre-arranged Hartley set out the tone for the meeting, 'Good afternoon Miss McClure, have you had a good journey down from Yorkshire?'

Mhairi nodded as she replied, 'Yes, I came down last night but the guards wouldn't allow me a night out on the town.'

The other three smiled at her relaxed sense of humour before Hartley continued 'I received your letter and I can assure you I did not need reminding about the microchips you are carrying around with you. The reason for my delay in ordering the removal of the technology is I have been reviewing your contribution to the Elke Kohl murder. I have been discussing your performance with McFaul and Anderson who admired how professional you were in adapting to the plot to capture her killers.'

Mhairi interrupted 'Are they now awaiting trial?'

Hartley was blown off his prepared script by the question, 'Eh, not altogether, Mohammed al- Basiri will be coming up for trial at the Old Bailey next year. The three Estonians made the mistake of turning a gun on Campbell, and in our defence they were eliminated. Your contacts Geordie McNab and his henchman Alistair McLagan will be tried in the Scottish Courts.'

'I'm glad it all came to a satisfactory conclusion.'

Hartley returned to the main event but was stopped by the arrival of a drinks tray offering coffee and soft drinks. Everyone helped themselves and turned their attention back to business.

'Miss McClure, I have managed to convince the inner cabinet at MI6 that we change the profile of the type of agents we recruit. In addition to the young graduates we source from universities, I think we should broaden our approach to employ the more mature professional person. People like you.'

Mhairi looked at the three intelligence officers, 'Well, apart from the term 'mature' I would like to hear a bit more about your change in direction.'

'Hugh would you like to explain further.'

'Certainly Sir, Ms McClure the department is constantly meeting challenges all over the world which we must be able to absorb and eliminate quickly to protect our citizens.'

'Academically you fit the role after obtaining a degree from Oxford and a post-grad at Harvard. You have considerable skills, not only are you an expert on financial affairs but possess extensive computer skills. In addition you used your time in the Vatican wisely becoming fluent in several languages.'

'We do not have a specific project at present but we would like you to consider moving from Askham Hall down to the London area where we would put you through a training course where you will be continually monitored to see if you meet our high standards both mentally and physically. Would this be of interest to you?'

'Absolutely' retorted Mhairi with a big grin on her face 'tell me more please.'

Hugh McFaul continued 'We shall make arrangements for you to attend our next training course. You will be in a team led by Campbell Anderson, who you already know from your last venture and Lydia Tomlinson, one of our young bright experienced officers. Your identity will not be revealed to Miss Tomlinson, who has been working abroad on a top secret assignment which has taught her to be very discreet so don't expect much in the way of idle chit-chat.'

'The course will be held in Hereford where the SAS are based although you will be kept quite separate from them. Their disciplines are different from MI6 in that they plan uniformed assaults based on the intelligence information they receive from us. The next course will be held in three weeks time which will give you time to tidy up any loose ends at Askham Hall.'

Richard Hartley, who had been quietly observing Mhairi McClure's body language took over the conversation, 'I would like to go over a little housekeeping with you Ms McClure to avoid any confusion affecting your survival within MI6 which are:-

1. You sign the Official Secrets Act.
2. You tell nobody including your mother about this arrangement.
3. You will continue to be known within the Department as 'Veronica Benson' which I feel is a bit of a mouthful so we will shorten it to 'Roni Benson.' If you use 'Veronica' when calling one of your team that will signal to us you are in danger.
4. You will continue to use Askham Hall as your residence and any mail delivered there will be

forwarded to a new address which we will give you at the completion of the course.

5. You shall not have any visitors unless they have been sanctioned by this department.

6. The microchips placed in your body shall remain there. Do not attempt to have them removed as they are very finely tuned and the slightest alteration to their mechanism could be lethal.

7. At the satisfactory completion of an assignment you will qualify for a review of your prison sentence. Any reduction will be decided upon by the Department and not subject to any appeal procedures.

'Do these terms which will not be put in writing meet your approval Ms McClure?' asked Hartley.

Mhairi shrugged her shoulders 'As usual Assistant Controller Hartley you are holding all the aces. I will not go into specifics as to how much further you will reduce my prison sentence as to date you have always honoured our arrangements.'

Hartley looked the former Irish terrorist in the eye 'I appreciate your last comment but warn you not to take anything for granted as your life will continue to be in my hands.'

A cold silence descended over the proceedings until Cam Anderson broke the ice 'Mhairi, I look forward to us working together again and this time I will have Lydia to protect me from your advances.'

Mhairi felt her face going red thinking about how she had blatantly solicited Anderson when they were in Edinburgh. Hartley noticed Mhairi's embarrassment and stepped in.

'I think that will be all for today. I have to attend an important meeting this afternoon. Commander McFaul and Anderson will see you off the premises. I doubt if you will see much of me in future Miss McClure but I will be kept constantly in touch with your progress. Good afternoon.'

Chapter 5

Mhairi was excited with the outcome of the meeting at MI6 headquarters but did not compromise herself by discussing the proceedings with anyone. The morning after she arrived back at Askham Hall the Governor sent for her to come up to the office.

'Morning Mhairi, did you have a good time in London?'

'Yes, if you call looking at four different walls a good time.'

'Don't be flippant Mhairi, I am responsible for all the prisoners in my care at all times, so I will ask you once again what were you up to at MI6 headquarters?'

'Governor Smith I am not allowed to say but MI6 will be in touch with you shortly.'

'So you are leaving us again?'

'That's for MI6 to decide. If that is all Governor Smith, I'll get back to producing financial projections for your office.'

Mhairi got up and left the room with Governor Smith still fuming at the fact she had lost control over a prisoner, 'That girl is too clever for her own good' she concluded to herself.

Fifteen days later, earlier than expected, an unmarked car arrived at Askham Hall and whisked Mhairi McClure down south to a safe house in Chesham. The car was driven by Campbell Anderson who took the opportunity to talk with Mhairi during the three hour drive to Chesham.

'Morning Mhairi have you packed everything you need?

'Yes let's go'

They approached the car and Mhairi searched for an accompanying security guard, 'Looks like your back-up has gone to the loo Cam.' she smirked.

'Mhairi there are no guards with me. I wanted to talk to you privately and besides there is no chance you will run away and force me to activate the microchips in your body.'

'As usual Cam you've thought of everything.'

The Audi moved off and Cam gave Mhairi ten minutes to settle down before he started serious conversation.

'Mhairi, I wanted to make sure you are happy about going to SAS headquarters in Hereford as it was a sniper team from there who were responsible for shooting your fiance'.'

'Cam I am well aware of that but Matt was killed over twenty years ago and his death did change my life. However, since my last outing with MI6 I have come to the conclusion that I need a fresh start. I can't go back to Ireland as the IRA will be after me; I have been excommunicated from the Roman Catholic Church after being held responsible for the death of three Swiss Guards. I do still believe in God and hopefully he will pardon my sins when the day of reckoning comes.

I enjoyed working with you and I hate being in prison so the only future for me is to sell my life to the devil, which in my case is MI6, knowing I can be assassinated anytime soon.'

'My! My! Mhairi' exclaimed Cam 'you have been doing a lot of thinking, good for you. The only person known to you at the safe house in Chesham is Beverley Thomson who you should talk to if you have any problems. Lydia Tomlinson will join us in the next few days and she will be completely unaware of your previous record.

'What is she like Cam?'

'She's young, bubbly and quite ambitious. She is still trying to make her way in the Service and by all accounts should succeed.'

The rest of the journey passed quickly as they chatted about the scenery and current affairs. Before they knew it they came off the M1 and were soon in Chesham. Mhairi was no stranger to the property which she had occupied on her previous assignment for MI6. She was given the same room in the large Victorian villa and after emptying her suitcase went downstairs to the office. She met the staff who, in line with MI6's staff rotating policy, had all changed with the exception of Beverley Thomson. The staff were totally oblivious as to why she required the use of a safe house.

During the next two days Mhairi read about any recent changes in procedures which could affect her role whatever that turned out to be.

The day before leaving for Hereford Lydia Tomlinson phoned Mhairi to make the final travel arrangements. 'Morning is that Roni Benson?, Lydia Tomlinson calling, just wanted to touch base before Cam Anderson and I pick you up tomorrow. We haven't met before but I am looking forward to meeting you. Cam has spoken highly of you, so I am sure we will form a good team.'

'That's very re-assuring for me to get a good reference from Cam' replied the Irishwoman before thinking to herself 'I wonder what he has been saying?'

Lydia continued 'We are there for the week so make sure you have a few changes of clothing for night time. During the day we will be issued casual clothing as there will probably be some physical training or role playing but I expect Cam will take us to some nice hostelries at night.'

Roni responded, 'I'll go and pack my tiara now and look forward to meeting you tomorrow. Bye for now.'
Roni put down the phone and rushed downstairs to Beverley Thomson's office. Beverley had been her chaperone when together between them they had snared Geordie McNab, the Edinburgh drug lord.

Beverley looked up at Roni, 'You seem in a bit of a rush. What can I do for you?'

'I have just been talking to Lydia Tomlinson who I am going to Hereford with tomorrow. She is expecting to go out for meals in the evening and I don't have anything to wear!'

Beverley smiled 'I wondered when you were going to ask. That prison gear you arrived in won't get you a

Prince Charming. I'll take you into Amersham this afternoon and kit you out.'

True to her word Beverley, accompanied by a plain clothes security officer, took Roni on a shopping spree in Amersham. She was soon suited and booted appropriately as she anticipated the arrival of Lydia and Campbell Anderson.

Next morning a metallic silver Audi 6 came up the driveway and stopped at the front entrance. The two security officers exited the car, stretched themselves as they surveyed the Victorian villa before entering the building and making their way to the foyer. Lydia Tomlinson was smaller than Roni had imagined, but very attractive with shiny black hair and a smooth skin. Her brown eyes danced around as she spoke quickly with a polished Cambridge accent. She wore a racing green cotton dress which hugged her contours and her figure was further enhanced by a pair of beige high heels. 'Hello Roni, Lydia Tomlinson' said Lydia holding out her hand 'I'm looking forward to working with you; Cam has been giving me glowing reports on you all the way down in the car.'

Cam smiled, 'Morning Roni, are you ready to be scrutinised closely by the boffins in Hereford?'

Roni answered confidently, 'With you to look after me it should be a piece of cake. My luggage is here for a big strong boy like you to load into the car.'

'See Lydia I told you how she orders me around! Nothing changes. C'mon let's be on our way.'

Chesham is almost one hundred and forty miles from Hereford and a part of the world Roni was not familiar with. She sat in the back of the car and listened mostly to Lydia and Cam talking about MI6. Their route took them through Oxford where Mhairi had studied after leaving school and where she got a first-class degree in computer studies prior to doing her post-grad at Harvard. Much of the town centre remained the same but on the outskirts there were industrial estates spun from the discoveries of the Oxford boffins. After Oxford it was not long before the car began to wind its way through the Cotswolds one of the most picturesque areas of England with its succession of beautiful little villages. Roni had not been in the Cotswolds for years and it brought back memories during her time at Oxford of long lazy Sunday pub lunches in male company. It was not long before the car was entering Cheltenham where the majority of the security records for the U.K. are held along with any threats to the United Kingdom. The Government Communications Headquarters (GCHQ)was established in 1919 and is the chief security establishment used by both MI5, MI6 the Police and the Army to maintain the security of the country.

Passing the modern circular building set the tongues wagging in the front seats of the Audi as Cam and Lydia relayed their experiences of the building which is the high temple for all security employees. Roni had been to Cheltenham several times in the past to watch the Cheltenham Gold Cup, one of horseracing's classic meetings, where it seems the whole of Ireland had descended on the town. Her banishment from the Irish Republican cause readily indicated she would not be able to join the festivities in the future.

They stayed on the A40 as they circled through Gloucester then headed through the countryside until they reached Ross-on-Wye changing to the A49 at Bristow for the last few miles of their journey to Hereford. Cam turned the Audi into Credenhill Barracks, a former RAF training station which the SAS had transferred to from their original base in Worcestershire. After a stringent security check they proceeded to the main office block. They decided to leave their luggage in the car and approached the foyer where Cam introduced himself and asked for Dr Roderick Walton, MI6's Head of Operations at the base.

Five minutes later a thin wiry man supporting himself with a walking stick got out of the lift opposite the front desk and approached the visitors. Walton was not what any of them had expected having read his CV. He had obviously come off second best in one of his exploits and now had a stiff leg. He was just short of six foot and had a head of thick black hair above his ruddy complexion a face containing staring brown eyes behind his solid framed bifocals.

Roderick Walton was a career soldier who had been involved in several actions. He was probably most famous as a member of the SAS team which stormed the Iranian embassy in London in May 1980 to free the hostages who were being held by Iranian terrorists. The intervening thirty years had taken their toll on Roderick who after he was pronounced unfit for any physical sorties went to St. Andrews University to study military strategy and ended up with a PhD. The army held him in such high regard that they paid for his studies. He returned to Hereford and took over the role of Senior Strategist and Training Officer. His good work was noted by the security services who promoted him to be their Head of Operations.

He was wearing a military uniform of light fawn slacks and an open-neck dark brown shirt, ideal for a warm summer day.

'Did ye have a good journey down?' he enquired in a Cornish accent 'Dr Roderick Walton, welcome to Credenhill.'

Cam stepped forward, then stood back to introduce the girls, 'Dr Walton, meet my colleagues Lydia Tomlinson and Roni Benson. I'm Campbell Anderson.'

Walton did all the handshakes and commented 'Roni, that's an unusual name for a girl.'

Roni smiled back 'Short for Veronica, sir.'

'Come along, we'll go upstairs to one of the lecture rooms and have a chat but first I will organise some coffee and biscuits from the canteen. We have to take the lift as my stiff leg doesn't work so well on the stairs.'

Everyone got out at the second floor and followed their leader to lecture room 12 which was set out like a classroom to accommodate twenty four students. It was an extremely modern lecture theatre with all the very latest sound and visual effects. The three security staff sat themselves down in front of Walton who positioned himself behind the lecturer's desk.

'Prior to us starting I'll tell you the housekeeping rules. MI6 staff are obliged to stick to their own areas and do not mix with the SAS. We do not have many women at the base as they were only admitted into the regiment a few years ago. Two attractive ladies like you would prove to be a distraction. We are as you know a very secretive organisation and the same applies to the SAS, many of whom don't even inform their close families what they are up to.'

'This week we shall be alerting you to the current enemies of the State and I shall be monitoring you to see if you are suitable for the challenges should we decide to use your individual talents. This will include being prepared physically and mentally, instructed in strategy and the use of disguise to fool the enemy. We will not start until the morning so you can take the rest of the day off.'

'Thank you sir' they chorused but Cam added, 'Do we have to stay on the base tonight or can we go out for dinner?'

Walton replied. 'It's up to you but it would be best you do it tonight as we may carry on later in the next few nights. I would recommend 'The Silver Spur' which the officers regularly frequent. If you want I will get Betty Jones my P.A. to make a booking and arrange for a car to take you there and pick you up later. We prefer guests to be escorted, as accidents involving the SAS could attract a lot of bad publicity.'

Roni spoke up 'Well Cam, no excuses now for you not to come up with the champagne.'

At 7.45 the diners were picked up from the foyer and whisked away in a Range Rover for the short journey to the Silver Spur. The hostelry was very grand, full of oak beams and real leather sofas leading through to a dining room with wood panelled walls. The majority of the round tables were laid out to host groups of four seated at carver chairs with red and silver silk striped cushioned seats. They had no sooner sat down when a young waiter wearing a white shirt and a dark red bow tie approached their table.

Cam pre-empted what was about to happen and beat the girls to the punch 'A bottle of Bollinger for me and two glasses of sparkling water for the girls please.' He waited until the mouths of the two opposite were closing before he added 'Only joking, bring us three champagne flutes.'

The waiter returned shortly and was accompanied by another waiter to hand out the menus whilst his colleague popped the champagne cork prior to handing out the three glasses.

Lydia held up her glass 'Cheers here's to a good week!'

Half an hour later they entered the dining room which was quite busy for a Tuesday night -with mostly male diners . It was noticeable all the diners stopped eating to give the new arrivals the once over. This did not go unnoticed by Roni or Colonel George Blackstock sitting at a nearby table, who felt sure he recognised the woman with the blond short hair but he could not put a name to her.

'Well Lydia if that's the reaction we get when we have dresses on up to our necks I think I'll wear a little off the shoulder number next time.'

The others chuckled and concentrated on the food for the next two hours accompanied with some excellent wines. During the meal the three officers discussed their experiences in MI6, which was awkward for Roni who covered herself by saying her past assignments had been so secret she was unable to speak about them. Cam smiled to himself and thought 'What a clever answer for someone to give, considering they have been in prison for the last 'X' number of years!'

Chapter 6

The next morning after breakfast the visitors made their way to a small meeting room where Dr Walton was already busy passing papers out round the table set for the three officers. After they were seated Walton began his formal address:

'You have all been sent here by Assistant Commissioner Hartley to prepare for an assault on enemies of the State who even I have no knowledge of at the present time. This does have the benefit of making our lecturing cover a broad field and once Hartley decides on his strategy you should have sufficient knowledge to go into the field anywhere at short notice.'

'In the next few days you will undergo some physical training or should I say survival assistance. The SAS has a reputation for dare devil attacks to diffuse awkward situations but we also put great emphasis on protecting our team. To that end you will learn how to put procedures into practice which will stand you in good stead.

Regarding your mental health there will be psychology sessions to establish how strong your resistance will last should you be detained by an enemy. These tests will be carried out by Professor Sebastian Pollock and his team.

I think that covers the curriculum for the programme. I do remind you once again not to mix with the troops who like yourselves are being prepared for action and need no distractions.'

Walton pressed a button on his desk and a map of the world came down from the ceiling. 'Let's see now, where will we begin?'

Dr Walton stood up and stood beside the map with a ruler in his hand 'Europe has gone through change since the Berlin Wall came down in 1989. The Soviets are still active in Eastern Europe mostly to the north where they have old contacts in Poland and Finland. Vienna and Budapest also feature often in spy circles as Moscow tries to infiltrate the West. Equally we have agents operating in Russia as we play our never ending game of chess.'

'Moving south, the area around the Mediterranean is becoming interesting. At the eastern end you have the Muslim countries and their 'Blot' in the landscape, Israel. This has always been a bit of a powder keg with Israel being able to contain itself with the help of the United States and their superior weaponry including nuclear warheads. Further up the coast you have Syria who are engaging in a civil war which will result in millions of refugees making their way to a better life in Europe. The lack of proper stable administered governments clears the way for al Qaeda to influence the region and impose their cruel regime upon the local population. This will be a true cause for concern in the future.

'The ports down the eastern Med could become crucial in the future as a means of transferring some major weapon systems into a volatile political arena if Iran is involved. However, the main concern in the short-term is along the North Africa coast including Egypt, Tunisia, Libya, Morocco etc. In recent months these governments have become de-stabilised and the worrying aspect to all this is how friendly they are going to be in their future relations with the west.'

Lydia intervened, 'Dr Walton do we have many agents in these areas and would I be correct in saying there will not be many women involved as they are very much male dominated countries.'

'Yes definitely more suited for Cam rather than Roni and yourself.' Dr Walton continued 'the threat is not immediate as the sudden changes of government in these countries will have left them short of funds for acquiring sophisticated weapons of the type they require to upset the West, if that is what they decide to do. Where I see MI6 acting is to find out who is prepared to bankroll the new regimes and at what cost to them. China has been making strides in Africa by buying up commodities like most of the maize production in Zambia.

Many of the deals are organised in the South of France in Monaco or the other tax havens like Luxembourg or Lichtenstein. We do not have the expertise here to analyse the structure of these deals and know where the funds for these transactions are coming from but I understand from HQ that's where you come in Roni?'

Roni was not ready with a reply but took a drink of water to buy time for her response, 'Yes I have plenty of experience of tracking funds which I used to do in my youth prior to joining MI6. My expertise has already proved useful to the Service and I am glad I have kept abreast of the financial markets. I am confident we can challenge any threats provided we can penetrate the gangs organising the shipments of weapons.'

'Very impressive Roni' piped up Lydia 'I wouldn't know one iota about international finance. I will be watching you closely to see what I can learn from you.'

Roderick Walton continued 'Intelligence have identified one man who would be of interest to us - Roland Christophe Canault. Canault has been living in the South of France for a few years, Canault is not his real name. Sources in Serbia are convinced he is Milo Malkovitch who was a hidden face in the Serbian Government. We cannot be certain it is Malkovitch, as a burned-out corpse with his identification tag on it was found in eastern Serbia.

If he is, who they think he is, as a young officer he served under Radovan Karadic who disappeared after the war ended for twelve years after the war ended. Along with Ratko Mladic, Karadic has now been brought to the International Court of Justice in The Hague to stand trial for war crimes. Before the war ended Serbian nationals shipped huge amounts of arms to safe havens possibly in Russia and elsewhere plus billions of dollars to Switzerland. This would have given Malkovitch a base to set himself up as an arms dealer.'

'Canault has set up home in the South of France where he has registered companies in Monaco for tax purposes. He resides forty miles along the coast at Valescure a couple of miles inland from the port of St. Raphael. Now in his late forties Milo leads a very active social life especially now that his two sons have gone to finishing schools in Switzerland. His wife Jana and he live under the same roof but have separate tastes in lovers.'

'Do any of you play tennis?' enquired Walton.

The three 'pupils' were taken aback by the sudden change in conversation and looked at each other before answering.

Lydia responded first 'I haven't played since school'

Cam added 'University was when I last played in the reserve side at Oxford.'

All eyes turned to Roni who beamed thinking about what she was about to reveal 'I played in the Northern Ireland Girls Championships but stopped when I went to Oxford. I took up the game again when I was at Harvard as a means of trapping my boyfriend which I have to admit worked. However that was twenty years ago so I would need to get a few games in before reaching any reasonable standard for my age.'

'Good two out of three. Canault is a fanatical tennis player and has his own courts but goes regularly for coaching to Valescure Links & Raquette Club where he has an eye for the female tennis players. Leave it there for now but it may be a way of getting close to him.'

The briefings continued for the rest of the day with only a short break for lunch. Just before they broke up for the day Dr Walton laid out the agenda for tomorrow; 'In the morning you will all be going to the gym to get some self-defence training and shooting practice. In the afternoon you will join our special effects team who run through disguises which could come in useful.'

Cam was uneasy about Roni having any guns in her hand so he spoke up immediately 'Roni, you can be excused from the shooting gallery on the grounds of your perforated eardrum which could be damaged further by the noise of the range. Is that okay with you Roni?'

Roni knew she was not in a position to argue if she wanted to keep out of jail so she smiled and answered, 'Thanks Cam for bringing my condition to Dr Walton's attention.'

The trio met for dinner in the Officers' Mess which was a bit downmarket from the Silver Spur and devoid of any alcohol. The conversation was mainly about their course and they were so engrossed in it that they failed to notice a tall figure approaching their table.

'Good evening, I'm Colonel George Blackstock' he announced to all and sundry in an upper-crust English accent, 'the mess is a bit different from the Silver Spur where I saw you all enjoying yourselves last night. Apologies for my intervention but I wanted to ask this young lady', pointing a finger at Roni, 'if we had met previously or if she had a twin?'

Roni had prepared for this scenario, 'No Colonel I don't think so, my name is Veronica Benson.'

By using 'Veronica' she put Cam on alert and he reacted 'Colonel we are all MI6 officers and I can assure you Veronica has been involved in, how can I put it, 'Clandestine' operations abroad for a number of years.'

The embarrassed Colonel went red in the face, 'Apologies again, when I think about it the lady I am referring to was a nun I met in Rome.'

They all laughed at the thought and Roni added, 'No Colonel that's not a habit I would like to get into if you pardon the pun!'

The Colonel turned on his heel and rejoined his friends who also laughed out loud at their colleague's mistake.

Lydia announced she was going to the powder room which gave Cam time to talk to Roni 'That was close Roni. You handled that situation perfectly as it could have been a game changer for you if you had shown any sign of weakness.'

Chapter 7

Next morning after breakfast Roni, Lydia and Cam dressed in army issue jogging suits reported to one of the smaller gymnasiums to meet Staff Sergeant Fred Dunn for some unarmed combat training. On the way there they were passed by a platoon of SAS soldiers running in the opposite direction. Roni was surprised that they were, in the majority much smaller than she had imagined. It was men like them who had gunned down Matt O'Reilly all those years ago and changed her life forever. The one thing they all had in common was a deep display of concentration on their faces as they prepared for what they did best – exterminating anyone who crossed their paths!

Dunn, dressed in a dark green t-shirt with matching jogging pants, was a fine physical specimen who looked like he had been a physical training instructor for years.

He smiled and shook hands before speaking 'Good morning I'm Sergeant Major Fred Dunn, call me Fred, my task today is to show you how to defend yourself from assailants who may be physically bigger and stronger than yourself. What you will learn today is how to attack the nervous system's pressure points which will weaken your attacker and remove his aggression. Have any of you been on this course before?'

Campbell Anderson raised his arm.

'Good Campbell, I will be able to use you to demonstrate to Lydia and Roni.'

Rolling down a screen from the blackboard featuring an outline of the human body he continued 'Basically there are nine pressure points identified here by the red spots at different parts of the body. By exerting pressure on any one of them you can render your attacker senseless for a short time enabling you to escape or inflict some aggression of your own.'

'Some of these are fairly obvious like gouging eyes or kneeing someone in the groin. When considering an attack in the optical area I would advise women to assist their assault by carrying a small perfume spray which if used correctly can be extremely effective. Moving down, a sharp hit on the jaw with the back of your hand can render someone unconscious the same way as a boxer would.'

'Another useful defence if you are being held tightly is to press firmly behind the ear lobe on the lymph node which will cause temporary paralysis. Equally a similar effect will take place if you press down hard on the soft tissue between the thumb and forefinger on the hand.' Fred continued, 'Any sharp blow in the solar plexus has a winding affect on any opponent and allows you the split second you need to re-adjust your offensive position.'

'Other places you may consider which are probably not so obvious to you, are giving someone a sharp blow to their biceps which also has the response of temporary paralysis. Equally by attacking the sciatic nerve in the inner thigh will lead to your attacker suffering from dizziness.'

'Oh, there is one form of defence I have missed if all else fails – 'The Glasgow Kiss' which means head butting your assailant on the nose which will break his nose and possibly concuss him, but watch out for the blood from his nasal area!'

Staff Sergeant Dunn concluded 'That's just a quick oral background to self –defence. What I would like to do now is go over what I have just spoken about in demonstration mode. Campbell, you can attack me and I will show the girls how to put theory into practice. Don't worry I will not exert enough pressure to damage you in any way. At the end we will reverse our roles and you can get your own back. By that time we shall need a rest and we can sit back and see if Roni and Lydia have learned anything from us.'

The two men faced up to each other and grappled for a few seconds with Cam using his judo skills to keep the instructor at bay, because he was no match for him. Almost as soon as they made body contact Dunn located the pressure points calling out the various parts of Cam's body as he reached them - soon it was Campbell's turn to assault Sergeant Major Dunn who did not make it easy for Cam but he did congratulate him on finding all the pressure points after several minutes. Both men were glad of the rest at the end of the combat which had lasted three times as long as a boxer does in one round in the ring.

Now it was the girl's turn. Roni, being the taller of the two, role played the part of the attacker. She had developed an aggressive streak which she had acquired during her time in prison which she implemented as Lydia fought off her advances. The pair crashed on to the rubber matting as Lydia, smaller but very wiry, fought like a devil and eventually found her targets. Both girls were physically exhausted after their efforts. After a short rest Roni set about Lydia using the protection skills she had picked up in prison to overwhelm Lydia very quickly. Dunn was very impressed as he had not expected the older woman to be so aggressive and reveal another side to her character.

'That concludes the unarmed combat section for just now. We shall go through to the shooting gallery. You can try out a variety of weapons and decide what best suits you. Roni, I know you have been excused this duty so you can stand behind the glass over there' he said pointing to an observation room, 'and you will find a coffee machine. Just help yourself.'

Chapter 8

Roni made herself comfortable with a coffee and a biscuit while watching her two compatriots go through their manoeuvres shooting rapidly at targets in the shape of humans, which were coming towards them at all different angles. Roni reflected 'What a change from the last IRA firearms course I attended which was held in a windy barn on the West coast of Ireland. Here the military had all the latest technology in operation to keep their men as safe as possible and their enemies exposed as the easiest of targets.'

Cam and Lydia were having a shooting contest and it was Lydia who portrayed the quickest reflexes and came out on top. They had removed their ear protectors and goggles by the time Roni offered her congratulations 'Well done Lydia, good shooting which must be worth a few drinks from Campbell this evening.'

Looking embarrassed Cam replied, 'Okay you win but I will get my own back later.'

Staff Sergeant Dunn rejoined them 'That was excellent shooting drill, you both scored well so not much room for improvement. Now, I will escort you along to our special effects/psychology department where Sebastian Pollock will put you through your paces.

A couple of minutes later the party arrived at double glass doors which could only be entered by pressing a security bell. A receptionist opened the door then escorted them along a long corridor to a laboratory. At that point Sergeant Major Dunn bid them farewell.

When they entered the laboratory a small rotund man in a white coat stopped his conversation with two colleagues and rushed to meet his visitors. 'Welcome to my world. It's not quite Disneyland but you will see some magic which will make your survival last longer!' he laughed excitedly in a squeaky high- pitched voice.

Sebastian Pollock was the epitome of the mad professor, bald head with long grey wisps of hair hiding the legs of his thick-rimmed spectacles. His florid complexion was supported by two double chins the lower one appearing to be choked by his red and white spotted bow tie.

'I will give you a short tour of the facilities and you will see how we are constantly using technology to give us field advantage over our enemies. Some of them are catching up fast. Put on the white coats and ear protectors I have laid out for you and we'll tour the shop floor.'

The 'Shop Floor' was reached by going through a large metal door into an outdoor area containing a number of different shaped dwellings which you would expect to find in the middle east or eastern Europe. Several exercises were taking place some using live ammunition and being directed by officers using heat-seeking technology to direct the soldiers through the buildings. Others were on ambush manoeuvres where they exerted their unarmed combat skills.

The visitors were impressed and although what they were witnessing was not relevant to their security role it made them appreciate the backing available should they require it. After half an hour Professor Pollock signalled for them to return to the calm of the laboratory.

'I hope you enjoyed the tour. A lot of the technology on display was supplied by my staff in here' said Pollock waving his arm in the direction of ten white-coated scientists who were sitting on high stools, some processing computers while others had their eyes down microscopes. 'If you follow me I will supply you with your own little survival kits.'

'In your line of work it is surprise and disguise that is necessary to keep you one step ahead. In these bags you will find a variety of wigs in different colours and styles which I appreciate will be of more use to Lydia and Roni than yourself Campbell. A supply of contact lenses in different shades will add to your appearance. There are also inflatable body parts to complete your transformation.

We even supply the ladies with jewellery. Take this little brooch or tie-pin for example. It is only three inches long and can used as a clasp or on your lapel, looks harmless enough, but if you slide the back of it along you then have in your possession a mini Stanley Knife which slices through skin with the greatest of ease.'

Professor Pollock handed the assembled company one each and they were impressed how simply it transformed into a deadly weapon.

Sebastian carried on 'There are other little gadgets in your goodie bags which I would advise you to familiarise yourselves with. However, time is moving on and I know my psychiatrist colleague Howard Ramsay wants to interview you individually after lunch. I hear you missed out on the shooting Roni so you will be first to see Ramsay when you come back.'

The trio bade farewell to Professor Pollock and headed for the Officer's Mess where they enjoyed a light meal on the basis they would be going out to eat that evening. After they got themselves sat down Cam started the conversation.

'Well, that was an interesting morning apart from Lydia beating me to the draw on the shooting range! Professor Pollock is an interesting guy and you wonder what is his ratio of kills versus lives saved.'

Roni answered 'He didn't come across as someone who would lose many battles. If his hit rate didn't come up to the targets set by his bosses he would be back in Oxford or Cambridge lecturing physics.'

Lydia spoke up 'Roni you surprised me with your aggressive streak during the unarmed combat. Your moves were not out of any text book, more what I would associate with a street fighter.'

Cam thought to himself 'Or a prisoner in a high security jail.'

Roni smiled 'Sorry if I was a little rough on you Lydia but in Ireland we were taught from an early age it is all about winning!'

Roni arrived first at Howard Ramsay's office to be told by his P.A. Abigail Heywood that Dr Ramsay was running late. She picked up a copy of 'Army News' and had almost finished reading by the time the psychiatrist arrived out of breath.

'Terribly sorry Miss Benson I had gone home quickly to sort out a domestic problem and got stuck in traffic on my return. Please accept my apologies and come this way. Abigail, can you organise some coffee?'

'Yes sir.'

Ramsay's large office was fitted out with very modern furniture in pastel shades to match in with the calming wallpaper. The medic ushered Roni to an armchair before disappearing to his desk to pick the papers he needed for their discussions.

'Where are we? You're Roni Benson who has been sent down from MI6 in London for a refresher course to prepare you and the other members of your team for a mission - the title of which is still to be disclosed. It says here you have been in the field carrying out special projects.'

The psychiatrist hesitated then continued 'I received a phone call this morning from MI6 confirming that you are in fact Mhairi McClure an Irish terrorist serving twenty years in prison for numerous atrocities. I should say Roni that I am the only person who knows

49

your identity apart from Campbell Anderson who you have worked with in the past'

Roni felt herself going red with anger, 'What's Hartley playing at? He assured me I would have complete anonymity. How many other people will find out about me?'

'Nobody if they value their career. When Richard Hartley tells you something in confidence you keep it that way. Hartley is a very ruthless individual who has put the fear of God into many staff members. Now, let's move on. How do you feel about acting for a regime you used to hate with a vengeance?'

Roni replied, 'You will see from my personal file I am a professional woman who lost her way years ago and allowed myself to be drawn into activities which were alien to my upbringing. I have been wasting away in prison doing menial tasks so the opportunity to enlist in MI6 activities has given me a new lease of life.'

Ramsay made notes before resuming the conversation 'You have been responsible for a number of deaths in the past.' Staring into her eyes he added 'Do you think you could kill again? I am talking in terms of following a command telling you to eliminate a target with a happy family life and possibly someone you have dined with in their home. In another scenario it could be someone you have experienced and enjoyed sexual relations with. How would you react?'

'Mr Ramsay, my priorities are to survive and keep out of prison life for as long as I can and if that means killing some people then so be it. My past has left me devoid of any moral fibre and I see myself now as a monster murder machine operated by evil men in their pursuit of doing what they consider right for their political aims. This is maybe a long answer to your question but the short answer is YES!'

Howard felt guilty about having to ask such direct questions but his job was to decide whether candidates were suitable for field work and whether they would falter in the face of the enemy. By her answer Roni Benson confirmed she was one of the most callous women he had ever encountered and he would have no hesitation in endorsing her for field duties. The only reservation he might have was that if she ever suffered a nervous breakdown. Her mind could revert back to the loss of her fiancé and she could turn her gun on her colleagues, killing Lydia Tomlinson and Campbell Anderson in the process. This could be a long shot but one worth mentioning in my report.

Late in the afternoon after Lydia and Cam had been in front of Howard Ramsay they met up.

'I'm glad that's over' Cam announced.

'Me too', agreed Lydia 'Ramsay doesn't hold back when it comes to asking you personal questions.'

'Well girls we have a couple of hours before dinner. What do you fancy getting up to?'

'It's a nice warm afternoon and I see there are some tennis courts vacant over there. Let's go across and see if we can get rackets and balls. This could be the start of some early preparation if Hartley sends us down to the South of France.'

Their equipment request was confirmed and it was agreed that Cam would take on the girls which proved a bad move. Cam was high in the physical attribute stakes but his co-ordination was somewhat lacking. Roni on the other hand got into the swing quite quickly and after the first set she swapped places with Cam and made it more of an even contest. Roni concluded to herself after the game that she couldn't wait to go to Valescure to resume more than just tennis.

Chapter 9

'Well played Roland! You are now serving for match point' shouted Gigi Montalban a girlfriend of Roland Canault.

Canault steadied himself wiped the perspiration off his brow with his left sweat band before bouncing the ball three times. He tossed the yellow ball high in the air then unleashed a huge serve down the centre of the court for victory. His opponent Guy Fontaine raised his racket to acknowledge defeat before arriving at the net to shake hands.

'I finally got him Gigi. That's the first time I have beaten Guy. I must go and tell my coach Pierre De Feu.', announced a delighted Roland after receiving a congratulatory kiss from his lady friend.

Gigi had been sitting watching the match from the comfort of the sidelines under a large white umbrella which offered protection from the sun while she and her friend Michelle Dupree enjoyed a bottle of cool Chablis. The match had been staged on one of Canault's private tennis court in the grounds of his magnificent chateau a few miles in from St. Raphael looking out on the hills of Massif de l'Esterel.

Chateau Rose Blanc was the former home of a British aristocrat Lord Plomley who had it built in 1902 but had to abandon the thirty acre estate temporarily when The First World War was declared in 1917. Lord Plomley died at his baronial home in Yorkshire before

World War 1 was concluded and it was 1921 before his descendants returned to the South of France to mix with other members of the British aristocracy. It was not only the British who flocked to Valescure as it was here that the famous American writer F. Scott Fitzgerald finished composing his famous novel 'The Great Gatsby.'

There was a repeat exodus when France was taken over by the Nazis in 1940 and the local Nazi commander General Wolfenstein occupied the chateau as his base to govern the St. Raphael and Valescure areas. Germany concentrated their main war efforts on northern France and the Atlantic Coast, leaving the rest of France to be governed under the Vichy arrangement negotiated with the German invaders. The allies launched an often forgotten offensive called 'Operation Dragoon' on 12th August 1944 which involved five hundred ships, including eight aircraft carriers, and one hundred thousand troops who had sailed from their base in Corsica. They took the Germans by surprise as they had expected them to attack Genoa but instead at the last minute they headed for the Cote d'Azur. The whole area including St. Raphael / Valescure was over-run quickly and the offensive's main objective - to control the ports of Toulon and Marseille - achieved. Victory did not come cheaply with the loss of many soldiers on both sides but it paved the way for an earlier conclusion to World War II.

Roland Canault was born Milo Malkovitch in Vrsac a manufacturing town in eastern Serbia. Milo was a bright student and studied economics at Belgrade University coming out with a first-class honours degree in 1989 just when his country was pursuing wars against the other states which previously constituted Yugoslavia. He joined the civil service and was seconded to the ministry of defence where he controlled a large procurement section to keep the military machine advancing at all times.

Weapons were rife throughout the Balkan states due to the manufacture of weaponry, which in some cases was the second largest industry after tourism in the Sarajevo region. Indigenous companies such as Solo built aircraft based on Russian and French designs while Igman produced the popular range of Lastava small arms.

When it became obvious to Malkovitch that Serbia was losing the war and fearing he could face war crime charges he planned his disappearance. Serbia, being a land-locked country was used to transporting their imports by air freight and in many cases the planes flew home empty. This gave Milo the opportunity to negotiate with an air charter company to load weapons onto the planes and deliver them to Russia where they were stored prior to being sold on to terrorist groups in the Middle East and North Africa. Several flights had already left before Malkovitch made his way to his home town Vrsac. From there with the added protection of three bodyguards he was able to cross over the border into Albania driving an armoured vehicle. On his way across Albania they stumbled upon a burned out jeep whose occupants were unrecognisable. Seizing the chance to vanish for good they switched identification discs with the corpses and took their credentials. No more Milo Malkovitch. After taking a quiet country route the group exited Albania in favour of Russia where Milo had already established business contacts.

During the next two years he created a new identity with the blessing of his Russian masters in the shape of the KGB. They were anxious to have a presence in the South of France to support oligarchs who were residing in the tax free haven of Monaco. He acquired Chateau Rose Blanc a property which ticked all the boxes: thirty rooms including eighteen en suite bedrooms, a large swimming pool, tennis courts and stables which he converted into offices. The chateau was positioned overlooking Valescure and looking down on the port of Frejus and the Mediterranean Sea. The high position of the chateau made it conducive to installing the latest security systems. Roland had brought his three bodyguards with him to Valescure which aided his desire to sleep soundly at night.

Roland Canault hid behind the façade of being a wine broker and established Valescure Vineries and engaged himself in supplying French wines to countries all over the world. Simultaneously the dark side of his empire left him free to supply arms to the unsavoury side of society which usually meant political activists.

Chapter 10

Roni had been back in Chesham for a week when she got the call from Cam 'Roni we are sending a car tomorrow to bring you up to H.Q. Assistant Controller Hartley wants to see Lydia, you and me.'

'Will I pack an overnight bag?'

'Nobody has mentioned it. I get the impression this is a briefing with a view to moving into action soon on an assignment.'

'That's good news Cam, I'm in need of a new challenge and it will be good to get out of sleepy Chesham and into the buzz of London.' Roni replied laughing as she spoke.

'Is it you who is picking me up Cam?'

'No it will be one of the more mature drivers to make sure you don't try to seduce him.'

'Cam Anderson, you have a low opinion of me!' retorted Roni.

Cam chuckled, 'No Roni just an accurate one based on my personal experience!'

Next morning a metallic blue Ford Focus drew up at the Chesham safe house and an elderly gentleman struggled out of the passenger seat. He entered the building where Roni, dressed in a grey business suit, was waiting for him.

'Miss Benson I presume. I'm Harry Parker your escort. Pleased to meet you.' he continued, 'Jim Hill our chauffeur is waiting in the car.'

They made their way out to the car to find Hill cleaning his windscreen. Both men were dressed identical and both looked over retirement age, weighed down by the bulging revolvers under their jackets. Roni smiled to herself 'MI6 obviously don't operate an age discrimination policy.'

It was a lovely hot sunny morning with not a cloud in the sky and the journey passed quickly helped by Parker's quick wit and Hill's running commentary on the bad impatient driving practices of vehicles weaving their way through the traffic. Hill and Parker dropped Roni off at the front entrance to MI6 where, after clearing security, she sat at reception until Campbell Anderson and Lydia Tomlinson appeared to take her upstairs.

'Morning Roni how are you today?'

'Feeling good Cam, have your recovered from our tennis match?'

'What tennis match was that again?' he joked, 'a distant memory now. Come along we'll take you up to meeting room 1 to meet Assistant Controller Hartley and Commander Hugh McFaul.'

'So both the usual suspects are still working together.'

Cam replied using a serious tone 'Roni, I would ask you to remember that your freedom is in Richard Hartley's hands. I have seen his ruthless streak and believe me you wouldn't like it. If you don't want a quick return to Askham Hall I would cut out the flippant remarks and play along with him at all times. Understood?'

'Yes!'

Meeting Room 1 was designed to make the occupants feel relaxed with large windows looking out over the River Thames. The walls were wood panelled sporting numerous art deco paintings which surrounded a large oval teak table with twelve matching fawn velour-backed chairs with armrests. Each placement had a writing pad and coffee mats which matched the crockery beside the coffee machine. Hartley was standing making polite conversation with Hugh McFaul and his personal assistant Freddie Sharpe when they entered the room. He came forward to greet them before introducing Freddie Sharpe.

'Come on, get yourselves a coffee and we will get on with the briefing. Freddie, can you set up the screen for me?'

'Yes sir.' Sharpe moved across to a nearby wall and pressed a button which resulted in the ceiling opening up and a large screen lowering itself down in front of the windows followed by the window blinds shutting out the daylight.

Hartley addressed the others 'Good morning formally, I have received reports from Hereford that the three of you conducted yourselves very well and have been considered suitable for the task ahead by Colonel Walton and Sebastian Pollock. The Hereford staff's task was to ascertain if you could operate as a successful team in the face of adversity.'

'Now, turning to today, Walton mentioned to you during his talk, a gentleman known as Roland Canault.' Harley pressed a remote control he was holding and an image appeared on the screen, 'This is Roland Canault.'

The three visitors fixed their eyes on the tall tanned athletic figure in his mid- forties, blond hair receding at the temples with a smattering of grey at the sides. He was wearing sunglasses to hide his blue eyes but this did not detract from his good looks which got both Lydia and Roni's approval.

Hartley continued 'Canault lives on the outskirts of Valescure at Chateau Rose Blanc the thirty acre estate in the next slide. The grounds are very well protected by all the very latest surveillance systems so the only way to go there is by invitation.'

Roni couldn't contain herself, 'Nice pad.'

Hartley gave her a stare and continued 'Canault's weakness, if he has one, is tennis. He loves having tennis parties which are played on his two floodlit courts in the grounds of the chateau. I would like you three to befriend Canault and his associates and if possible get invited to Chateau Rose Blanc. It is vital we find out more about his arms dealing activities.'

'Why? Because we are concerned about the future political map along the North Africa coastline where all the countries tied up in the 'Arab Spring' could become, in the years ahead, a major threat to Europe. What we want to do is penetrate Roland Canault's base in the hope we can find out where he is storing his supply of weapons and more importantly who is he acquiring them from, and to which organisations is he selling them?'

'We have arranged accommodation for you in two apartments on the Esterel Golf Complex in Valescure. Roni will have one to herself whereas Campbell and Lydia will share as I am proposing they pose as a couple – Mr and Mrs Graeme Doncaster. However, you will be able to join each other for meals as we will be keeping your identity as before i.e. representing Farrer Financial Services. As you know there are no records at Company House for FFS so it will be difficult for the opposition to find out about you. If the occasion arises when someone does want a reference we have rigged up telephone numbers and senior contacts in fictitious financial organisations who will all give you glowing reviews.'

The company around the table smiled at Hartley's last remark.

'I have had Freddie put together a dossier for you on everything we know about Roland Canault plus a booklet on the Cote d'Azur which you should familiarise yourselves with. The British ambassador in Marseille which is our nearest embassy to Monaco will provide contacts in Monaco's financial district which will enable you to get to know the Principality. Embassy staff will also furnish you with weapons which they will deliver to you at your hotel.'

'Go out and buy yourselves tennis shoes and shorts. Wear the trainers as much as you can to distress them and give the impression you play regularly. Don't bother with rackets as you will be able to hire them from the Valescure Tennis Academy and anyway they are awkward luggage to carry with you. I understand Roni has shown the most talent for the game so I would recommend she approaches the tennis centre on her own. Lydia and Campbell can take a day trip to Monaco and explore the lay-out and how if necessary, they can make a quick escape, should the necessity arise. Initially you will be down in France for two weeks and depending on your progress, making repeat journeys to the Cote d'Azur in the future.'

'You should be ready to leave for France in three weeks time which will allow you a period of time to familiarise yourself and know everything you should about Roland Canault and the Cote d'Azur. That concludes the brief, best of luck everyone.'

Campbell asked a final question 'Excuse me Assistant Controller where and when is our flight time.'

Hartley smiled. 'Flights Anderson? You are booked first-class on the Euro Star changing in Paris to the TGV which stops at St. Raphael. Remember not too much claret at lunchtime!'

The spy-catcher excused himself and returned to his office taking Freddie Sharpe with him. Hugh McFaul who had been observing the proceedings approached his colleagues 'Well it sounds like you have got yourselves a nice little assignment to the South of

France. Sunshine, smart apartments, tennis schools coupled with good food and wine. What more could you wish for?'

Lydia responded first 'How about that we all return in one piece!'

Chapter 11

Freddie Spence's dossier on Roland Canault was very detailed and for the next two weeks Campbell, Lydia and Roni met regularly at the safe house in Chesham to discuss its contents. It was far more private there than being in MI6 headquarters where they would be subject to interruptions.

Along with the detailed report on Canault himself, there was also useful information regarding his three bodyguards who had accompanied him from Serbia. They were all from the elite special services unit who carried out the most fiendish crimes to protect their Serbian Leaders. Most likely they had also been cited for war crimes but as yet were resisting arrest behind the new identities Roland Canault had purchased for them.

The MI6 trio spent hours on a Satnav simulator learning all there was to know about the South of France. To prevent boredom they began testing each other on the best routes to use in an area famous for long traffic jams with the losing contestant picking up the wine bill at the evening meal.

It was a relief for them when Commander McFaul phoned and told them they were leaving in two days time for France from Paddington Station on the 9.00 a.m. Euro-Star to Paris. After giving Roni all her documentation for the journey which consisted of a passport, EHIC health card, credit cards and cheque book, Beverley Thomson joined Roni on the train journey into London. The last thing MI6 wanted was Roni getting cold feet and missing the train.

Lydia and Cam were waiting outside W.H. Smith's newsagents in St. Pancras International Station, as pre-arranged both dressed in casual gear reminiscent of holidaymakers going on a jaunt to France.

Beverley handed out the first-class tickets wished them all the best and disappeared into the throng of commuters. All three of them had large suitcases and the girls were delighted to have Campbell to load them on to the luggage rack. Everyone settled into the first-class compartment where they had seats facing each other when they were joined by a young student who spread his laptop over the table, encroaching on his fellow passengers' space.

'Sorry about this' he declared 'I have a dissertation to complete for my PhD which has to be handed into the Sorbonne in two days time.'

Cam exclaimed 'Ah, now those were the days girls where your whole future was tied up in a manuscript which you had grave doubts about. Look we don't mind you working away as long as we have enough room for our drinks, but when lunch is served you will have to take a break.'

As if on cue a waiter sporting a black bow tie and maroon jacket arrived with a bottle of Veuve Clicquot champagne and some nibbles Cam had ordered in advance.

'I thought we should get used to the high life sooner rather than later.' he said, the others nodded their approval.

The Euro-Star got up to one hundred and sixty miles per hour only stopping at Ashford before entering into the dark chasm of the Channel Tunnel where it slowed down. The waiter returned, issued the lunch menus and waited for their selections. The student lifted his head up from his studies to say he had a packed lunch in his bag. Within minutes the waiter came back with trays of readily prepared food which was considerably grander than the usual British Rail fare - especially as it included a half-bottle of red wine each.

Two and a half hours after leaving London they were in the centre of Paris where they had to transfer stations from the Gare de Nord to the Gare de Lyon. It was only a short journey and Cam suggested they take the subway but Roni intervened 'Cam, the Paris subway has a bad reputation for pickpockets and the three of us would stand out a mile with this luggage. Let's get a taxi.'

Lydia nodded her agreement and they piled into a people carrier to Gare de Lyon. They only had to wait a short time to board the TGV where again the carriages were very comfortable and there was a bar for the first-class travellers to enjoy. The TGV sped even faster than the Euro Star through the French countryside until it reached Aix-en-Provence. From there the train slowed down considerably as it wound its way along the Mediterranean coast before stopping at St.

Raphael only seven hours after leaving London. A fifteen euro taxi ride deposited them at their apartments at the Esterel Golf Hotel.

The apartments were practical rather than palatial, spotlessly clean two bedroom accommodation with balconies which overlooked a twenty-five metre swimming pool and the twilight was filled with the sound of the uniformed staff preparing the tables for their diners. Cam looked at his watch.

'Girls we have been travelling all day. I think we should eat here tonight. I'll go downstairs and book a tablet – is eight-thirty okay?'

Lydia replied on behalf of the girls 'Fine Cam. We can retire to our rooms which are all en-suite and pamper ourselves before meeting in the bar at say eight o'clock.'

Roni retreated in the direction of her room, 'I'll leave you two to work out your sleeping arrangements. See you at eight.'

Following years of sharing a prison cell, having her own room was, to Roni one of life's luxuries. She ran a hot bath and soaked in it for the best part of an hour planning how she could get close to Roland Canault.

A couple of minutes after eight Roni stood at the bar wearing a loose pale green cotton dress which floated over her white sandals. She ordered a gin and tonic with ice and lemon then moved away to a nearby table. Cam and Lydia were not far behind her, Lydia having decided to wear light–blue culottes while Cam decided on a black shirt and cream slacks. They sat down at the table and did not disturb Roni who was reading a magazine entitled 'What's On in Valescure.'

'Anything interesting Roni?' enquired Lydia.

'Yes there is an advert for the Tennis Academy or to give it the correct name 'Valescure Links et Raquette Club.' It gives you all the opening times and information on hiring equipment. Apparently it is within walking distance of Esterel Golf which will save any car hire. How are you going to go into Monaco tomorrow? From what we hear about the traffic I think the forty mile journey would be best covered by the train. It says here there is a direct service which runs twice a day, Monday to Friday.'

Cam gave his approval to Roni's suggestion 'That's settled then Lydia, I'll get the times of the train going to Monaco tomorrow and arrange for a taxi to pick us up in plenty of time. Right, come on it's time for dinner.'

All three were showing signs of weariness so they settled for a two course tableau d'hote meal and retired to their rooms by eleven o'clock.

Chapter 12

Next morning Roni was up early for a dip in the swimming pool before the others surfaced. It was a beautiful warm sunny morning making the water very refreshing and giving her the perfect start to her day. Roni returned to her room showered and dressed before joining Lydia and Cam on the terrace for breakfast.

'Everybody sleep well?'

Lydia pointed at Cam 'He did but I couldn't get to sleep for his snoring in the next room. I had to get up at three o'clock during the night and sit out on the balcony.'

Being mischievous Roni commented 'It is probably better if you slept in the same bed then you could give him a kick every time he snores.'

Lydia protested 'Well, we'll give that suggestion a miss for now!'

The continental breakfast was excellent very much in the French style with a good selection of bread, cheeses, cold meats, fruit juices and a glass of sparkling wine to accompany the coffee. The quality of the food was reflected in the silence which followed as everybody gorged themselves.

Over coffee Cam laid out the plans for the day. 'Lydia and I will be leaving shortly for Monaco which we should reach in just under an hour and be back late afternoon. Roni, I know you are heading for the tennis academy but could you be on the look-out for restaurants we could frequent this evening?'

'No problem Cam, subject to my exertions on the tennis court not affecting my culinary needs.'

Cam smiled 'You're only going for a knock-up, not three sets with Serena Williams!'

The conversation concluded with Cam's jovial remark and everyone retired to their rooms to prepare for their day. In Roni's case she changed into white shorts, a pale blue t-shirt, put on her tennis shoes and lastly her white baseball cap with her sunglasses perched on top. By the time she went down to reception Cam and Lydia had left by taxi for Gard de St. Raphael to catch their train for Monaco.

Roni approached reception and asked for directions to the Valescure Links et Raquette Club.

The receptionist asked, 'Are you in a hurry to get there madam?'

'No not really.'

'The tennis club is very close and if I were to order you a taxi it may take longer than it would you going on foot. Let me show you.'

He guided Roni to the front door 'The best way is go over the golf course.' Pointing with his finger he added 'If you walk down the first hole to the green you will see a sign for the next hole which is a par three. At the back of the green you will see a gate which takes you out on to the main road. Turn right and the tennis academy is only two hundred metres on your right. It will only take you about twenty minutes.'

Roni crossed the road and headed off down the fairway following four golfers who had just teed off in two golf buggies. She knew enough about golf not to encroach on the golfers or make a noise. By the time she reached the green they were lining up their putts. One of the golfers shouted across 'Are you looking for someone?'

'No I am heading for the tennis academy via a gate behind the next hole'

'Just carry on; you'll be out of range by the time this lot take to putt out!'

Roni enjoyed her walk and found the gate which took her on to a main road and within a few minutes she was climbing up the stairs into the tennis centre.

The outer façade of the sandstone building had a Victorian look about it, but inside possessed all the features of a modern tennis academy. There were six courts, four red clay and two hard courts so players could practice on different surfaces. Down the side of the courts there were warm-up areas where players could hit balls at a wall containing a line painted the same height as a tennis net, or equally face a machine which fired out balls in all different directions for the player to return over a net. At the opposite side of the court there was an open-air stand consisting of ten rows of seats which ran the length of the two courts it overlooked. Behind the stand there were a number of flag-poles adorned with the national flags of players who had graced the Valescure court. All the facilities were covered by floodlighting. Tables with sunshades which lined one side of the courts were served by a waiter who weaved his way back and forward from a small bar in the corner.

An attractive receptionist dressed in a green and white dress smiled as Roni approached the desk.

'Brigitte Lamar, how can I help you?' she asked in French.

Roni decided not to reply in French 'I am living in Valescure for two weeks and would like to hire a tennis racket and have a game. I am on my own today. Is there anyone looking for a game?'

'Sorry my apologies, you are English. I am unable to fix you up with a partner just now but one of our coaches will be free in an hour if that would be suitable. Are you a beginner or do you play regularly?'

Roni replied 'I used to, but I have only taken it up again recently.'

'Don't worry - Maria Milagro D'Andrea is a very patient young woman who is very popular with her students.'

'Ms D'Andrea sounds just the sort of coach I need. I'll be delighted to play with her.'

'Tres bien, I will book court number five. You are welcome to sit here and have a drink or some food or go for a walk and come back later.'

'Is it possible to get a racket just now and I will go over to the warm-up area for a short session hitting balls against the wall.'

'But of course!' Brigitte exclaimed standing aside to give Roni a view of the tennis rackets laid out in rows behind her 'Which one would you like?'

'Wilson Staff please, that's what I used when I lived in America.'

Brigitte handed over a red Wilson racket, some yellow balls and Roni headed off to the warm-up area. She was glad of the practice as her game was a bit rusty, to say the least, but after ten minutes she was able to anticipate how the ball would rebound as if she was hitting returns to an opponent. Due to the heat of the day it was not long before she worked up a sweat making her decide it was prudent to stop and enjoy a bottle of water as she awaited the arrival of Mademoiselle D'Andrea.

She did not have long to wait. She was intrigued watching two players fighting a duel on a court, so much so that she failed to see Maria arriving at her table.

'Miss Benson? I am Maria Milagro D'Andrea – pleased to meet you. My friends call me 'Milagro'. Are you ready to go on court?'

'Milagro – that's an unusual name.'

The tennis coach replied 'It is Spanish for 'Miracle' and when I was on the tennis circuit my fellow competitors all referred to me as Milagro and it just stuck.'

The girls shook hands. Milagro was in her early thirties and had the physique of someone who earned her livelihood exercising. Facially she reminded Roni of

Natalie Wood who played Maria in the film version of the musical West Side Story. Her brown eyes portrayed a bubbly personality and Roni took to her immediately. Milagro had played on the senior tennis circuit when she was younger but retired early when she failed to recover from a major back injury. They commenced playing with Milagro going through the motions and competing within herself, but recognising how good Roni was for a woman in her mid-forties. Roni produced a variety of shots but it was her ground strokes and back-hand that were most impressive.

After forty minutes Roni went to the bench and lifted up a white towel in surrender. Breathing heavily she gasped before taking a long slug of water 'That's enough for today Milagro, I'm exhausted.'

'A wise move Roni. You've done well but don't overdo it. Let's find a seat under a parasol and enjoy a drink.'

Roni was still sweating profusely when the waiter arrived with a large jug of soda water and lime. Milagro poured the drink as Roni posed the questions. 'Have you been a coach for long?'

'Two years'

'And always at Valescure?'

'Yes'

'Are there enough customers to keep you busy?'

'Oh yes Roni, in the summer we have the holiday-makers and as the weather is good in the south of France we have a long season. In the winter we go indoors.'

'I would imagine the social scene is very vibrant around here.'

'Yes Valescure is a very wealthy community so someone is always throwing a party and as their tennis coach I normally get an invitation.

'Are the residents quite cosmopolitan?'

'Yes but it is changing. There are a lot less British and Swedes and far more Russians and East Europeans. They seem to have the money and are constantly buying up large properties in the area. One of the most wealthy men in Valescure is Roland Canault who adores tennis and he comes here for his lessons from my boss Pierre de Feu despite having his own courts at Chateau de Rose Blanc.'

Roni eyes lit up and she couldn't resist asking 'How often does he come for lessons?'

'Every week, in fact he will be here tomorrow.'

'He sounds like a bit of a character. I have taken an apartment for two weeks at Esterel d'Golf along with my colleague Graeme Doncaster and his wife Lydia who have gone into Monaco for the day. We are involved in finance and will be calling on some of your wealthier neighbours in the area during our stay. We'll all come down tomorrow for a game. Could you make up a mixed doubles?'

'Let me look at my diary' Milagro replied stretching into her sports bag 'I have to be here to help Pierre with Monsieur Canault's visit at 10.30 but I could fit you in at 1.00 p.m.'

'That is excellent Milagro. We will look forward to seeing you in the morning.'

Chapter 13

'When do you want them and where will we be delivering them!' Roland Canault shouted down the phone 'sorry for shouting but it is a bad line. Yes I understand you are phoning from the middle of the Sahara. It can't be easy for you. I'll read out what you've ordered once more:

200 HS Produkt HS-95 semi automatic pistols
200 Zastava M91 Sniper rifles
200 Zastava M80 Assault rifles
50 Rocket Launchers
1000 Hand Grenades
Supply of sufficient bullets and missiles for the above.

We shall get them ready to be despatched from our stores the minute your payment clears our bank in Monaco.'

The voice on the other end of the Phone asked 'Do we get a discount for cash?'

'No Tariq, margins are tight enough so our prices remain as quoted. Get back to me when you have transferred the money to my bank. Good afternoon.'

Roland placed the phone on his desk and turned round to talk to two of his bodyguards Spiridon Natalic and David Andelic 'Do you hear that guy! He's leading a small bunch of camel bandits in the middle of the Sahara and he expects to get a discount on this puny little order. David, send a coded email out to Moscow and get them to have the order ready for despatch to Libya. The consignment will be picked up by the Libyans but only once their payment has been received. The only problem dealing with Libyans is they want to pay in cash – usually US dollars- but that's cumbersome and not so easy for us to dispose of. I can see this 'Arab Spring' becoming a problem for us if it continues to be so fragmented with each little group setting up their own little private armies.'

The Serbian failed to realise that his phone was still live and Tariq Aziz had been party to Roland's derogatory comments and he thought to himself 'Bunch of camel bandits! Roland Canault you'll regret that comment!'

David Andelic joined the conversation in the chateau office 'Is that not what Moscow wanted us to do. Keep in with as many factions as possible rather than risk them consolidating into a central government which attracts huge subsidies from the West and the armoury which goes along with it.'

Roland replied 'I am getting a call from Uri Bardosky tomorrow when he flies into Nice and I will discuss our strategy at length with him over in the next a couple of days. In the meantime I will turn my attention to our Middle East customers, who are about to embark on major offensives in their area, and also the African states.'

Roland looked out the window and took stock of how fortunate he had been to have settled in Valescure. If he had remained in Serbia he would probably have been in prison by now, trying to defend the indefensible. It could be argued that he, as the Senior Procurement Officer for the Serbian Army, had contributed to the genocide which took place at Srebrenica where eight thousand men and boys were killed. All the officers responsible were cited for war crimes.

Here in Valescure he was leading the life of luxury keeping up with the Cote d'Azur jet set, many of whom had more money than sense. Their privileged backgrounds allowed them to hold lavish social gatherings where alcohol and drug abuse often loosened their tongues, allowing Roland and his staff to increase their intelligence bank.

Canault was surrounded by his trusted bodyguards who had defended him throughout the Serbian War. They were all highly trained security officers. Matija Zoric (nicknamed Zorro) came from a poor Slav family and witnessed his parents being killed by Montenegrin Muslim soldiers. The young Zoric could not wait to join the Serbian army and become one of its most ruthless officers who delighted in massacring as many enemy soldiers as he could. Some of his exploits were against defenceless prisoners whom he tortured regularly and allowed his platoon to force themselves on women. He was transferred from field duties to Milo Malkovitch's division partially for his soldiering qualities but also for his own safety from himself as he was becoming mentally unstable.

David Andelic (known as 'D.A.') was the complete opposite of Matija Zoric. Born into the wealthy home of a leading industrialist he attended college in Pancake an industrial town only eighteen kilometres from Belgrade where his family owned a successful pharmaceutical company. David had studied history and politics and saw his future in politics but when he witnessed how Yugoslavia was being divided up he settled for a career in the military. He was very athletic, good at all sports especially the martial arts, both judo and karate, so was attracted to the Serbian Special Services Unit.

Spiridon Natalic ('Spy' to his friends) was very close to Roland Canault principally because they were both from the same town and knew each other from primary school. Whereas Roland had gone to university Spy had found his niche in the military where his naturally aggressive nature was noticed by his superiors and earned him quick promotion to the rank of Captain. His good looks did not go un-noticed and Roland used him regularly to woo unsuspecting female personal assistants of important people in order to extract confidential information from them.

Addressing his bodyguard team Roland announced 'We shall be travelling along the coast on Thursday to meet up with Commissar Uri Bardosky in Cannes. He has a reputation for enjoying a good time and will not be travelling alone. He will have a least one young lady to attend to all his needs but don't be surprised if he also tries the local talent at the same time.'

Spy laughed 'Roland, are you trying to tell me I will be competing with a sixty-five year old overweight bald-headed pensioner to bed the most beautiful girl in the room?'

Roland stared coldly at his friend 'Spy, nobody competes with a Commissar for a woman unless you want to end up in a ditch with a bullet in your head!'

Chapter 14

Next day was another beautiful morning and after breakfast the tennis trio set off for the academy. Roni led the way through the golf course which Lydia and Cam enjoyed and it put Cam in the mood for a game later in the week. Roni continued her tourist guide role when they entered the tennis club and ushered them to a seat courtside. She looked around the courts at the players who were mostly in all-whites which made it difficult to see Milagro immediately.

'Ah there's Milagro over there on court four playing with the tall slim gentleman who I assume is Roland Canault as the man on the other side of the net is older. I presume he is the senior coach, Pierre de Feu, judging by the ease in which he returns the ball.'

'Roni our Mr Canault is a very attractive man who we must meet up with.' quipped Lydia.

'Milagro is very tidy too, do you know if she is married? asked Cam

'She never mentioned any man in her life but our conversation was very much trainer to pupil.'
The next hour passed quickly helped by refreshing soda water and lime and the snacks the waiter brought with the drinks. Action on court no.4 ended and the players exited the court. Milagro looked towards the refreshment area and when she saw Roni she smiled, waved and made her way to their table.

'Morning everyone, you must be Mr and Mrs Doncaster who Roni told me all about yesterday.

Cam butted in 'I take it was all good.'

'Of course! Let me say goodbye to Roland and I will be right back.' She turned away and nearly bumped into Roland who was curious to meet her new friends.

'Sorry Roland I nearly caused you an injury.'

Roland smiled 'I thought I would come over to introduce myself to the new players. Hello I'm Roland Canault.' he said holding out his hand to Roni who went to shake it but Roland gently lifted her hand and kissed it adding 'I prefer a French greeting.'

A slightly embarrassed Roni did the introductions 'I'm Roni Benson and these are my friends Lydia and Graeme Doncaster.' Roland shook Cam's hand and kissed Lydia.

'Are you here on holiday or business?'

Cam replied 'A bit of both. Roni and I are in finance and we are going to call on potential clients in Monaco. My wife thought it would be a good idea to come along for a holiday.'

'Good thinking Lydia' returned Roland 'Have you been to Monaco before?'

'Not until yesterday when we took the train in which is probably the best way to travel when you see all the cars moving tail to tail.'

'Yes it can be frustrating. When I first came here I thought about copying the American actor Orson Wells who, when he lived in New York, bought an ambulance to get through the traffic quickly. I have a more simple solution - I bought myself a helicopter!'

The quartet round the table laughed as Roland made his departure speech 'Perhaps we could have a game later in the week if you're available. How about the day after tomorrow in the morning at 9.30 before the sun gets up.'

'Sounds terrific Roland but I'm not sure we shall be up to your standard.'

Roland responded 'We can revolve the pairings and I'm sure we'll find the right balance.'

Roni beamed 'We're game if you are. Okay Roland it's a date!'

Roland moved off towards the exit followed by two very fit looking minders carrying sports bags open at the zip. Cam reckoned the reason for this was to allow quick access to the weapons they concealed. Returning from his thoughts he rejoined the conversation.

Lydia was speaking, 'Well that was a bonus meeting Roland and even better arranging a game for Thursday.'

'Yes' agreed Roni 'but let's get down to today's main event. We'll start with Cam and I taking on Lydia and Milagro.'

This match proved to be the best of the three paired matches as Cam and Roni combined well. Milagro offset the shortfalls in Lydia's game to keep the match close until Roni fired the winning blow, a cross court passing shot which whizzed by Lydia. In the end everyone enjoyed themselves and returned to the bar for a drink to celebrate.

Milagro asked 'What are you doing for lunch?'

Cam replied first 'Nothing planned what would you recommend?

'The full name of the club is Valescure Links et Raquette Club and the golf clubhouse on the other side of the road is attached to a four star hotel which serves good food. I am unable to join you as I have coaching commitments today but will see you on Thursday.'

Lydia replied 'Before you go Milagro I am not comfortable playing tennis and feel I could spoil the game for everyone. Would you be able to substitute for me?'

Milagro held up her hand while getting out her diary, 'Thursday, yes I can play as I don't have classes until the afternoon.'

The party remained chatting for another hour until Milagro had to leave and the others headed over the road to the golf clubhouse for lunch.

The clubhouse was a charming old fashioned wooden building on two levels, the upper floor being the staff quarters which had been constructed in the 1920s. Its most prominent feature was a covered veranda stretching fifty yards along its front where tables were laid out for lunch. In front of the veranda there were a number of round tables covered by parasols for the members who only wanted a drink after their round of golf or practice their putting and chipping on the beautifully manicured green. In contrast adjoining the clubhouse there was a modern four star hotel with an outdoor pool and a spa.

The British contingent found a table overlooking the scene and spent a few minutes watching the golfers passing, both male and female, dressed for a day on the links. After looking over the varied menu they attracted a waiter who took Cam's order of two croque monsieurs for the girls and steak for himself, all with French fries. To quench their thirst they asked for a bottle of wine accompanied with still water and Cam had a pint of lager after going into the attractive all wooden–lined bar to inspect the draught beer on offer.

Lydia spoke first, 'A nice spot to relax and get our breath back after the tennis. I don't think I will miss it on Thursday.'

Cam replied, 'I thought it was very noble of you to volunteer to sit out on Thursday which will present the opportunity for you to talk to Roland's bodyguards, acting all innocent of course.'

'It was good of Milagro to come on Thursday if nothing else to hide our tennis flaws.' confessed Roni.

Cam jokingly added 'Rubbish Roni you'll be up to the test against Roland Canault.'

At that point the food arrived and the bantering ceased.

Chapter 15

After an early morning swim Roni relaxed on the terrace reading the local paper until the Doncasters arrived twenty minutes later.

Lydia asked 'Morning Roni did you have a good swim? Cam and I were watching you from our balcony and were impressed by your straight armed backstroke.'

'Cam used to join me but I think he is scared I beat him.'

'Attack me is more like it! Lydia to let you understand the last time I went swimming with Roni I thought she was going to have the Speedos off me.' informed Cam.

'Well I was!' laughed Roni 'but anyway I came off best with a full massage from a young husky masseur.'

'That's enough Roni.' protested Cam 'Changing the subject, what do you fancy doing today?'

Lydia answered first 'I've always wanted to see Cannes. Over the years I have watched all the film stars attending the Monteux Film Festival and it looks fabulous.'

'Sounds good to me Lydia.' said Roni giving her approval.

Cam stood up 'Right I'll go to reception and see about getting a taxi. I don't fancy driving here and a taxi removes all the hassle about finding parking places.'

Thirty minutes later a Peugeot 607 rolled up at reception and the trio were off in the hands of their driver, Yves Lampard. He took them along the twisty coastal route with its hairpin bends, weaving along the cliff tops, past two thousand foot high Mount Esterel, before descending into Mandelieu-la-Napoule then into Cannes. He stopped the car at the Croisette where there was a lovely beach and plenty of bars and restaurants. Cam went to settle the taxi but Yves negotiated to remain with them for the day and gave Cam his card to call him when they wanted to return to Valescure.

Like children on a Sunday school trip the trio set off to explore Cannes. They walked the length of the Boulevard de la Croisette until they reached the harbour where they stopped for a cool drink and admired the beautiful yachts in the bay. They were seated near the Carlton Hotel, one of Cannes most famous tourist sites, where they could watch as the taxis and limousines made a never-ending parade to the door. Cam studied the security staff trying to identify their nationalities by the cut of their suits and the hardware they were concealing under them. He pretended to take photographs of the girls but the ladies were nowhere to be seen when he looked at the prints later.

A large Mercedes four-by-four stopped outside the Carlton, three security men all dressed in black linen suits jumped out and formed a guard round a small rounded figure in light casual gear sporting a wide brimmed straw hat and sunglasses. With the stranger was an attractive young lady accompanied by a tall slim character wearing a floral shirt and a white baseball cap which gave him protection from the sun. Cam clicked his camera and caught a few images of the mysterious guests before they disappeared into the hotel. It was difficult to recognise the man but Cam sent the photos to Hugh McFaul who would get the special effects department to remove the hat and sunglasses and perhaps reveal his identity. The trio finished their drinks and were continuing their tour walking on past the entrance to the Carlton when a vehicle drew up and three men stepped out.

Roni called out 'Roland! What are you doing here?'

A startled Roland turned round sharply after hearing his name shouted out 'Oh Roni it's you – is this you doing your tourist bit in Cannes?'

'Yes – and are you here for a nice lunch?'

A hesitant Roland replied 'Y...Yes a spot of lunch and we are meeting up with some old friends.'

Cam butted in 'Well bon appétit and we'll see you tomorrow morning. Au revoir.'

Once they were out of earshot they all started discussing their chance meeting with Roland and friends.

Lydia commented 'Lunch with some old friends. THAT WILL BE RIGHT! Who would go to lunch for a bite to eat carrying a bulging briefcase and surrounded by two professional security men. Did you notice that while Roland was speaking the other two were doing three sixty scans of everything around them?'

Cam agreed with Lydia 'I took that in as well. It took me back to when I used to accompany security chiefs to work every morning on the train. It must be an important meeting. What I would give to be a fly on the wall at that one.'

Leaving the seafront they travelled a couple of streets back to the main shopping centre which suited Lydia and Roni, but Cam decided it was time for him to have a rest, buy a newspaper and relax with a drink.

'I'll sit here and wait for you but don't be all day. Come back in an hour or so and we'll have lunch.'

Roni answered 'Okay see you later.' and they moved off.

Cam got out his phone and looked at the images he had taken. They were reasonably clear but would require some maintenance by the boffins. He dialled a number which was immediately answered 'Hugh, Cam here.'

'Ah Cam how are you? Lying back on a sun-bed and taking in the sun's rays no doubt!'

Playing along Cam replied 'No. I am sitting in Café Regal in Cannes reading a paper and enjoying a cool glass of Chablis. Seriously Hugh, I thought I would give you an update whilst the girls are at the shops. We have made good progress in the last few days thanks to Roni. She went down to the tennis academy the first day and met up with Milagro D'Andrea, a tennis coach. Milagro plays often with Roland Canault and we went to meet her the next day when she had just finished a match with our man. He came and introduced himself and would you believe it Hugh, we are playing with him tomorrow.'

An excited Hugh intervened 'That's fantastic Cam, you must let me know how you get on.'

Cam continued 'We were having a drink in Cannes outside the Carlton Hotel doing a spot of people watching when one party drew my attention - they looked to me like Russians - by their apparel. I am sending you photos to see if the boffins can throw any light on their identity. We were on the point of moving on when Roland Canault arrived with two minders carrying a heavy briefcase and nearly made me giggle by saying he was at the Carlton to meet some old friends for lunch. It will be interesting to know if we can establish a connection between the two parties I've mentioned.'

'I will get back to you Cam the minute I get a response from our technicians.'

Shortly afterwards the girls returned holding small carrier bags containing trinkets they had purchased. Cam did not inform them he had spoken to Hugh McFaul preferring to make his first priority getting a good venue for lunch. The 'Jardin Sur La Plage' proved to be the perfect spot, situated looking down on the harbour. All the white linen covered tables each with extensive menus, were protected from the hot sun by parasols. For the next two hours the trio relaxed, gorging the excellent meal and engaged in idle chat until Yves returned to take them back to Valescure. Everyone was feeling tired from the heat of the day so Yves suggested they take the much quicker route back along the motorway.

Cam was in the shower when he heard his phone ring but before he could get to turn the water off Lydia had entered the bathroom to hand it to him. She admired his physique as Cam tried to cover his modesty.

'Thanks Lydia. Hello who's speaking? Oh Hugh, give me a second while I get a towel round me. Right, did you find out anything?'

'I hope I haven't disturbed you having a good time?' McFaul laughed.

'No we have just got back from Cannes and I needed a shower.'

'I passed your photos on to the lab boys and once they stripped the hat and sunglasses off your target he bears a close likeness to Commissar Uri Bardosky, the KGB's European Controller. Now I suspect he is not there on holiday. Most KGB hierarchy tend to use the Black Sea resorts so what are he and Roland Canault up to? We have no record of his accomplices but suspect they are administrators rather than security staff.

'Interesting Hugh, I will see if I can find out more tomorrow at our tennis match.'

Chapter 16

Roland Canault waited nervously in the lounge of Commissar Uri Bardosky's suite in the Carlton Hotel while he assumed the great man was resting for half an hour after his long trip from Moscow. The truth of the matter was Uri Bardosky was using an old KGB tactic to make the interviewee feel uncomfortable and perhaps come up with additional information he would not normally reveal. He also used the time to go over his agenda for the meeting.

Uri only visited Valescure once a year to discuss how the KGB's clandestine operation in the South of France was performing and to discuss the strategy Moscow wanted implemented in the next twelve months. Roland was only too aware that Commissar Bardosky was there to mark his report card and if he got 'a Fail' he would find himself back in Russia doing some menial task. He was under the threat of losing his opulent lifestyle and may be faced with the choice of returning home or seeking political asylum in one of the NATO countries.

The double doors leading to the Commissar's bedroom opened and Uri strode out followed by a man and a young woman.

'Afternoon Roland' he said with a firm handshake 'let me introduce you to my personal assistants Elana Podescu and Gregori Rasputin. Elana will take the minutes and Gregori is here to witness our discussions and contribute advice should we need it. Come we'll sit down at the table over there and Elana will pour the coffee. How are Jana and the boys?'

'Very well sir. The boys are attending a finishing school in Switzerland.'

'Probably best if you start by giving us your assessment of how you are doing.' Suggested Uri
Roland opened his briefcase took out some papers which he placed on the table. After taking a sip of his coffee he commenced his summary.

'Our operation has been doing rather well this year. We have been able to increase our weapon sales to the usual suspects around Europe based both here in France but also the U.K., Germany and Spain. The sales in these countries are to terrorist organisations with grievances either against their own governments or in the case of the Muslims on religious grounds. The merchandise they require is very much at the lower end of the armament scale i.e. semi-automatic pistols, sub-machine guns and grenades. All this is conducted under the cover of our wine business which has also had an excellent year.
On a broader front the Arab nations, whether it is Hezbollah or the Arab Spring region, are always seeking heavier artillery, such as rocket launchers, mortar attack systems and drones both for surveillance or armed attack. We have used up most of the stock we flew out of Serbia into Russia so I need you to arrange to replenish our inventory. I have here a detailed list of requirements.'

Roland passed the list across the table to Uri who in turn gave it to Gregori to scrutinise.

'We are able to get the arms smuggled into countries, and I include France in my statement, by having them imported whilst hidden in the centre of containers carrying batches of fresh fruit and vegetables. If we are delivering to a client from here we shall transfer them into trucks full of wine cartons which are loaded carefully so the arms are in the middle surrounded by the boxes of wine.'

'Very clever Roland' complemented Gregori Rasputin, 'looking at your sales charts you should be very proud of your performance.'

'Thank you Gregori.' was Roland's satisfied reply.

Commissar Bardosky took the meeting to a new level 'Roland, how do you see the future and how can we continue to be a thorn in the side of the European Economic Community's larder?'

Roland hesitated before answering, 'I have given this some thought recently. We are in a far better position now than we were twenty years ago when the Cold War was in full swing and the West was wary of every move we made. Who would ever have thought that Russia would create a number of oligarchs by allowing individuals to buy up the nationalised industries of the Motherland and use the proceeds to live opulent lifestyles which are way beyond their wildest dreams? Many of them have invested in large companies on the stock exchanges around the world. Others are into property in a big way and a couple of them have bought into football clubs.'

'Yes there have been a lot of changes Roland, not all for the better but if we are being honest many of us have benefitted at the expense of the poor in Russia. Part of my remit while I am in the Cote d'Azur is to have meetings with oligarchs who have settled in Monaco where, of course, they lead a tax-free existence. For some of them it is pay-back time and our leader now wants his share of the spoils.'

'What if they don't see it that way Commissar Bardosky?'

'Then they won't sleep at night for fear of not waking up the next morning. My three security men outside the door are experts at persuasion and one of the little games they play amongst themselves is who can inflict death in the most painful manner. I don't think we shall have much resistance from the Oligarchs. Apologies Roland, we are deviating from the main event, please go on with your thoughts.'

'There have been a number of enquiries for more sophisticated weapons from the 'Arab Spring' countries who fear the threat of invasion from NATO and are desperate to install deterrents to prevent this happening. This would entail you having to smuggle effective defences into these countries but I am not technically qualified to say how we can achieve this. Commissar Bardosky, if you were successful in bringing their requests to fruition, it would go a long way towards improving Russian influence in the region and serve as a threat to Europe, which they do not encounter at present.'

Bardosky leaned back from the table to gather his thoughts 'I think what you are proposing has merit Roland but how we implement it may not be easy. Leave it with me and I will discuss it with the politburo when I return to Moscow. The only practical way I can think of is to transport missiles from northern Russia by sea through the Atlantic to North Africa. However transporting heavy weapons from there to face Europe is fraught with difficulties. I've taken a note. What else do you see happening in the region?'

'Certainly sir, Europe is a mixture of over twenty different cultures, with excellent economic performing multinational companies. What they did lack in the past was the labour to service them. At present they have a sufficient source of manpower from outwith Europe, but are wary about having any more as there has been quite a few instances of social unrest among the indigenous population who are looking for work. On a number of occasions terrorist activities have been Al Qaeda led and the authorities have been stretched to contain them.'

'Looking ahead, I'm talking twenty years ahead, I think we could upset their environment further by causing an immigrant invasion. Immigrants are desperate to come to Western Europe as they see that transition from life in the Middle East will provide a much higher standard of living. Equally those travelling from sub-Sahara Africa feel as though they have travelled through time. The Africans will bring, in most cases enlarged families who in the future, would provide the foot soldiers to be radicalised by the Muslim leaders. If we can adopt a policy of upsetting the European states then eventually this will lead to anarchy and reprisals based on revenge for their colonial past.'

'I must admit this is a very long-term strategy' judged Uri 'but a very interesting one nevertheless. I will give you a budget to finance the inflatables which will be used to transport the immigrants. All we have to control is to remain committed to protecting our own borders, and ruling with an iron fist, to make sure we do not end up with a deluge of immigrants ourselves.'

The talks continued for another couple of hours covering various aspects of how Roland Canault could continue to support the Russian cause from his base in Valescure.

As the meeting came to a close Roland issued an invitation to the visiting delegates 'This weekend I am hosting a tennis tournament at Chateau Rose Blanc to which you are all invited. It will give you an opportunity to mix with the Monaco jet set and get a feel for their lavish lifestyles which you will find to be quite an eye opener.'

Next day in the office Roland took cognizance of what Commissar Bardosky had said and called a staff meeting with D.A., Spy and Zorro.

'Commissar Bardosky was very pleased with our progress on the weapons front but as part of our long-term strategy he would like us to get more involved in people trafficking. It is an area I have never dealt in before but I would like you guys to source rubber dinghies and small boats suitable for transporting immigrants. The majority of the immigrants are coming into Europe from Libya and Tunisia so find out where they get the dinghies and what they cost. Bardosky is going to give us a budget to buy the merchandise. Our involvement will keep us on good terms with Libya and Tunisia who constantly ship bodies to Europe which Commissar Bardosky thinks will upset the European economies of the future.'

Next day the team reported back.

Spy had learned that the majority of dinghies are manufactured in Shandong province in China and shipped to Europe. They treat this activity as a normal commercial venture and their liability stops when the goods are delivered into port. D.A. followed the trading lines and was surprised to hear that Malta stored warehouses of dinghies. They moved them across the Mediterranean to Libya where the underworld were waiting to exploit the desperate people who had already travelled thousands of miles to find what they thought would be the promised land. D.A. had noted the name of the Maltese supplier who was part of the local mafia. Roland phoned him with a view to getting in touch with Libyan slave drivers.

Back in London MI6 were contemplating a strategy to interrupt the supply line of dinghy deliveries. One suggestion was to instigate a huge fire in the warehouses which were normally holding three months stock. The logistics of setting off an incendiary device was tricky as Malta is a Member of the Commonwealth and the European Union. Any evidence linking back to the United Kingdom could set off an international incident.

Richard Hartley took the decision that this strategy was not urgent and put all actions on the back burner for now, but wished to be notified of any future changes.

Chapter 17

Suitably dressed in their tennis gear, Roni and Cam turned up early at the tennis academy to knock a few balls out before the arrival of Milagro and Roland. Lydia preferred to relax at the hotel and join them later when the game would be in progress. Both players were happy with their preparation although the pair recognised their level of expertise would be way below that of their opponents.

Milagro arrived first after seeing to some admin in the office and five minutes later Roland strode in with his minders on either side of him.

'Good morning everyone, I hope you are all ready for our game today. What are the partnerships going to be?'

Milagro replied 'I thought we would start off with men versus women until someone wins ten games then split the pairings with Cam and I taking on you and Roni, Roland. If we still have time we can finish up Roni and Cam challenging you and me. Don't worry we'll give you a few games start to make it competitive!'

After a short warm up, Milagro took the first serve which she flashed across the net at Roland with such force that it caught him unawares and he hit it into the net, cursing something in Serbian as he did so. Cam noticed the change in his partner's temperament as Roland conveyed his aggressive nature which continued throughout the game as he openly blamed Cam for not returning forearm drives which he expected to go back over the net or stay in the court. The girls won the first game 10 – 7 and now it was up to Roni to bring some cheer in to Roland's life and she did not disappoint him. Over the last few days Roni's tennis had improved especially at the net where she was quick to intervene and even demonstrated the odd drop shot which frustrated the opposition. Cam tried to retaliate with some strong backhands which invariably turned out to be too long for the base line resulting in a 10 -5 victory for Roni and Roland.

Over refreshments Roland announced 'I am not used to losing two games in a row, so Milagro I do not want to see you showing any mercy to our visitors.'

'I always play to win but we shall give them seven games start so that we remain disciplined and concentrate on catching them up.'

Roland smiled 'Agreed. Now let's get stuck into them.'

Cam and Roni spent the next fifteen minutes flailing at shadows as the two opposite on the other side of the net hammered balls in their direction. With the score at 8 -7 for Milagro and Roland they did produce one scare when they got to deuce but were quickly disposed of by the home team who went on to win 10 - 7.

Lydia had arrived during the second match and joined the spectating bodyguards 'Good morning gentlemen, you like me, are here to see the big challenge match. That's my husband Graeme Doncaster partnering Roland. I'*m* Lydia Doncaster.' she said shaking hands with all the enemies 'Do you work with Roland?'

David Andelic responded' 'Yes we are all in business together looking after the wine company.'

'That must be fun if you attend all the wine festivals all over Europe!'

'No the boss does that. We're in involved in carrying out his commands.'

'What do you do yourself?'

'I work for the civil service in the Health Service but I am on holiday for two weeks so I have come down here for a break while my husband visits contacts in Monaco.'

David asked 'What sort of contacts?'

'Graeme and Roni are in finance - finding suitable homes for surplus cash which rich clients want to hide from the tax authorities.'

'Well you should find plenty of business down here.' The third game finished and the players joined the audience. Roland wiped the sweat off his brow and took a gulp of water before turning to the others.

'That was excellent. Milagro, you certainly kept me on my toes. By way of recompensing you for your losses everybody, I am staging a tennis tournament at my house this weekend and would be delighted if you would all come along. It is starting at noon and will finish when the last guest departs. For those who are not playing tennis there is a swimming pool, food and of course lakes of good wine.'

A beaming Cam replied on behalf of the others 'Thanks very much Roland for the invite, we'll look forward to what sounds like an excellent day.'

The group chatted for twenty minutes before Roland and his entourage left shortly afterwards as did Milagro leaving the British trio relaxing with a soft drink.

Cam spoke first 'Well done Roni, you must really have impressed Roland, as you did me, with your tennis performance for him to invite us over on Saturday.'

Roni looked across and smiled 'Yes I think he likes me and I think I could get on very well with him if the opportunity arises.'

Lydia had not been ready for Roni's suggestive comment 'How can you say that Roni, you hardly know him!'

'I am a bit more experienced in the carnal delights than you are Lydia. Roland was responding to my body movements during the game and displaying some of his own body language in return. I will go out of my way on Saturday to snare him – just watch me Lydia.'

'I'll look forward to observing how you get on but I will be surprised if you succeed!'

Cam intervened to calm the girls down 'If Roni can find a way to get under Roland's guard all to the good.

Lydia, I can assure you when it comes to seduction Roni is very good – it took me all my time to refuse her advances when we were in Edinburgh on a mission. Anyhow, after all that tennis I'm going back to the hotel to sit around the pool and decide what we should do tomorrow.'

It was decided after a poolside drink that they would go on an excursion to Monaco on Friday to let Roni see the outlay of the tax haven. Next morning dressed as tourists they got a taxi down to St. Raphael station and took the train into Monaco. Trains in the South of France are slow and it took ninety minutes to do the thirty-nine mile journey. After admiring a marina featuring millions of pounds worth of yachts tied up in the harbour, they moved round to see the Palais du Prince where the head of the Grimaldi family, Prince Albert, resides.

Cam insisted in touring the sports complex, which had been built on land reclaimed from the sea, featuring a football pitch on the fourth floor with an eight lane running track circulating it. Below the football pitch the trio passed an Olympic size swimming pool and an auditorium for major indoor sports such as basketball and boxing.

Roni was more interested on touring the corporate sector where all the financial wheeling and dealing took place. Outside a number of offices she took photographs of the names embossed on the brass plates listed on the entrance walls so she could identify the occupants later when she returned to her hotel and consulted her laptop. Next it was on to see the famous Monaco casino where fortunes had been won and lost over the years. The gaming halls were quiet in the afternoon apart from the humming of the slot machines.

On leaving the casino Roni spotted the equally famous Hotel de Paris and brought it to the attention of her companions 'What a lovely looking hotel. Do you think we should see if they do afternoon tea? I would like to see if there are any traders we could get to know.'

Lydia tried to put her off 'Roni we are not dressed in business garb and we would stand out a mile.'

'I disagree, my credit card is as good as the next person's as far as Hotel de Paris is concerned. Cam you have the casting vote.'

Cam had no hesitation 'I'm with Roni. We might as well see what the clientele look like and who knows we may meet some of them tomorrow at the tennis tournament.'

The Hotel entrance was very grand with high ceilings supported by pillars and bedecked with ornate golden crown mouldings. They strode in very confidently as though they frequented such establishments daily and entered a huge lounge, which was heavily populated. A waiter in a black dinner suit escorted them to one of the last available tables. For the next few minutes they scoured not only the menu but also all their fellow diners.

'It looks good to me. I will have a pot of Earl Grey tea. How about you?' asked Cam

'Cappuccino for me.' stated Lydia

'I'll settle for a cafetiere of black coffee.' confirmed Roni before adding 'what a beautiful room, the large paintings, expensive wall-coverings and furnishings, they must have cost a fortune.'

'Judging by the menu prices and the sartorial elegance of the diners they can afford it.' commented Cam 'I would love to know what they are all discussing. Take these four guys over there hunched over some papers on their table. What grandiose scheme are they concocting?'

'Well one way you can find out is to wait until someone in this room goes to the toilet and follow them, then start a conversation as you are washing your hands. You will be amazed how often people relax and talk freely to you.'

Cam laughed 'I'll leave that theory to you Roni – but please don't try to prove it by going into the gents!'

The afternoon tea was delicious featuring a good selection of French patisseries as expected and it was now time to get the train back to Valescure. The trio found some relaxation before heading out at night to 'The Le Fig' restaurant for their evening meal which was within walking distance from the hotel. Planning ahead Cam phoned taxi driver Yves Lampard, to arrange their lift to Chateau Rose Blanc for the start of the tennis tournament.

Over dinner Cam spoke mostly to Lydia briefing her to circulate extensively while Roni and he were competing on the courts and building up a dossier of Roland Canault's friends, with special attention to those men who were wearing Arab costumes. He and Roni would try to get close to their opponents over a drink at the end of each session and by the end of the day they may have a clearer picture of those who dealt in wine and those more interested in obtaining weapons.

Chapter 18

As requested Yves Lampard turned up on time and reacted when he heard his destination 'Chateau Rose Blanc! Oh Monsieur Davenport you are mixing with the elite today. I have taken guests there in the past and it is a beautiful location – would I be right in saying you are going there to play tennis?'

'Yes Yves, if you can call my flailing about tennis, but Miss Benson here will make up for me.'

Roni was embarrassed but managed to utter 'Let's hope so.'

It was only a short ten minute drive to Chateau Rose Blanc before Yves guided the Peugeot through the electric wrought iron gates leading to the long driveway up to the big house. Yves brought the car to a halt at the door, got out and opened the boot to retrieve his passengers' luggage which consisted of three sports bags. A slender black haired lady wearing a green silk jump suit which emphasised her body shape came to greet them.

'Bonjour and welcome, I am Gigi Montalban and Roland has asked me and my friend Michelle Dupree to be his greeters for the day.'

'Pleased to meet you' replied Cam 'I'm Graeme Davenport, this is my wife Lydia and my business colleague Roni Benson.'

Everyone shook hands then Gigi announced 'Follow me and I will take you through to the tennis courts and get you your first drink and thereafter call the waiters.' As they got nearer the house, they could hear a jazz band playing soft music on the main lawn near the swimming pool where some of the guests were enjoying themselves. Following on from there, Gigi directed them behind a large privet hedge and they started to hear the thud of tennis balls being exchanged rapidly from across the courts. The two hard-courts were in full swing with a ladies singles on one and a mixed doubles on the other watched by a crowd of fifty spectators, all sitting sunning themselves under parasols with drinks in their hands. Milagro saw the newcomers and waved to them to join her.

'Nice to see you all, this is my partner Robert Fouche who will be playing with me in the mixed doubles. Let me explain how the tournament works. There are thirty-two players in the singles and sixteen partnerships in the doubles. All the games are decided by the first players winning ten games. Sets would take too long. Players are seeded with the less able contestants getting a few games start. Here is the programme for today and I would suggest you seek out your doubles partners and introduce yourself.'

'Highly efficient programme' commented Roni 'is this all your work Milagro?'

'Good Heavens no, Roland is a control freak when it comes to his tennis tournaments. The nearest anyone gets to organising the tennis is making sure the courtside fridges are packed with new balls!'

The others laughed but curtailed their guffaws on seeing Roland approaching.

'Hello everyone, I know you are going to have a super time at Chateau Rose Blanc. Roni, I hope you are in good form as I have picked you to be my partner in the mixed doubles and I will be disappointed if we don't win.'

Far from being embarrassed Roni rose to Roland's challenge 'Roland, I don't do 'Lose' so it will not be my fault if we don't win, but if we are victorious you will be in for a good night.'

'Well that's the response I was looking for and I do like having fun. I must see to the other guests, see you later.'

Cam took Roni to one side. 'Well you laid out your stall there Roni. Roland will be unstoppable at the thought of spending time with you.'

The atmosphere round the tennis courts was very entertaining as each group at a table shouted encouragement to their friends and jovially mocked them when things went wrong. Cam was first to go on court against an older gentlemen, who on appearances looked as though his spindly legs would not get him through one game never mind ten! That was until he got a tennis racket in his hand. What he lacked in mobility he made up for in positional play and it did not take long to banish Cam back to the sidelines.

'That is embarrassing,' sulked a despondent Cam as he slumped down into his seat 'I mean look at him, he is old enough to be my dad!'

'Yes' chided Milagro 'but was your dad good enough to win the 1970 Cote d'Azur Men's Singles Tennis Championship?'

'No but he would have beaten him at darts!'

The others laughed at Cam's poor analogy but were interrupted when the announcer informed everyone 'The next match on Court 1 would feature our host and his British partner Roni Benson versus Marie St. Clare and Bernard Dubussion.'

Benson and Canault proved too good for the opposition and were quickly through to the next round. During the game on every point won Roni was conscious of Roland's congratulatory close contact touches which she encouraged, climaxing in the two embracing each other tightly after winning the final point.

Leaving the court he whispered 'That was excellent Roni. Allow me later to take you round the Chateau. I promise you will not be disappointed.' he smirked.

'And neither will you be Roland' answered Roni.

Chapter 19

After an hour Lydia became bored with the tennis and wandered back to the swimming pool area. She was standing watching guests frolicking about in the pool and was unaware of a tall figure creeping up on her.

'Mrs Davenport. I'm Spiridon Natalic, I saw you at Valescure Tennis Academy two days ago. How are you today?'
Lydia turned round quickly to face the handsome bodyguard who was wearing light-blue shorts with a red and white striped t-shirt.

'Are you going in for a swim?' he asked 'the water is not cold'

'I might, I have brought my bikini but I notice some of the women are topless.'

'In this part of the world that is not unusual. Would you like to join me in a drink?'

'Yes my husband is involved in the tennis but I don't play to tournament standard.'
The pair found seats nearby and Spiridon caught the attention of a waiter and ordered two glasses of champagne.

Lydia began her interrogation 'Spiridon.'

The Serbian smiled 'My friends call me Spy but I can assure my nickname does not match my occupation.'

Lydia went back to her original question 'Do you work for Mr Canault?'

'Yes we have a wholesale wine company. I split my time between arranging for the distribution of the wine and being in charge of the security.'

'Were you acting as a security guard at the tennis club?'

'Yes. I am one of three security guards who protect Mr Canault.'

'Oh, how exciting I have never met a bodyguard before! What sort of training do you need and do you live like James Bond flashing all sorts of gadgets and have beautiful women on your arm at all times!'

'Mrs Davenport, most of the time it is not exciting at all standing about waiting for your boss to finish his meeting. There are no college courses for being a bodyguard - it is something you aspire to. In my case I sought a military career but when the Serbian War finished Mr Canault gave me an opportunity to follow him here to the South of France.'

Lydia kept up the excited tone in her voice 'Spy call me Lydia. Do most wealthy businessmen down here in the Cote D'Azur employ bodyguards?'

'Look around you Lydia. See how many men here not dressed for tennis are standing about or sitting having a soft drink next to an open sports bag which I could almost guarantee you, holds their automatic pistol.'

'Really! I am getting my eyes opened today! I can't wait to tell Graeme what an exciting time I have had today. Have you ever had to use a gun?'

'Well I have told you all you need to know about my career, what do you do for a living?'

'Lead a boring life compared with you Spy. I am a civil servant and work for the Ministry of Health in the Senior Citizens Department just outside London in Basingstoke. We make sure everyone receives their entitlement and remove them from the lists when they pass away. I am a personal assistant to one of the senior managers which makes it a little more interesting. Changing the subject does Roland have a lot of tennis gatherings here at the Chateau?'

'Yes probably about three times a year. The tennis is his thing but the fun really starts after the tennis finishes and everyone launches into the free drink and disco music.'

'I look forward to that. I'm starting to feel a bit hot so I think I will go and put my bikini on, where are the changing rooms?'

'I will show you where to go and get changed and may even join you.'

'That sounds good Spy. I think this champagne is working, I will be back in a minute.'

Lydia made a brief return to Cam and Roni and picked up her sports bag after informing them of her exploits with Roland's bodyguard. Cam issued a cautionary note, 'Be careful Lydia the sharks in the pool are red-blooded and dangerous!'

Lydia stood at the edge of the pool in a white towelling dressing gown which she removed slowly to reveal a red polka-dot bikini which displayed her well proportioned figure. Spy, who was watching nearby, sneaked in behind Lydia, picked her up and despite her shrieking protests jumped into the pool with her.

Lydia emerged coughing and holding on to Spy tightly to avoid a further ducking 'You bastard Spy!' I did not see that coming. I'll get you back for that' she said as she tried to get near his well honed physique.

Spy held her off then brought her back in close to his body only this time she did not struggle but clung onto his shoulders. Spy toured Lydia's body while she reciprocated by rubbing her hand down the inside of his Speedo trunks. The other swimmers were too engaged in their own activities to take notice of the couple but Lydia became conscious of her actions and broke away.

'Stop Spy, it must be the champagne that's affecting me. I must go and find out how Graeme is getting on.'

Spy smiled 'If you change your mind you know where to find the chemistry that appears to be missing in your marriage.'

Lydia changed quickly and by the time she got back there had been mixed results in the tennis. Roni had been eliminated from the singles by a German billionaire's daughter who was about to join the international tennis circuit. However better news was to come for Roni who was back on court and about to be victorious in her mixed doubles semi-final with partner Roland Canault.

Cam welcomed back his colleague 'Hi Lydia, you've been away for a while, anything interesting to report?'

'Yes I've been having a drink and a swim with Spiridon Natalic.'

'A swim? Tell me more.'

'Cam if you were not here as my 'husband' I could have been whisked upstairs to one of the boudoirs by a handsome bodyguard. It's amazing what a couple of flutes of Bollinger will do for a girl's libido. I had changed into my bikini and didn't see Spy coming from behind, he picked me up and we both landed in the pool. When I surfaced I clung briefly to him then I remembered that I was a married woman.' Lydia laughed.

Just then a great shout of appreciation rang out signifying that the host and his partner were through to the final of the mixed and were shaking hands before leaving the court. Seconds later they approached their friends table.

Cam jumped up and kissed Roni on both cheeks and shook hands with Roland 'Fantastic Roni! Well done and all the best for the final.'

Roland spoke up 'On that form we showed in the semi-final I'm confident on beating anyone in the final which will take place in an hour or so. In the meantime I have to go up to the Chateau – will you join me Roni?'

Roni glanced at Cam and Lydia for guidance then answered 'Yes I would enjoy seeing your place.'

At that the tennis stars left and as he watched them go Cam turned to Lydia 'I told you not to underestimate Roni when it comes to men.'

Roni walked alongside Roland as they reached the entrance of the Chateau Rose Blanc where a waiter, wearing a white shirt and bow tie, under his beige jacket, stood handing out drinks. Their entrance was also recorded by Jani, Roland's wife, who looked away briefly from the young man who had been soliciting her for the past hour. She thought to herself 'Same old Roland, get the female up the stairs and try his luck.'

The pair stopped at the drinks stall 'Two soda and lime Angel, Miss Benson and I are through to the mixed final so no alcohol.'

The entrance hall was dominated by a huge staircase and beyond that a passageway with rooms leading off.

Roni moved around in a circle taking in all the pictures on the walls and the soft furnishings hanging beside the windows. Roland gave Roni a brief tour of the public rooms which brought them back to the foot of the stairs.

Looking upwards Roland announced 'I think I will go up and get a fresh t-shirt for the final.'

Roni smiled 'Lucky you, this is all I have with me.'

'Come on Roni let me see if I can find you something to wear.'

At the top of the stairs the couple took a right turn into what was a suite rather than a bedroom. A marble fireplace with two armchairs and a sofa in front of it overlooked by a four-poster bed with a door leading off to a large bathroom. Roland went into a dressing room just off the bedroom and picked out two t-shirts.

'Here try this for size' he suggested removing his sweaty garment as he said so.

Roni knew this was her chance and removed her top as she was facing Roland who been admiring her figure before moving closer. He kissed her gently on the cheek and she reacted by opening her mouth, feeling his exploring tongue. Quick embraces continued as she dug into his skin while he removed her shorts and pants and directed her over to a deep piled carpet in front of the fire. As he did so Roni opened the zip of his shorts and stroked his manhood. She lay back on the carpet as Roland whipped off his shorts to fully expose his erection which Roni quickly grabbed and plunged as much of it as she could into her body. She wrapped her legs round Roland's body and dug her nails into his buttocks. The next ten minutes, full of passion passed quickly, until they both reached a climax.

Roland rolled off Roni exhausted, trying to get a breath 'That was great Roni but a bit too quick.'

Roni ran her hand up his muscular thigh 'Yes it was. I think you would enjoy my full repartee!'

Roland kissed her on the cheek 'John F. Kennedy said 'The best way to relax before making a major speech was to have sex.' On that basis we should win the mixed doubles final with a bit to spare after what I have just enjoyed.'

Chapter 20

Roland eyed the young man on the other side of the net before unleashing his serve, an ace down the centre line. He had laid out his side's stall and this seemed to upset the opposition who found they couldn't cope with Roni's quick interventions at the net. The result was they won in straight sets 6-2 6-2 in under one hour.

After receiving all the congratulations from everyone round the court it was time for the prize-giving ceremony which Jani Canault carried out. Shaking Roni's hand she kissed her on the cheek and whispered 'Nice t-shirt I suspect Roland gave you that and a lot more upstairs!'

Roni's felt her face reddening but Roland helped her out by stepping in and kissing his wife while Spy simultaneously popped a bottle of Bollinger to fill the cup. The tennis crowd made their way towards the pool area where there was a barbecue serving food. The jazz quartet were packing up their instruments and making way for the discotheque which began setting up their lighting and audio systems. Now all attendees mingled together and the networking began.

The MI6 trio spread themselves out to take in as broad a gamut of the guests as possible to increase their intelligence banks which they would compare notes on later. Cam managed to get into a conversation with Uri Bardosky who was holding court in the company of two beautiful German women who appeared to be ignoring their escorts in favour of the Russian. Uri's three minders stood guard a few yards away.'

Cam asked innocently 'What brings you to the South of France Commissar Bardosky?'

'I am on holiday and needing a rest from Vladimir Putin!' he laughed 'it has been a busy year for diplomats who have been straining to keep up with the government changes brought about by the Arab Spring.'

'Do you see trade advantages for Russia along the North Africa Coastline? ' Davenport asked.

'Yes Graeme, these countries have been torn apart by the aggression they have experienced, and will require to be re-built which Russia will be only too happy to assist.'

Cam pushed Bardosky further 'Do you think they will require any military help?'

Bardosky looked at Cam quizzically 'That would be for each individual government to decide.'

Cam backed off at this point. He sensed the Commissar did not like his line of questioning and Bardosky's unease was filtering through to his bodyguards who were taking a closer interest in the inquisitive Englishman who announced 'I better go and see where my wife is.'

Roni had become a sporting personality after her success in the doubles and she was feted by all and sundry, thanks to Milagro. The tennis coach knew anyone who was anybody and when they approached she introduced them to Roni. The admirers ranged from sporting personalities to wealthy businessmen who were keen to know more about the tennis star. Roni took advantage of the situation to make notes on the guests, promising to make contact with the ones she thought would be useful to her MI6 assignment.

Lydia concentrated her networking on the younger element and as the night progressed she was seen enjoying herself on the dance floor with several different partners. Roland spent his time setting up meetings with different contacts as he balanced his business enquiries between arms dealing and fine wine supplying.

The tennis tournament was soon forgotten and the party atmosphere continued for several hours with alcohol taking its effect resulting in guests ending up in the pool, some of them having abandoned all clothing.

Roni asked Milagro 'Is it always like this?'

Milagro surveyed the scene before replying 'Yes everyone tries to outdo each other in the hedonist stakes and the men usually end up sending bouquets of flowers the next day to the women they had offended. The women who have over dallied with the males are not seen in town for a few days!'

'I suppose it all comes down to too much disposable income.' Roni observed.

Milagro smiled 'Yes it does, but long may it continue as it keeps me living comfortably.'

Roni paid particular attention to Jani and Roland who were touring the guest tables making sure everyone was having a good time and appearing to be the perfect hosts. It was only when Roland left Jani's side for a moment to go into the Chateau that he stopped briefly to talk to Roni.

'Thank you for giving me an excellent day Roni, which I would like to do again before you return to England. In two days time Jani is going to Switzerland to visit the boys, so I will be at a loose end so why don't we get together for a knock?'

Roni was a little surprised by Roland's forward approach but had no hesitation in taking up his offer 'Yes I would like that Roland who will make up the four?'

Roland smiled 'This match will only be between you and me!'

Chapter 21

'Morning Roni, I had a quick word with Lydia before I came down for breakfast and suggested we get our heads together and talk about everyone we networked with last night.'

Roni replied 'I had my mobile attached to my belt all last night and managed to record all my contacts as I met them so I'll go back to the room and get my phone.'

Cam settled down to an excellent continental breakfast and thought out his strategy regarding the potential intelligence he was about to discuss and how he could make the most of the data. Roni's contribution will be interesting as Cam was aware that she had gone up to the chateau with Roland Canault and had returned wearing a different t-shirt.

Knowing Roni as he did he would not be surprised if there had been a short carnal exchange. Lydia was different. She had kept her tabs on the younger attendees by engaging them on the dance-floor of the disco and joining in their drinking sessions which accounted for her fragile state of mind this morning.

After everyone had seen to their culinary needs the trio found a quiet spot in the corner of the terrace and began the debrief. Cam set out the agenda outlining that he felt the trio had to spend more time in Monaco talking to the contacts they had made last night 'I had a brief encounter with Commissar Bardosky which made me even more suspicious of the Russian who has, in my opinion, come to the South of France to arrange some sizeable transactions which I would imagine on behalf of the Arab League countries.'

'Another interesting character I had a conversation with was the young Saudi, Sheik Abdul al Mushasa who is known to MI6 as being responsible for funding terrorists in different parts of the world. He is someone who would definitely make use of Roland Canault's services and make payments discreetly through Monaco's banks.'

Roni butted in 'Yes, we need to get into Monaco and find out more about the workings of the banks. I have an invitation from Giles Normand of Verte Banque who is involved in supplying funding for green projects such as wind farms etc. but I suspect there is more to it. I mentioned Farrer Finance's role in the financial services jungle and that's when he invited me to his office.'

'Good work Roni when do you think we can go and see him?'

'Not today obviously as it is Sunday and tomorrow I have been invited back to Chateau Rose Blanc for a match with Roland.'

'Nice one Roni!' exclaimed Lydia 'Are we all going?'

'No it's a private game' she replied struggling to conceal a smile.

Her colleagues reacted immediately 'You conniving devil, you've got Canault eating out of your hand already.'

Cam continued his attempt to embarrass Roni 'I noticed you returned from the chateau wearing a different but dry T-shirt as did your new friend Roland. As I said to you yesterday Lydia, Miss Benson here is not slow at coming forward.'

Roni protested her innocence 'Cam our orders from Assistant Controller Hartley was to get close to the enemy and as you know I always obey orders!'

'So why has he invited just you to Chateau Rose Blanc?' asked Lydia.

'Well it may be something to do with the fact that his wife is going off tomorrow to visit their two sons in Switzerland.' answered Roni brazenly.

'Hopefully this will not be your last trip to the chateau. If you can gain Roland's confidence, he might reveal how the different aspects of Canault's business empire operates. I have a plan I would like to put into operation but I will have to contact Hugh McFaul before we can take it any further.'

'Lydia what progress did you make with the guests last night?'

'Cam I was a little over the top last night and I'm suffering for it this morning. I did in my own way achieve some useful surveillance as I spent a lot of the time with Roland's security men and learned a lot about their history and their daily routines. They have all adjusted to life in the South of France which is worlds apart from Serbia or Russia where they were latterly. Spy told me that Roland is a very nervous individual and he was quaking at the thought of a visit from Commissar Bardosky who has a reputation for making non-performers disappear.'

'Did he say how the visit went?' interrupted Roni.

'Yes Bardosky is pleased with Canault's performance but wants to expand the Russian influence in the region which he can achieve by being closer to Sheik Abdul al Mashasa – his name is a bit of a mouthful so why don't we precis it to 'Sam,' '

The other two nodded their approval.

'Okay it's Sunday so why don't we have a day out. I will call Yves Lampard and see if he can take us somewhere interesting. I suggest if we meet in the foyer in half an hour we can begin our Magical Mystery Tour of the area. '

Yves was still in his bed when Cam called after a late night in the taxi 'Morning Yves, Campbell Anderson here. Is your taxi for hire today? We thought we might take a trip out to St. Tropez today.'

Lampard rubbed his unshaven chin before answering as he wasn't really wanting, to spend Sunday, his normal day off, stuck in the Riviera traffic jams. 'St. Tropez?' he questioned 'If I can make a suggestion Monsieur Anderson, the best way to get to St. Tropez is by ferry. The ferry leaves from St. Raphael and sails to St. Tropez in just under an hour whereas it could take you two hours plus by car. I'll take you down to St. Raphael and if you phone me when you are on the return ferry I will pick you up when you come off the boat.'

'That sounds perfect Yves. Can you come and pick us up in half an hour?'

'But of course!' agreed the taxi driver 'See you soon.'

Cam wasted no time in informing his colleagues who were preparing themselves for their day out. 'I have spoken to Yves and he will be here in half an hour to take us to St. Tropez.'

'St. Tropez!!' they both shrieked before Lydia added 'We're right in with the jet set now!'

Cam raised his hands in a calming motion 'Can I suggest you pack a bag with your swimming costumes, hats and suntan lotion in it as we are going there by boat.'

'How wonderful Cam, you'd make a good tour rep.' complemented Roni.

'It was Yves idea and if I say so, a bloody good one.'

True to his word Yves arrived thirty minutes later and took his passengers the three miles down to St. Raphael where they boarded a sleek modern ferry for the one hour journey to St. Tropez.

Their two hundred plus fellow passengers were mostly holidaymakers heading for the town made famous by Brigitte Bardot in the sixties. It had maintained its place amongst the high rollers domiciled in the South of France. Everyone disembarked when the boat docked alongside Quai Jean Jaune and all dispersed in different directions. Some of the passengers headed for the beaches while others settled for doing some people watching by sitting in one of the expensive cafes on the quayside opposite the hugely impressive yachts in the harbour.

'Well here we are in one of the world's most expensive holiday towns so what do you suggest we do ladies?' asked Cam.

Lydia summarised the options 'We are only here for six or eight hours so let's divide our time equally. Before the sun gets too hot I suggest we walk along the front to a beach where we can relax and have a swim. If we feel we have to cool off later we could go into the backstreets where there are places of historical interest including a naval museum. In between times we can enjoy a good lunch.' turning to face Cam she enquired 'has our tour rep managed to book lunch?'

Cam surprised them both by replying 'Yes as a matter of fact I have. I was going to go to Auberge de Maures the best restaurant in St. Tropez but it only opens in the evenings so we are going to Café Sud which is recommended in my guide book.'

'Glad to see you're keeping up your standards as a holiday rep Cam,' congratulated Roni.

The day went to plan - they had topped up their suntans and enjoyed a long lazy lunch outdoors under a canopy in the courtyard of Café Sud. After lunch they disappeared into the quiet and welcoming shaded backstreets of the town. The modern art museum proved to be of more interest to Roni and Lydia. The navel museum caught Cam's attention as his grandfather had been a tank commander in the

Operation Dragoon allied landings in Southern France during World War II. Leaving the cultural centres they emerged out into the main square of St. Tropez when Roni suddenly stopped in her tracks.

'That's interesting' she observed 'if you look across the square there is a large gathering sitting round two tables that have been pulled together. Commissar Bardosky and his entourage are sharing their space with one of the bankers I met last night, Giles Normand of Verte Banque, as though they were long lost friends. Last night, I do not recall them going anywhere near each other. This makes me think that this is the real reason for Bardosky's visit to France if I am not mistaken he is negotiating to move funds to be transferred to Monaco possibly to be distributed for some dubious purpose. Verte Banque operates on a policy of only being interested in funding ecological projects aimed at saving the planet so could it be the perfect cover for a Russian undercover arms aid project for dissidents to utilise in Western Europe terrorist attacks?'

'How can you possibly prove such an obscure theory Roni?' asked Lydia.

'Proving it may be difficult but eliminating it from our investigations may not be. There are two areas I can seek out, one during my close encounter with Roland Canault and the other taking up Giles Normand's invitation of a visit to Verte Banque. If Monsieur Normand is open to illegal transactions then he could be the passport Farrer Financial Services have been looking for to open up opportunities in Monaco. A telephone call first thing tomorrow morning inviting myself to take up his offer will be our starting point.'

'Great thinking Roni, I'm sure Richard Hartley will be proud of you. We should be making our way back to the ferry, the last thing we want is to miss it and have to spend the night here.'

'How do you think Bardosky will get back to Monaco Cam?'

'Probably on board one of those luxury yachts, or if he is in a hurry hitch a lift on Canault's helicopter!' suggested Lydia.

Chapter 22

Yves Lampard picked up the returning party as promised and whisked them back to their hotel. It had been a long sweaty day Roni and Lydia were in need of a shower and a lie down. Cam said he would get a beer on the terrace and read the Sunday Times which had just been delivered so he could catch up with events back home.

Five minutes later having assured himself that the ladies were resting he phoned Commander Hugh McFaul 'Afternoon Hugh, sorry to disturb you on a Sunday afternoon.'

'Good to hear from you. Amy and I are sitting in the sunshine enjoying the afternoon barbecuing our evening meal in the company of two bottles of the finest South African Beaujolais. What can I do for you?'

'Nothing serious to worry about, everything is going quite well here. Yesterday we were at Roland Canault's Tennis Tournament where Roni won the mixed doubles with the host after, I suspect, having had a brief liaison with him prior to the final.'

Hugh laughed out loud 'You've got to admire her Cam - she never misses an opportunity to have a bit of 'La Dolce Vita!' Sorry I interrupted, carry on.'

'Today we made a trip across to St. Tropez by boat and just as we were getting ready to leave Roni spotted Commissar Bardosky having a close conversat - ion with Giles Normand of Verte Banque. They were both at Roland's tennis tournament on Saturday but seemed to ignore each other. Roni thinks Verte Banque could be the Commissar's reason for being down here. She has an invitation from Normand to visit his bank and is hoping to arrange her visit in a couple of days time.'

'I was thinking it could be an opportunity for us to place listening devices into both Verte Banque and Chateau Rose Blanc. I know that our laboratories were working on a new range of undetectable devices – have they been approved yet?'

'I'm not sure they have but I will make a call to the boffins and find out' assured Hugh.

'If the answer is yes Hugh, can you get some sent over to me tomorrow in time for Roni to plant them during her visits?'

'Cam I'll make a phone call now and get back to you later tonight.'

Four hours later Cam's mobile rang as he was sitting at dinner with his colleagues. He looked at the mobile's screen then apologised 'Excuse me I have to take this call, it's my mother. Moving out of earshot he spoke into the phone 'Sorry about the pause Hugh, I was at dinner with the girls with whom I have not yet discussed our plan. How did you get on with the lab boys?'

'Good News Cam. All the tests on these devices which are the size of a pin head have been passed positive so I have arranged for them to be sent in a diplomatic courier bag to you overnight so they should be with you in time for Roni's proposed visits.'

'Excellent Hugh I'll confirm their arrival tomorrow, apologies to Amy for ruining your afternoon.'

'No problem' replied McFaul 'it gave her time to read some of her British Medical Journals. Bye for now, speak to you tomorrow.'

Cam returned to the table with a spring in his step – now all he had to do was convince Roni to go along with his tactics.

'Everything okay at home Cam?' Lydia asked.

'Yes couldn't be better she's improving with the help of modern technology all the time.'

'What's been her problem?'

'Communicating with the outside world!' a smiling Cam answered.

After dinner they retired to a quiet corner of the bar well away from a party of holiday revellers gyrating to piped disco music.

'What's the plan for tomorrow Cam?'

'You and I will go to Cannes and see if we can meet up with Georges Du Pont who runs a car hire company. I had a long chat with him and he seemed like a useful contact as he supplies limousines to most of the dignitaries who fly into Nice including Sheik Mushasa. Roni, you will have to phone Giles Normand for an appointment at Verde Banque before you go off for you match with Roland Canault. What time is he picking you up?'

'He's sending a car for me at one o'clock.'

'Good that should be late enough for me to supply you with something for him. My call at dinner was actually from Hugh McFaul who sends his regards by the way, confirming that we shall receive a batch of the latest listening devices tomorrow morning. Roni I would like if you get the opportunity, to place them if possible in Roland Canault's office. This will be a risky exercise as Canault has very good security systems but I am assured by the boffins that their latest invention is undetectable by the current warning systems.'

'Are you positive metal detectors will not pick them up?'

'Yes I'm told they are only the size of pinheads and are made of minutely thin layers of silicon.'

'Do you know where his office is situated in relation to the lay-out of the Chateau?'

Cam replied confidently 'Yes he has converted the stables into offices and from there he runs both the wine and arms dealing. If you are successful it would mean we have penetrated his operation and will be party to all his transactions. Not only would we be able to get the names of his contacts it would allow us to know when and where weapons were being delivered for planned terrorist atrocities. If you can pull this off Roni your street credit within MI6 will be sky high and could result in personal benefits to you, and your contribution could well be recognised by Richard Hartley.'

Roni understood what Cam meant and she was determined to return to London with a successful result which could reduce her prison sentence dramatically and edge her nearer to freedom. 'I'll take up the challenge. If Roland reacts as I think he will to my advances, he will show me everything he's got!' she laughed.

Chapter 23

At 9.30 next morning a delivery man arrived at the reception of The Esterel Hotel and asked for Mr Anderson.

'Who shall I say is calling?'

'Monsieur Preston from Marseilles.'

Cam picked up the message and bounded down to reception where Mr Preston was waiting for him.

Preston shook hands and handed over the small parcel 'Mr Anderson I was told to tell you that all the instructions are inside the box.'

'Thank you very much for handing these in. I'll take the parcel up to my room and read the guidelines. Have a safe journey back to Marseilles.'

At that Preston tipped his cap and left to start the ninety mile journey back to Marseilles.

Cam returned to his room and opened the parcel which contained a dozen electronic listening units all carefully placed in separate plastic compartments in the shape of lipstick tubes, with activator switches for company. The boffins at MI6 had provided an idiot's guide for the surveillance equipment which Cam read extensively before calling the girls to make their way to his room.

Roni made her call to Verte Banque and was given a good reception from Giles Normand who said he would be delighted to meet her and Graeme Davenport. Furthermore he suggested that her visit included an invitation to lunch which she delighted in accepting.

Lydia was first to arrive at Cam's room having been down at the hotel store replenishing her suntan lotion and Roni followed her a couple of minutes later.

Cam seated them on his bed and produced the brown box containing the technology 'I'm glad to say that our little box of tricks has arrived safe and well.'

The two women watched as Cam opened the lid of the container and laid its inner contents, cocooned in bubble wrap, on the bed. Cam picked up one of the boxes and handed it to Roni.

'This is what I want you to place in Roland's office at the chateau if you get the opportunity. As you see they are transparent and adhesive so will blend in with the surface you attach them to. Do not place them on any surface that is moveable such as a plant pot. Rather go for the rear leg of a piece of furniture that is out of sight. Once you have placed the listener you can activate it by pressing the 'On' button. This can be done from some distance so I suggest you make an excuse to visit the toilet and activate it from there. If you have time between your romantic engagements with Canault put additional devices into operation if the opportunity presents itself.'

'I'll try my best. If that's everything I better go and get ready, Roland's driver will be here in an hour.'

'If you are successful with your assignment, we will consider repeating it at Verte Banque when we meet Giles Normand. Good luck.'

Chapter 24

Roland Canault had been at his desk since 6.00 a.m. attending to all the wine deliveries and taking armament orders from German based customers. He was looking forward to his afternoon with Roni Benson. He had enjoyed the brief encounter with her prior to the mixed doubles final, which seemed to fire up both of them and inspired them to victory. Roni was more mature than some of the women he had seduced in recent years but her body was still toned and she certainly knew how to excite men.

His wife was away to visit his sons in Switzerland leaving her husband to philander with whoever he chose in the full knowledge that he would be at home when she returned. His bodyguards were familiar with his loose behaviour so Roland did not have to be coy in front of them.

David Andelic was given the task of picking up Roni but before he left Roland had a chat with him, 'David I am always cautious of making advances to a lady I know very little about. When you get to the hotel ask at reception what room Miss Benson is occupying. Bring Roni here, then return to the hotel on the pretence that she has left something in the room and when you get the key, search it for anything suspicious.'

The metallic blue Mercedes Sports Convertible arrived, with the roof down and an excited Roni Benson ran down the steps of the Hotel and jumped into the passenger seat. David put her sports bag in the boot before pressing the accelerator hard and the car shot away in a cloud of dust. For the next twenty minutes David's driving skills round hairpin bends with sheer drops down to the sea hundreds of feet below made Roni feel like Grace Kelly in the Hitchcock film 'To Catch a Thief'.

Roland heard the car approaching and went out to welcome Roni 'Good Journey?' he asked.

'Exciting to say the least' replied Roni 'not the best preparation for our tennis match.'

'Come into the house we'll go out on the terrace and relax with a drink.'

Roland led the way out on to the terrace which overlooked the tennis courts which had manicured lawns on either side. One of the chateau staff appeared without being summoned and took the drinks order - fresh orange with ice all round.

'What a gorgeous setting Roland, it really is magnificent.'

'Do you have a garden in London Roni?'

Roni hadn't expected the question but managed to produce the first lie of the day 'No I live in an apartment twenty miles outside London in a village called Godalming. Have you been to London Roland?'

'No I have only been in France after coming from Serbia via Russia. From what I am led to believe only the very rich Russians get to settle in London.'

Roni laughed, 'Well Roland, I never read about any poor ones in the newspapers. Can we get on court soon – if you can provide me with a tennis racket?'

'No problem my dear, I noticed when we played in Valescure you had a Wilson racket so I sent Spy down to the sports shop to buy one for you. I keep all the tennis equipment in the stables next to my office. Bring your bag and follow me and I will get you kitted out.'

The couple moved off in the direction of the stables where Roni changed her shoes and picked up the tennis racket before entering the tennis court to begin their warm-up. Roland's natural competitive spirit was in evidence as he made Roni run about the playing surface chasing his returns as he fired shots across the net. As their duel progressed Roland relaxed the power on his strokes which allowed Roni to get into a rhythm and make Roland run for the corners of the court. The game lasted just over an hour when Roni raised her racket to acknowledge surrender. The players came to the net and instead of the usual handshakes Roland leaped over the net and took Roni in his arms and kissed her passionately several times.

The love juices were now in full prominence and Roland guided Roni back into the stables where there were further passionate exchanges accompanied by the removal of each other's clothes. Lying on her back as Roland engulfed her, Roni spotted the CCTV camera and brought proceedings to a sudden halt.

'Roland! Go and turn off the CCTV system, I am not in the habit of performing for the masses!' before thinking to herself 'or let anyone witness me planting the listening equipment.'

An embarrassed Roland replied 'Apologies Roni I will turn the system off at the control switch on my desk.'
Seconds later he returned and reconvened his pleasure on the thick carpet in the centre of the office and was set about by Roni who went about satisfying her man as only she knew how. In her previous life, the years in prison as Mhairi McClure had terminated her natural yearning for sex and frustrated her terribly, so she valued every opportunity to enjoy herself. After fifteen minutes they both came to a climax and lay back smiling as they breathed deeply.
Roni had begun to appreciate Roland as a lover. His athletic body and middle-age good looks appealed to her as they were probably born into the same era.

'Roland that was lovely and a good start to the day as once is never enough for me.'

Roland leaned over Roni, stroked her body then answered 'That sounds interesting.'

'So this is where you run your wine empire Roland. I take it you have given the staff a day off.'

'It is a very tidy operation which I control with the help of my bodyguards who also run a distribution warehouse in St. Raphael where we dispatch wine all over Europe.'

'I wondered because there are only a couple of desks in here.' Roland was proud of his wine business and spent the next half hour explaining how he had developed the company. Roni stopped the conversation by placing her finger on his lips, 'Enough of this idle chat, time for your second lesson on how to please a nymphomaniac is now due!' Roni laughed as she got astride her man.

Chapter 25

As the orgy continued Spy had arrived back at Roni's hotel and approached the reception to ask if Miss Benson was available.

'Miss Benson?' the receptionist replied 'Let me see she is in room 23, I'll give her a call.'
She let the phone ring for 20 seconds, of course to no avail, but at least it told Spy what room she was in. He went back to his car to review the situation and spotted a cleaner coming out the rear door of the hotel to dump trash into a waste bucket. The cleaner moved off back through the open door and Spy grasped the opportunity to access the hotel and moving quickly up to the second floor and into room 23. Breaking in to hotel bedrooms was second nature to the bodyguard and he was quickly inside his required destination. Roni had kept her room tidy so it was easy for Spy to do a quick search which did not reveal anything untoward. In the wardrobe there was a wall safe and Spy tried to open it by using different combinations but Roni had sealed it with a code only known to her.
Back at Chateau Rose Blanc, act two of the love match had concluded with the two participants to be found showering together. One thing was beginning to puzzle Roni was how she was going to attach the two listening systems without Roland finding out? She dried herself and like Roland put on a big white towelling dressing gown with deep pockets.

'Roland I want to dry my hair and put on some make-up so if you have something you want to do for the next ten minutes carry on.'

'Well I could do with catching up with Spy up at the chateau so I'll leave you to titivate yourself for my return. Be back soon.' and off he went in the direction of the house.

Roni wasted no time in getting the small electronics out of her sports bag and rushed back through to the office where she looked for the best hiding places. Roland had a large oak desk with three drawers down either side with a space in the middle for his chair and his long legs to stretch out Roni crawled under the desk, removed the plastic outer cover on the listening device and attached the spying bugs – one under the desk and the other attached to the base of the desk not visible to anyone sitting in front of it. Returning to the changing-room she went into the toilet, locked the cubicle door and activated the electronics, praying that the signal would not set off any alarms.

Up at the chateau Roland sat facing Spy 'Did you manage to search Roni's room?'

'Yes but nothing untoward to report. Miss Benson appears to be a very orderly individual, there were a few papers lying about on the bureau but they were all relating to Farrer Financial Services. The room has a wall safe but I was unable to decipher the code to open it.'

'Thanks Spy that's what I wanted to hear.'

Spy smiled 'How is your afternoon going?'

'Very well and I don't think it has finished yet.'

'Oh there you are Roland I wondered where you had gone?' asked Roni still wearing the towelling dressing gown with Chateau Rose Blanc motif on the left breast pocket.

Roni moved towards Roland 'I was just admiring your beautiful desk. A solid piece of wood capable of supporting both of us.' she moved towards Roland and undid the belt of his dressing gown and slid her hand inside it 'Come on climb on board your desk. Let's finish this session with something different.'

Roni smiled to herself 'I wonder what HQ will make of the first communication they receive from Chateau Rose Blanc!'

Cam was in his room when Commander McFaul phoned 'Congratulations Cam, I have just had control on the phone. The devices Roni planted are coming over loud and clear even if the initial message will require an X Certificate!' Hugh explained the content before continuing 'Cam I think for her own safety you should get Miss Benson out of there as soon as possible.'

The phone in Roland's office rang startling the two lovers. Roland picked up the receiver and passed it over to Roni 'It's for you.'

A surprised look came over Roni's face before she answered 'Hello.'

'Hi Roni, Graeme here, I've just had a Mr McFaul on the phone and he wants to meet up with you to discuss what could be a very good deal for us. He wants to see us tonight so I will send a car for you. See you soon.'

'Sorry Roland a business opportunity has come up. Unfortunately I will have to leave right away. Graeme is sending a car for me. Thanks for a truly wonderful afternoon, which I will not forget in a hurry. I hope every time you feel bored sitting at your desk you will think of the good romp we had on it.'

Roni kissed Roland for the last time, dressed quickly and was ready to go when the car arrived to take her back to the hotel.

Cam was waiting for Roni when she returned and gave her an unexpected big hug quickly followed by Lydia who kissed her on both cheeks.

'Congratulations! I hope I didn't spoil your afternoon Roni but Commander McFaul was concerned that something might go wrong and you would take a one-way helicopter trip over the Med which is one of the Russian KGB's regular practices. What you achieved today could be mammoth in the West's fight against terrorism globally, both in terms of Islamic fundamentalists and East European Nazis. It is immeasurable at the present time to calculate the number of lives you could save. Once the signals commence picking up the arms sales orders, the military can concentrate on laying traps for the dissidents and detaining them prior to them standing trial.'

Lydia changed the subject and brought some light relief to the conversation 'How did the match go Roni?'

'Very well.' replied Roni 'Roland won the tennis and I got the better of him three times during the après tennis! It was a very successful day.'

Roni's remarks left her two companions flabbergasted as they followed her to the bar for a celebratory drink.

Chapter 26

Everyone was smartly dressed for the trip to Monaco to visit Giles Normand at Verte Banque which was situated facing the Palais du Prince where the Grimaldi family reside and rule the principality. Lydia was not involved in the financial transactions but would spend her time fruitfully, visiting hotels owned by guests she met at the tennis barbecue.

Verte Banque was housed in a beautiful modern building where the paintings and tapestries adorning the walls reflected the wealth of its clientele. Roni and Graeme reported to an imposing receptionist perched behind her marble desk and were told Monsieur Normand would be with them shortly. The couple sat down in the leather bucket chairs surrounding a glass coffee table and Roni picked up a French version of the Investor's Chronicle and began to look at the most recent news in financial circles. She went into her handbag pretending to the watching eyes of the receptionist to take out a handkerchief which was already wrapped round one of the listening devices. She deftly removed the device from her handkerchief and clamped it securely down the side of her leather chair and taking out a lipstick tube she activated it. Now, at least MI6 Communications Department would know who Giles Normand was receiving calls from at all times.

Five minutes later the diminutive figure of Giles Normand appeared dressed in a smart light grey pin stripe suit over a pink shirt and a navy blue and white spotted tie. Giles was blessed with thick black curly hair above his friendly blue eyes and a skin which radiated the lifestyle of a wealthy banker who spent much of his time outdoors.

'Good morning!' he cried rushing towards his guests, 'Sorry to have kept you but now that little problem is solved I will make sure we are not disturbed. Follow me this way to my humble abode.'

There was nothing humble about the manager's office which had huge floor to ceiling windows looking out towards the Royal Palace at one end while taking in a view of the harbour at the other.

Roni gasped 'What a fabulous place to work! I am inclined to ask if you have any vacancies.'

Giles smiled and joined in Roni's banter 'Who knows? Maybe if our discussions go well today I could find a position for you Miss Benson. Have a seat and I'll organise some coffee.'

Once the drinks order was complete Giles got down to business 'Tell me about Farrer Financial Services.'

Graeme fielded the initial question 'FFS has been trading in the, shall we call it 'The Shadow Market' for several years but you won't find anything about us at Companies House. We started the business after having numerous approaches from organisations who wanted to get rid of 'Hot Money' quickly. These were invariably funds which the tax authorities were unaware of and had they discovered them the proprietors would have found themselves behind bars.'

Roni continued the FFS presentation 'I have built up a network of contacts around the world and we have become skilled in making money disappear into untraceable destinations where it could be transformed into property or re-invented as the principles being shareholders of a new venture. The directors named in these companies are in reality only paid puppets on comfortable retainers in return for risking their freedom should they be exposed.'

The illegal activities described by Roni and Graeme did not seem to bother Giles as he spoke 'When I spoke briefly to you at the tennis tournament I got the impression you dealt in facilities that sailed close to the wind. In Monaco we have characters that fit comfortably into your remit and I am interested in finding a home for these transactions for customers which Verte Banque cannot assist directly.'

'I expect you have a cosmopolitan clientele at Verte Banque?' enquired Graeme.

'Yes Monaco attracts all manner of tax exiles in particular the nouveau riche who have escaped from Russia with boodles of money.'

Roni piped up 'We met a prominent Russian at the barbecue - Commissar Bardosky – do you know him?'

'No.' Normand lied.

'We also noticed some prominent Arabs present at Chateau Rose Blanc.' continued Roni.

'That would be the young Sheik Mushasa. He does a considerable amount of business with Roland Canault. He has acquired a large chain of wine shops based throughout Europe where Canault distributes fine wines to.'

Cam looked at Roni who nodded her head to inform her colleague she recognised the connection between the Sheik's wine empire and Canault's opportunity to deliver weaponry to enemies of the state all over Europe.

'What proportion of your business is ecologically friendly Giles?'

'The vast majority of it, many of the wealthy citizens of Monaco love to be seen as charitable overlords which takes the attention away from their scurrilous activities like raiding worker's pension pots and leaving the poor devils with a bleak future. Behind the principality's posh exterior there lies a sizeable sector of questionable activities.'

Roni observed 'Farrer are used to transacting under these conditions so if you have any situations where we can help out please keep us in mind. You may have clients for instance who are at their bank overdraft limits but are still in need of working capital to take advantage of cash strapped suppliers by offering to pay them quickly in return for additional discounts. This is referred to as supply chain finance and by using our services we take some of the burden away from Verte Banque and make our return by charging your client a service fee for the additional cash he so badly needs. We pay introductory commissions for successful leads, so there is an income stream for your bank Giles.'

'That sounds interesting I'll keep it in mind.'

Graeme was next to ask a leading question: 'I take it your presence at Roland Canault's Tennis Tournament was because he is a customer of Verte Banque?'

Giles laughed out loud 'If only Mr Davenport, I have been courting Roland for years but he continues to be banked by one of my competitors Ruski Bank. Ruski moved into Monaco thirty years ago when Boris Yeltsin decided that Russia would move over from a command economy to a commercial one. By doing that they removed the barriers on the sale of oil, amongst other commodities which coincided with the creation of the oligarchs who brought great wealth to Western Europe when they transferred large portions of their capital. Mr Canault is a very shrewd operator and his wine business appears to be very successful. '

Roni interrupted 'Judging by the guest list at the Tennis Tournament Roland is very well connected.'

'Monaco is such a small place Miss Benson it is hard not to be.'

The trio chatted on for a further twenty minutes about exchange rates and money supply which Roni conducted on behalf of FFI. Graeme was sweating that Giles would not spring a question on him which would expose his limited financial knowledge. The meeting ended with Roni saying they had further meetings to attend and would unfortunately have to forego his offer of lunch. They had found their discussions very useful. There was no harm in being aware of the channel Roland received his funding through and it was up to MI6's cyber division to see if they could hack in and put a tracker on Canault's money movements.

As a parting shot Graeme made one last request, 'Can I use a toilet?'

Giles smiled 'Of course. Use my personal facility which is behind that door.' he added pointing at the door behind his desk.

Graeme headed for the toilet. Once inside the room he checked for cctv cameras and took out one of the listening systems and placed it on the inside surface of an air vent which also served the bank manager's office. He was uncertain whether it would be successful but it was worth a try. He ended his visit by flushing the toilet and washing his hands. After they were well away from Verte Banque's office Cam confided to Roni about his successful trip to Giles Normand's toilet.

Chapter 27

Roni and Graeme completed another four similar calls and their heads were buzzing by the time they met up with Lydia for a drink. She had been moving round the principality ticking off her list of contacts as she visited them. They all remembered her dancing performance at the barbecue and were pleased to hear she had had no long-term hangover. Over the day she had picked up snippets of intelligence which could be useful in the future.

'Ah the Davenports and Miss Benson how are you?' a voice called out from behind them.

Spy and David Andelic were both dressed in smart business suits giving the impression they also had been having important discussions.

'Have you had a successful day amongst the financial community of Monaco?'

Roni replied 'Yes it has been very interesting. What about yourselves?'

David smiled before answering 'We were delivering some packages for Mr Canault to his bankers which Roland wanted to make sure they arrived safely. Are you off home now? We came in on the helicopter and if you like we can give you a lift back to Valescure.'

Graeme was wary of the offer and made an excuse 'That's extremely kind of you but I promised the girls a gambling session in Monaco's world famous casino but only after we have something to eat as we are all starving. Maybe we can take up your offer later in the week?'

Spy and David accepted Graeme's story and moved off down the road in the direction of the helicopter pad.

Once they were out of earshot Roni burst out, 'What a spoilsport Cam! I've never been in a helicopter and the thought of getting home in fifteen minutes appealed to me rather than an hour in the train.'

Cam held up both his hands in defence 'There was no way I was going to get into a kite with two professional hit-men who could open the doors of the aircraft at will and rid MI6 of three agents in one fell swoop! – but it looks like they've cost me a meal and a visit to the casino.'

The casino did not disappoint the tourists and although it was early evening there was a buzz about the place. Elderly couples, all dressed up for the occasion, placed piles of high value chips on to the various numbers on the roulette while others had little baskets of money which they fed into the slot machines. Lydia came out best in the gambling stakes which was just about enough to pay their taxi back to Valescure.

It was late when they got back to the hotel. Roni and Lydia went straight to their rooms but Cam stopped for a drink which he had served in a quiet corner of the lounge. He looked around to make sure no one could overhear his conversation before phoning Commander McFaul.

'Evening Hugh. Cam here, the girls have retired for the night so I'm taking the opportunity to keep you up to date.'

'Great to hear from you Cam you have had a very successful trip and it may be time for you to consider returning home.'

'You may be correct Hugh. After I spoke to you earlier Roni and I had a meeting with Giles Normand at Verte Banque. He confirmed three things for us; the first thing is he is a liar, he denied knowing Commissar Bardosky despite us seeing him socialising with the Russians in St. Tropez. Secondly, he is willing to get involved in underhand deals with the likes of Farrer Financial Services. Thirdly, he confirmed that Roland Canault banks with Ruski Bank but he would welcome the chance to do business with Roland Canault. However on the plus side I have left a listening bug under an air vent which is shared with the manager's office. '

'Very good Cam, Lyndhurst from communications told me they picked up your signal which is not quite as strong as the one in Chateau Rose Blanc but it will be very useful to keep tabs on Giles Normand. From what you say it is all the more reason for you to get Roni and Lydia back to London. I will brief Richard Hartley in the morning and suggest that Roni stays at Chesham and works with the techies monitoring Roland Canault. I would leave your departure until the day after tomorrow so as not to cause any suspicion and it will give you all another chance to hone your tennis skills.'

'No amount of honing will improve my tennis but I'll make sure Roni says her goodbyes to Milagro the tennis coach as she regularly knows Canault's whereabouts and Roland Canault himself who she has closely befriended to say the least.'

'I get your meaning. We'll leave it at that for now. Speak to you tomorrow. Goodnight.

Chapter 28

'Morning ladies did you sleep well?'

'Very well' replied Lydia. She was looking stunning in a white t-shirt with a silver sequin pattern on it and a pair of red shorts.

'No, I tossed and turned a bit during the night' admitted Roni 'I kept thinking how someone like Giles Normand could sit there in his office and deny any knowledge of Commissar Bardosky. Why would he say that? – unless Commissar Bardosky has some means of blackmailing him, either by holding a video of him in an uncompromising situation with a partner who is not his wife, or he has proof of a financial transaction which is not kosher. I think we need to do a full intelligence search on Giles Normand.'

'That's what I like to hear Roni, an intelligence officer who never switches off! Last night after you went to bed, I briefed Commander McFaul on yesterday's developments which pleased him no end. He wants us to return home tomorrow and suggests today we relax and say goodbye to our contacts in case we should need them in the future. Roni, that means you speaking to Milagro or going along to the tennis academy for your last game of tennis where you can see her personally and don't forget to say 'Au Revoir' to Roland Canault.'

Roni responded, 'I'll do what you suggest Cam but tell me - is this the end of the mission?'

'No far from it. We will all be involved in the future, monitoring developments in Valescure. Hugh McFaul is reporting our success to Richard Hartley this morning and I have suggested that you be based in Chesham for the foreseeable future Roni.'

Roni smiled at Cam 'Thanks, there are worse places.'

Two hours later Roni entered the tennis academy and spotted Milagro talking to a couple of women with whom she had just finished their booked lesson.

'Roni! How nice to see you. Do you want to have a game today because I will be available in thirty minutes if you can wait?'

'I wasn't looking to play today but have come to tell you we are leaving for London tomorrow and I didn't want to leave without saying goodbye. We have all appreciated the last few days and the tennis skills you taught us. I'll give Roland a call to thank him for his hospitality.'

'You can do it personally as he has just arrived for his tennis lesson with Monsieur de Feu.'

Roni was taken aback by her last remark as she had wanted to avoid meeting Roland in person as she had developed feelings for him during this week.

'Look Roni, here he comes now.'

Roland was in his tennis whites ready to do combat with de Feu and was very happy to see Roni.

'Good day Miss Benson I did not expect to see you here today. Did you manage to get the business deal the other day?'

Roni did not get his meaning at first and stumbled into an answer 'Y....Yes it was not as urgent as Cam made out but we are still in discussion with our client.'

'Can I ask who the client is as I have a lot of influence in Monaco and could maybe make it easier for you to succeed with your transaction.'

Roni was not going to be loose with her tongue and replied 'Sorry Roland we have strict rules never to disclose the names of our clients. Why I am here today is to say goodbye as we are travelling back to London tomorrow and thank you for everything. I have really enjoyed your company.'

Roland's face saddened and he struggled to find words 'I did not expect you to leave so soon and I will miss you dearly. If I am in London, which I have never visited as yet, can I phone you?'

'That would not be advisable Roland as like you I have a partner waiting for me. It would only lead to making things difficult for both of us, better just to think of the good times we had together. I better be off before I start getting emotional. Goodbye.'

Roni could feel tears coming as she kissed Roland on the lips for the last time.

Chapter 29

Five days later.

Richard Hartley looked up from his last observation in Commander McFaul's detailed report on his colleagues visit to Valescure. Gathered in front of him sat Hugh McFaul accompanied by Roni Benson, Lydia Tomlinson and Campbell Anderson.

'Congratulations team to all of you, especially Roni Lydia and Campbell. When we set you the task of finding out about the activities of Roland Canault, I don't think anyone thought you would get positive results so quickly. We spotted tennis as Canault's weakness and Roni meeting Milagro D'Andrea paved the way to an introduction to Canault which you exploited to the full. Campbell you did well to identify the Russian security men and who they were protecting. Commissar Bardosky ranks highly in the KGB and has a reputation for being ruthless with both his enemies and his staff.

Roni you have to be admired, for your bravery in planting listening devices around Canault's desk which our intelligence staff are recording twenty-four hours a day. Our linguists interpret the messages and we can be on alert to prevent attacks anywhere in allied Europe and beyond.

The chances are nothing major will happen for several months but I want you to remain at the Chesham safe house for the foreseeable future, answering all calls made to you as 'Farrer Financial Services.'

Roni smiled on the news that she would not be returning to HMP Askham Hall any time soon, 'Thank you sir, will I have Beverley Thomson working alongside me?'

Hartley hadn't thought that far ahead but quickly covered himself 'Of course Thomson and you have always worked well together.'

'Getting back to the report, Giles Normand at Verde Banque seems like a slippery customer once you delve into his background. From the outside, one would expect all his funding to be involved in developing ecological projects. Monsieur Normand has a weakness for the ladies and often retires to Spas on the pretext of recharging his body from the stresses of banking life when in actual fact he makes reservations for young women to join him in sexual activities. Recently he slipped up and we believe Bardosky had one of his sessions filmed and is now blackmailing him by threatening to go public, which means he will transact any financial movements they deem necessary.'

'Lydia the trip to Valescure was difficult for you as you were playing the role of the doting wife and having to stand by and watch as your colleagues took a more active role. Nevertheless you managed to gather intelligence on Canault's bodyguards, which is now on file along with other contacts you made at the tennis tournament. Your future role in what will now be referred to as 'Operation Valescure' will be minimal but I have recognised your qualities and arranged for you to join Commander Stavert's team on the Asian desk.'

Lydia nodded before replying 'I will miss working with Cam and Roni but look forward to my new role. Can I ask sir, will I be based at home or abroad?'

Hartley replied 'Probably abroad, but that is for Stavert to decide.'

'Cam, you will remain under Hugh's command at his request and will be a senior liaison officer for other members of the team. To conclude, I think that is all for this morning and once more thanks for a good job done.'

Roni and Cam left MI6 headquarters after saying farewell to Lydia for the time being. Hugh McFaul remained behind in Richard Hartley's office to discuss future strategies for 'Operation Valescure.'

Cam gave Roni a lift to the station and she told him how delighted she was to be remaining at Chesham and asked some leading questions 'Cam did you have an influence in the decision for my remaining at Chesham?'

'I thought you were excellent in France and stated so in my report to Commander McFaul and he must have agreed with me and passed on my sentiments in his report to Hartley.' Cam commented.

'Well many thanks for doing so. I have something to confess. During my short involvement with Roland Canault I found myself becoming very attached to him and I even fantasized about making our relationship permanent as he told me his marriage to Jani is over. What would you have done if I had decided to stay?'

'The service would never have allowed it.'

'And what would have happened if I got protection from Roland's bodyguards?'

Cam looked across at the passenger's seat 'Roni, you are forgetting one thing. I could kill you whenever I wanted by activating the microchip in your body as I was carrying the detonator with me at all times when we were in France!'

Cam's last remark brought a cold silence into the car which lasted for the five minutes it took to reach the underground where Roni caught the train to Chesham.

Roni reflected on what Cam had said and although severely disappointed with his comment she cheered up before she reached her destination where Beverley Thomson was waiting to pick her up.

'Did you have a good meeting with Assistant Controller Hartley?' Beverley inquired.

'Yes, full of good news,' replied Roni with a half-truth 'I am continuing to work at the Chesham safe house until further notice. You will be my closest colleague as both of us will be working on 'Operation Valescure' the code name Hartley has put on our project. Our remit is to destroy the Russian policy of supplying arms to terrorists through Europe.'

Beverley exclaimed 'Well done! We'll go out tonight and celebrate your work extension Roni and do a toast to future success!'

The monitoring of Roland Canault's activities had started immediately Roni Benson had placed the listening device under his desk. The initial calls were of interest to MI6 who listed all the weapon movements and confirmed that Canault was engaging with some very dubious characters. Each case was reported to Richard Hartley for further action but the Assistant Controller assessed the threat to human life and decided to let the weapons be delivered. Most of the early business involved supplying small splinter groups who were more involved in burglaries and bank robberies.

Five months passed before Hartley received word of what he was waiting for:-

Sheik al Mushasa had returned to his desk completely fulfilled after his afternoon session with three of his wives.

His personal assistant Khalid Bin Kassilly was waiting for him 'Sire I have received word today that our brothers have sent twenty of their finest and most trusted warriors to the destinations we suggested. They are now awaiting the delivery of a consignment of weapons to implement our plan.'

'Twenty men would equate to five per venue in Paris Brussels, Berlin and Rome all targeting famous tourist attractions.

In Paris we have to choose between the Louvre or Versaille which is an easier target but unlikely to attract the same notoriety as a threat to some of the great art treasures of the world.

Berlin's Brandenburg Gate represents both a grim reminder of Hitler's wartime speeches but to many Germans it is still seen as a focal point for rallying the nation. An explosive device aimed at the middle pillar with the chariots above it will destroy much of this famous landmark.

Brussels handles legislation for twenty-seven countries throughout Europe, three quarters of whom are Christian and they are wary about allowing any Muslim influence which is best demonstrated by their continuing refusal to admit Turkey into their club. A rocket launch attack on their main building will affect all of Europe.

Rome has many attractive targets but if we are going to upset the Italian population then our objective should be the Vatican on a Sunday.'

'I don't have to remind you Khalid that what we are implementing here is our commitment to keep up our Jihad threat which conventional military armies struggle to cope with. Get in touch with our commanders and place the order for whatever they require with Roland Canault. Do not pay him directly, rather put the transaction through our friend Giles Normand at Verte Banque' laughing out loud the Sheik added 'The size of this transaction will represent some amount of wine.'

Khalid finished taking down his master's orders and started a series of phone calls round Europe.

Chapter 20

Roland was discussing the weekend football results which including Monaco's 4-2 defeat of Marseille, which Spy and D.A. had attended in Monaco on their day off, when his phone rang.

The caller opened the conversation with a broken English accent which Roland recognised immediately 'Good morning Roland, has the week started well for you?'

'Yes we have shipped two large orders this morning but something tells me Khalid that what you are about to tell me will make things even better.' Roland joked.

'Glad I find you in such a positive mood Roland. Your observations are correct as I do indeed have a very important piece of business for you to get your teeth into. Sheik Mushasa wants me to arrange for a large order of arms to be delivered to his stores in Paris, Berlin, Brussels and Rome. As usual you will conceal them in an area within the load so if any suspicious custom officer opens the consignment up the first two of three rows will appear to be crates of French wines.'

'Yes that is not a problem Khalid. We can even create more storage space by raising the floor of the trailer, flat-packing the weapons into boxes and placing them into the newly created space and seal it. When the consignments arrive at their destination we shall take them to a secure warehouse and dismantle the false flooring before passing them to your contacts.'

'Excellent Roland, payment will come to you via Verte Banque as Sheik Mushasa wants to distance himself from the payment. We have spoken to our contacts in all the cities I have mentioned. I will send you an email confirming the range of weaponry we need plus the delivery addresses for the consignment and the shipping dates we require once you have the goods in stock. I think we are talking weeks rather than months as the offensives we have in mind will have greater impact during the summer rather than in the winter.'

Roland was excited by the potential size and range of arms which might be required for the proposed attacks and how his involvement would put him in Commissar Bardosky's good books.

'Usually it takes about three weeks to put together an order of the magnitude you are describing. Is there anything unusual you will need to implement the attacks?'

Khalid answered 'Yes the plan is to create some diversions which will entail our men releasing some drones armed with small explosives which will be directed at targets miles from the main objective.'

'Khalid, to supply the appropriate drones we have to know what weight of explosives they are expected to carry and what distance they will be covering to reach their destination.'

'I will talk to our commanders and get back to you with the specifications.'

Roland reacted 'I look forward to your emails but in the meantime I will have our vehicles altered to accommodate the consignment.'

'Yes Roland better to be prepared well in advance in case the order comes through to implement the attack quicker than expected.'

'Don't worry Khalid, we will be ready at short notice provided your money is in our bank and cleared in plenty of time. You have my word on that. Say hello to Sheik Mushasa for me. Bye for now.'

Roland put down the phone and punched the air 'Boys, we are going to be busy. The Arabs are planning big attacks all over Europe and we shall be responsible for supplying the hardware. I don't have the details yet, but we shall have to do some preparation. Zorro, as our maintenance man I want you to design false bottoms in our vehicles along with a cage within the vehicle suitable for storing weapons.'

Zorro rubbed the stubble on his chin before replying 'That shouldn't be too difficult to construct but to keep it confidential I will need D.A. and Spy to assist me.'

The other two bodyguards nodded their acceptance of Zorro's suggestion and Spy smiled at Roland 'Will you be able to look after yourself on your own Roland?'

'No problem Spy I will have my wife Jani to protect me and if she's out Gigi Montalban will see to my safety in the comfort of my bed!'

'Roland you never change, always after a bit of skirt when the wife's not here.'

The communications department at MI6 headquarters in London were 'all ears' at what they had just heard from Valescure. They quickly put a full recording of the transcript on to a CD and passed it up to Commander McFaul's office. Hugh listened intently and made notes to outline any problems the message could prevail which would affect them apprehending the threat to the European capital cities. Once he had heard the conversation several times he sat down to hear it one more time in front of Assistant Controller Hartley.

The CD terminated and Richard Hartley remained silent for thirty seconds 'Christ, Hugh this could be very serious for our colleagues across Europe. Let's analyse what we know before putting anyone on high alert;

1. We know what cities are being targeted but not when or specifically the whereabouts the attacks are to take place.

2. The supplier of the armaments is known to us and we have access to their movements by way of listening devices.

3. The potential level of destruction is unknown until such times as our contact receives his order for the range of weapons from Sheik Mushasa. Even then, if the confirmation arrives by email we will not know the full extent of it unless someone reads it out loud!'

'Hugh please arrange to have linguists for you and me to be at our disposal once this operation kicks off. We shall be operating on four fronts and we will need to know that everyone is treating this threat with the same level of seriousness. Mhairi McClure has opened up a big can of worms for us and I think we should keep her in the loop as we may require her to contact Canault in the future. She is fluent in French and Italian so I would let her have access to the communicators dealing with Valescure as she may have some inside knowledge which could be useful in interpreting the data they have accumulated.'

'If I may say so sir your opinion of Mhairi McClure has mellowed considerably.' Hugh suggested.

Hartley stared at his junior officer and removed his spectacles before issuing a cold reply 'No McFaul, my opinion of Miss McClure remains the same. Mhairi McClure is a dangerous woman who is fighting for the repentance of her sins from the only man who can save her – Me! Her survival is still in my hands and she knows any failures on her part could be terminal.'

Hugh apologised for his miscalculation of his superior's view 'Sorry sir I got that wrong.'

'A word of advice Hugh, in this job there is no room for sentiment as that will be taken by your superiors as a sign of weakness. Here it is very much a case of kill or be killed!'

Hartley's tone softened, as he went into planning mode 'I will contact all the heads of security in France, Germany, Belgium and Italy and suggest we have a summit using a video link initially. Once Canault has received the weapons we will arrange to monitor the attackers' movements from a central office somewhere in Europe. The military in the targeted countries will also have to be consulted. I would rather keep all our information confidential at the present time and restricted to the respected security services of these countries. Hugh, please keep me informed if there are any further developments.'

'Certainly sir.' replied Hugh standing up and heading for the door out of Assistant Controller Hartley's office.

Chapter 31

Colonel Tariq Aziz was in a good mood. He had just received a communiqué from Major Said al Benzani his commander leading the invasion of Tarhuna, a town of fourteen thousand inhabitants in the Msallata Region. Al-Benzani confirmed they had captured the town from the National Liberation Army (NLA). The victory he hoped would pave the way for him to attract more conscripts to what remained of disposed leader Muammar al-Gaddafi's army.

Tarhuna is only forty miles from Tripoli, Aziz's next military target but in order to achieve that, he knew he needed a whole new strategy which may include joining up with one of the other splinter groups. His band of merry men would be no match for the considerable strength of the NLA and his only hope for the future would be the re-appearance of Said al Islam Gaddafi who had fled into hiding following the death of his father.

Tariq decided to cease his offensive for the time being, but would use his time wisely and train the new recruits into being a fighting force ready for the onslaught of Tripoli. In order to do this professionally he knew it would require ordering up a whole new arsenal of weapons. The best person to help him in that department was Roland Canault.

'Hello Roland, it is your little camel herder calling from Tarhuna which we have just captured from the

Libyan National Army using the weapons you supplied.'

'Oh Tariq! Good to hear from you.' he lied 'How are things in Libya since Gaddafi was removed from office? Do you think his followers will return to power?'

'Yes if me and my soldiers have anything to do with it. I am calling you after taking control of Tarhuna, a small town only forty miles from Tripoli. I am consolidating my attack here in Tarhuna and implementing a recruitment drive. This could, in our estimation increase our numbers four-fold with the attractive financial packages we are offering assisted by the local high unemployment rate especially amongst the eighteen to twenty-four year olds. I shall send you an email listing all the stock we need. Payment is not a problem as Gaddafi has dispatched trainloads of U.S. dollars to South Africa for safe keeping and I will get them to send a payment straight to your bank once I get a price from you.'

Canault replied 'Well Tariq you seem extremely well organised and set to continue the Gaddafi dynasty in Libya. Once I receive your order I shall talk to Commissar Bardosky as the level of assistance you require is, I would imagine, above my remit. Russia sees Libya as an ally with whom they want to have closer ties with so getting you the supplies should not be a problem. Have you taken control of an airport capable of taking delivery of our supplies?'

'No unfortunately not. The two main airports are in the Tripoli region so we would have to think of how we can logistically transport such a big consignment without drawing attention to ourselves. I thank you Mr Canault for being so sympathetic to my request. I will transmit our order in the next few days. Goodbye.'

Roland ended the call and started thinking about the consequences of supporting what was left of the Gaddafi regime now that the public had so brutally murdered their former ruler. Based on what Tariq Aziz had indicated Roland wasted no time in phoning Uri Bardosky. When he called, Bardosky's P.A. Elana Podescu told him that her boss was in tri-part discussions with allies and could not be disturbed. In reality he was enjoying a threesome with two finely tuned young ladies who were extorting the life out of the portly official in the fear that failure to satisfy him could result in their disappearance.

Four hours later Roland was contacted from Moscow 'Good day Roland I heard you were looking for me earlier. What can I do for you?'

'Good evening Commissar Bardosky, earlier today I received a call from Colonel Aziz in Libya who had just captured Tarhuna which is only forty miles from Tripoli. He is supporting the effort to restore sympathisers of Gaddafi to seize back control of Libya. To do this he will require a massive support programme and I would like to know if you are in agreement with their demand?'

'Not an easy question to answer Roland. Currently we are trying to keep up diplomatic relations with all the interested parties as we are uncertain how the balance of power is going to work out. We could respond positively to Colonel Aziz's demands but that might pigeon-hole Russia as a Gaddafi sympathiser. My advice would be to wait and see how detailed the Colonel's order is then we can make a decision on our level of support.'

Roland hesitated then replied 'I would concur with your analysis of the situation and report back to when I have more information from Libya.'

The head of communications at MI6, Reg Lyndhurst, was overjoyed with the report he received from one of his junior officers, Ian Hogg, about the impending arms purchase for Colonel Tariq Aziz. He contacted Freddie Sharpe who arranged a meeting for him with Richard Hartley.

Hartley had listened to all the conversations firstly between Tariq Aziz and Roland Canault then Canault's discussion with Commissar Bardosky. He smiled to himself before addressing his two colleagues Reg Lyndhurst and Commander Hugh McFaul 'This is fascinating Reg, your team have done exceptionally well. We now have first class knowledge of an imminent attack by forces favouring the deposed Gaddafi regime and a pre-emptive notification of Russian involvement. I know both the Prime Minister and the Foreign Secretary have put their weight behind the National Liberation Army. Your intercepted communiqué will allow them to approach the new leaders in Libya and bridge some of the diplomatic tensions which have existed since the Lockerbie Air Crash in 1998.'

'I'm not sure that the Russians will give all the supplies they are seeking as Russia has taken a position in Libya where they are being amenable to various groups in the country. Until they see who is going to win the power struggle they shall continue with that policy before implementing an aid programme to get Libya back on its feet. Nothing new here, the West will be employing the same policies in the hope of securing good trade relations with Libya which has huge stocks of minerals.'

'In the meantime I will prepare a paper for the Foreign Office who will decide if we need to take any military action. One thing we have to establish is what method the Libyans are going to implement to pay the Russians. As you heard on the tape they usually pay in dollar bills and they will need cash in lorry loads for them to pay for the arms shipment. They could send them by boat into Marseille then by road transport to Monaco which is cumbersome and risky but if needs must they will do it.'

'Hugh, get a hold of Mhairi McClure and see if she has any experience of currency being transported in this manner. Also she could have a word with this chap Normand at Verte Banque to see if he is involved in assisting the Russians.'

'Thank you gentlemen for your excellent contributions today, I think that is all for now. Until we know when Colonel Aziz has a date for his next offensive we cannot warn the official Libyan Government and assist them in setting a trap to destroy Colonel Aziz's army.'

Roni took off her head-set when Beverly tapped her on the shoulder and signalled she was wanted on the phone. She crossed the office and picked up the phone on Beverley's desk 'Hello, Roni Benson speaking.'

An equally Irish accent spoke 'Hello Roni, Commander McFaul here. Richard Hartley has asked me to call you to get advice on a potential money laundering transaction which could involve Roland Canault.'

The very mention of Roland's name sent a sense of excitement through her body. Hugh outlined his earlier meeting with his boss and waited for an answer from the Irish financial wizard.

'Afternoon Hugh, moving cash about is not as easy as many people might think. Small amounts can be money laundered quite easily which is what drug dealers do all the time but large amounts take time to be dissolved into the money chain. I would suspect that the volumes you are talking about will be loaded on to a container ship and sent straight to Russia and re-introduced into the system to pay suppliers in third world countries who prefer to trade in U.S. dollars.'

'I will pay a courtesy call on Giles Normand at Verte Banque and see if I can find out how the Russians normally transmit funds.'

'Thanks Roni,' said Hugh avoiding addressing Roni as 'Mhairi' he changed the subject 'how are things in leafy Buckinghamshire? Are you being looked after?'

'Yes I much prefer it to my previous residence at Askham Hall and my role is interesting working with the International Communications Department.'

'Good. Long may it continue, let me know if you have any positive feedback from your banking chums in Monaco. Bye for now.'

Hugh McFaul pondered for a few minutes after his talk with Roni Benson and made another call to his best friend John Johnston in South Africa. John had moved recently and was now a consultant at Groot Shuur Hospital in Cape Town where Christiaan Barnard carried out the first heart transplant in the world.

A receptionist at the hospital put the call through to Dr Johnston 'Hughie! Great to hear from you, is this you and Amy wanting to return for a holiday to one of the most desirable holiday retreats in the world?'

'I wish to hell it was John but we will be coming down to see you soon if Amy has anything to do with it. The London weather doesn't suit her but she is enjoying her work at St. Thomas' Hospital.'

'The reason for my call is MI6 related John. What I am about to say is highly confidential but if I can trust anyone, it is you. We believe that sometime before he was assassinated, General Gaddafi, the deposed Libyan leader arranged to have billions of U.S. dollars sent to South Africa for safe keeping as he had a distrust of banks.'

'A situation has now arisen whereby his followers in Libya are attempting a coup against the National Libyan Army. In order to do so they have placed an order for what could be a huge consignment of arms which they will have to pay for in advance so they need money quickly. As the money is in hard currency they will need to transport it most probably on a container ship. I don't want to alert the South African authorities as they themselves could secretly be holding this large cache. They would move it on if they thought a foreign government knew where it was for fear that it could be impounded by the United Nations.'

'Sorry to be so long-winded John. My question to you is – South Africa export regularly to Russia but do you know what port they are likely to use most frequently?'

'Very interesting Hugh but as you know I don't travel in maritime circles but one of my neighbours Ed Barker works for the South African Chamber of Commerce so he will certainly have data on movements of shipping to and from South Africa.'

'I'm not keen to alert your friend in any way. You could put the question to him in more general terms by saying what is the most used shipping route for exporters sending goods to France and Russia?'

John Johnston replied to the suggestion 'Okay Hugh I will try that. My own thoughts are it is more likely for a consignment, such you are describing, to be loaded in Durban as it is the closest shipping route through the Suez Canal to Europe.'

'Will you be meeting Ed Barker anytime soon John?'

'Yes Hannah and Ed's wife Clara are close friends and we are due to have them over to the house next week for a barbecue and a few drinks. We often discuss what's happening in our ever-changing environment here in the Cape so I can throw in your subject matter.'

'First class John. We'll speak soon and I will get Amy on to looking at flights to Cape Town, goodbye for now.'

Chapter 32

'Hello Roni, very nice to hear from you. Did you have a good journey home?' asked Giles Normand

'Yes Giles, but I am missing your good climate.'

'What can I do for you Roni?'

'I was following up on our meeting to see if any opportunities for our services had come up and to discuss with you an opportunity which you can perhaps give me some advice on. An organisation based in the Far East has approached Farrer Financial Services to see if we can assist them in moving a large amount of used dollar bills to a safe haven. The notes are stored in a warehouse which I am unable to give you the address for at present. Have you ever had any experience of this type of transaction in the past?'

The banker was silent for a few seconds 'Roni, it depends what level of transaction we are talking about.'

'At this stage I cannot give you an accurate figure Giles but knowing the people I have been in discussion with I should think we are talking about one hundred million U.S. dollars plus.'

'Wow Roni, that's a lot of paper to move around. We have transacted smaller amounts for drug cartels. Usually they come into Marseille on a container ship, a route the Russian oligarchs used in the early days when they had robbed the State-owned industries. They brought their currency along here by the truckload, re-packaged and disguised the contraband before entering Monaco and putting it in a safe place. Here we can arrange property deals all over Europe for our clients, many of which can be settled in cash especially in Eastern Europe in what was previously the Soviet Bloc. A lot of dollar bills are also washed through the casino.'

'Giles you are a man after my own heart – always trying to find new solutions for your clients. Your information has been very useful to me for solving the little predicament I am working on at present. If we can resolve it and find a route for bringing my client's funds to Europe I will recommend Verte Banque as the first place he should be looking to deposit his haul.'

'Thanks Roni if you need any further information do not hesitate to call me.'

'I won't Giles. Au revoir.'

Roni put down the phone and wrote a short email to Hugh McFaul describing her conversation with Giles Normand. She had come to the conclusion that it was possible the Libyans could move the currency from South Africa to France if they got the logistics correct.

When Hugh received her message he immediately relayed it to Richard Hartley. Hartley contacted the British South African ambassador in Pretoria Sir George Elwood. He asked Elwood to alert his contacts at all the ports in South Africa and monitor closely every container ship destined for either Russia or France and Marseille in particular.

Chapter 33

Two days after receiving the initial enquiry from Colonel Aziz, Roland received an email stretching several pages containing specific details of the Libyan's request. He printed off two copies of the email and passed one to David Andelic.

'D.A., Tariq Aziz has sent me this list of what he needs to embark on further military assaults in Libya. Before I send this procurement request to Commissar Bardosky I want to accompany it with a report from ourselves. You are the man who deals with securing the arms from our suppliers and although this particular order is likely to be delivered direct from Russia. I still think we should check it for clarity before it goes off in case there are items here we can't supply or, what is listed has any technical ambiguities which could lead to Aziz receiving a wrong order. Cast your eyes down the email and point out any discrepancies you find.'

'My God Roland, they are serious about this assault!' Flicking the pages in his hand he added 'This will cost them a fortune and will have to be air-lifted in or sent by sea which could take a few weeks. Okay let's get started and see what we find.'

The two colleagues engaged themselves for the next two hours and found to their surprise the order was very accurate apart from a couple of minor velocity issues regarding bullet sizes.

At MI6 headquarters in London the communication department were ecstatic about what they were hearing. The two Serbians who were oblivious to the fact they were being overheard, did not go through the order line by line but the items they did discuss in detail gave a picture of the scale of the operation.

When they had completed the inventory Roland phoned Colonel Aziz to discuss the logistics of transporting such a large consignment of arms.

'Hello Tariq we have checked over your order and we are able to supply what you have requested. However delivery could be a problem transporting it to you undetected by the National Libyan Army. Do you have any suggestions as to how we can deliver it safely to you?'

'Leave it with me. I shall talk to contacts in neighbouring countries and find a safe haven for you to deliver the goods. Most likely it will be a disused military airstrip where they can land under the cover of darkness out with Lybian air space, so as not to alert the Libyan Air Force.'

'I should remind you Tariq that we require payment before we can release the weapons. '

'Send me a secure coded email featuring a detailed invoice of our account with you and I will arrange for the funds in dollar bills to be sent to a bank of your choice.' replied the Colonel.

Roland concluded 'I shall inform you in my email as to where I want the funds delivered. I have to get sanction for that from Moscow. We should be able to confirm the cost of your order by tomorrow, then the ball is in your court to get the money to our bank.'

'You still use tennis terminology even in business Roland. One day I will come across to Valescure and have a game with you. Goodbye for now.'

After a quick discussion with D.A. they both decided it would be pointless wasting time working out an estimate for Tariq when Commissar Bardosky would have the final say. Instead he picked up the phone and spoke to his boss after being connected by Elana Podescu. 'Good morning Commissar I have received a request for a large supply of arms from Colonel Aziz in Libya who is carrying out offensives on behalf of what was previously Gaddafi's army. I am sending you an email with a detailed list of his requirements which are way beyond my sanctioning authority so I would like to respond with a total costing. I have informed Aziz that no delivery can be made until we have received his payment into our bank.'

'Payment brings me on to another problem with his request. He wants to pay in U.S. dollars which we would have to 'wash through the money chain' so I need you to tell me where you want the dollars delivered?'

'Nothing's easy Roland. I will have Aziz's order calculated and the result sent to you to post to Libya. Regarding where to deliver the cash, I would not want it put into Ruski Bank as my superiors have given me instructions never to upset the Monaco banking system for fear of being thrown out of Monaco by the Grimaldi Regime. Good work if we can pull it off but I will have to seek clearance from our Foreign Office who may limit their exposure to one side of the Libyan domestic conflict. Leave it with me and I will get back to you promptly.'

'Thanks Commissar Bardosky, I look forward to hearing from you.' Roland ended the call and relayed his last conversation to his anxious colleague D.A. Now all they could do was to wait for Moscow's response.

Over the weekend the Johnston family hosted a barbecue which they invited the Barkers to attend. Ed Barker loved to do the cooking so John was able to corner him into a conversation as he barbecued the steaks and hamburgers.

'Ed, can I ask your advice? A friend of mine wants to send a container from South Africa to Marseille in France – what port would you suggest he uses?'

Ed hesitated before replying 'John, Cape Town or Port Elizabeth would be your best bets. I hope your friends are not in a hurry as it can take up to twenty-five days for deliveries to land in France.'

'Really I'll let him know, he might decide to airfreight which will be more expensive but he's a wealthy individual.'

Later that evening John relayed Ed's advice to Hugh McFaul who shared his surprise at the delivery time 'Twenty-five days would set the assault plans back so I should imagine they will definitely use airfreight. They will not get access to any new arms until the funds are cleared in the banking system. This will make it harder to trace as they may use a private cargo plane which could land anywhere in France, most probably at an abandoned military base. '

'Thanks John I will have to go and think about this one.'

Hugh quickly came to the conclusion that his only hope of confirming a delivery time was MI6's communication sector. He took the precaution of alerting Reg Lyndhurst to brief his staff to be on the lookout for any conversations emanating from Chateau Rose Blanc that made any reference to travel arrangements.

A week later Lyndhurst's staff documented an exchange between David Andelic and Colonel Aziz which was 'Good Day Colonel nice to hear from you. Did you receive our quote for your order?'

'Yes and bloody expensive it is too. Can I speak to Roland?'

'No, he has gone to Toulon with his wife and won't be back until tomorrow. He has left me in charge so how can I be of assistance?'

Tariq hesitated before answering 'It is about the payment. We are loading it on to a cargo plane which is landing on a small private airstrip alongside Aix en Provence Airport. We would like you to have a truck ready to pick up a container of fresh fruit with the dollars concealed inside it and deliver it to Verte Banque in Monaco.'

'When is it arriving?'

'Next Thursday evening October 2 at 20.00 hours when the airport is at its quietest.'

'Leave it to us Colonel Aziz, we shall be there to bring your load into Monaco. Today I will email Commissar Bardosky who will be in touch with you regarding the shipment of the weapons you require. Goodbye for now, speak to you again soon.'

Richard Hartley read the communiqué then called Commander McFaul and Campbell Anderson to his office. He issued them both with a copy of the recorded conversation and asked them for suggestions as to what their next move should be.

Cam Anderson spoke first 'This is good news. We now know when the cash is arriving and where it is bound for. We could mount a covert attack on the truck as it journeys to Monaco using the SAS or the French equivalent. This would bring a halt to the Arabs receiving any weapons to escalate the civil war threat in Libya. Colonel Aziz would immediately become suspicious that Roland Canault and his bodyguards had arranged for a third party to steal their money and would take revenge which could result in Russia's cell in the south of France being disrupted for the time being.'

Hartley peered over the desk at Anderson 'Interesting thoughts Anderson, but you are forgetting that we are currently sitting with the trump card in the form of the bugs Roni Benson attached to Canault's desk which has been sending a great amount of useful information. If we upset the running of the Valescure office Bardosky will smell a rat and could find our equipment. Remember we are still awaiting a date for the terrorist attacks in four major cities in Europe which must remain our priority for now.'

'I much prefer to let the transaction take place at this stage until we get a date from Sheik Mushasa's office confirming the terrorist attack. As you say Campbell, we know the funds will be stored at Verte Banque and the manager Monsieur Normand likes women so he would prove easy to blackmail should it become necessary. Let's be patient gentlemen and let the Arabs show their hand.

Chapter 34

The five Al-Qaeda commanders sat round a table in the tent of their leader Ahmed Fadhi in a remote location in Northern Iraq where before them lay the plans for their impending terror raids.

Ahmed opened the meeting 'Brothers the time has come for us to continue our fight against the enemies of Allah. I have received word from Sheik Mushasa that all the weapons you require to implement our plan are now ready to be despatched to the respective target sites. This will be our final meeting before our strikes which will take place very soon, but for security reasons I am not releasing the date today. Instead I have brought you here today to go over each assault in detail. Imad how are your plans for Paris?'

Imad Atwa was a very experienced operator in acts of terror and was, like his fellow commanders, on the United States wanted list. At thirty-five he had twenty years service to the Islamic cause which meant he was constantly on the move. He began 'We have spent six months studying the movements of the security staff at the Louvre who, as you might expect, are very competent. However, like all large tourist attractions they are reliant upon public services for the smooth running of their operation. Waste disposal is carried out daily by the same workers, as are food deliveries, to satisfy the high demands of the tourists. One of my men will pose as the bakery delivery man replacing the usual employee who we will have intercepted at the transport café he stops at every morning. He will be ordered to drive to a quiet area where unfortunately we will assassinate the innocent man before hiding his body.'

'We will gain access to the art gallery by telling the security guard at the gate that the driver has phoned in sick. Using the driver's phone we will dial the office of the bakery and get them to confirm the changes but the actual number dialled will be to a mobile of one of my men who is already inside touring the building as one of the holidaymakers. When we get to the delivery drop-off point four of us will come out of the van wearing Louvre staff uniforms, pushing two trolleys bedecked in Louvre livery - one packed with explosives, the other with our automatic guns and hand grenades on board. We shall leave an explosive charge in the abandoned bakery van which we will detonate ten minutes later as a diversion to cause chaos.'

'This should allow us time to reach the entrance area of the Louvre and demolish the iconic glass pyramid which will result in heavy casualties as the occupants of the art gallery attempt to exit the building. It is unlikely that any of my team will survive the raid but we shall get our reward in Heaven, brothers.'

Ahmed nodded his approval to Imad's plan 'Thank you Imad for sharing your detailed explanation of your plan. My only reservation would be that you spare the life of the innocent van driver but sedate him heavily so he does not wake up until after your attack is finished. May Allah recognise your sacrifice in his name.

Moving on, Hassan is your attack on the Brandenburg Gate on schedule?'

Hassan Yasin, like everyone round the table was a bearded man whose sturdy body echoed the fact he enjoyed the good life. He had learned his skills in Iraq during the two Iraqi Wars against the West and was highly skilled in the use of modern armament technology.

He began his presentation 'Our attack on the Brandenburg Gate is more technology based as opposed to Imad's Paris venture. We shall drive up to the Brandenburg Gate and fire two rocket launchers from the back of a high curtained vehicle. Our target is the centre pillar featuring the chariot statue. Driving past the monument, simultaneously we shall direct three drones carrying explosives all guided to damage the other pillars. It will happen so quickly that the element of surprise will be in our favour as we drop the canvas curtain down and continue on our way.'

Ahmed intervened, 'What happens if you miss the targets?'

'We won't, the targets will be electronically locked on to our weapons.

'Very clever Hassan, we wish you every success but what if you are seen by a member of the public – is there a plan B?'

'We will be armed and would head in search of a densely populated area, gather as many hostages as we could and negotiate our way out of Germany.'

'I think that will be difficult as the Germans do not like being dictated to.'

'My men are under no illusions so if there is a fight to the death it will be an honour to die serving Mohammed.'

Ahmed moved the meeting on 'Thanks Hassan, Abdul is it all systems go for our assault on Rome?'

Abdul Ezz–al-Din was a small wiry figure who displayed a nervous disposition and wore heavy-rimmed spectacles covering eyes which twitched constantly.

He wrung his hands together before addressing the others 'Rome or should I say the Vatican is proving to be a little difficult being protected as it is by the efficient Swiss Guards. It would be too difficult in my opinion to get a suicide bomber into St. Peter's Square anytime near the time of the Pontiff's speech. I would recommend we detonate a device at a location in Rome itself and I am undecided between The Pantheon and The Colosseum but will probably go for the latter as it attracts more media attention. It was where the gladiators fought to the death and we can describe ourselves as the modern equivalent.'

Ahmed sniggered 'I like your line of thinking as our warriors are indeed like gladiators fighting to the death. How will you carry out your attack Abdul?'

Abdul sheepishly replied 'We will use three human bombers at different areas of the Colosseum which will bring down some of the pillars which have stood for many centuries.'

Ahmed shifted uneasily in his seat then dropped a bombshell in the direction of Abdul 'I am unconvinced at this late stage by your uncertainty about how and where you will launch your offensive in Rome so we shall postpone your involvement at this stage. Call off your men and get them to return to base.'

Abdul was deeply upset by Ahmed's decision and launched his defence 'Ahmad, I was just pointing out my possibilities for attacking Rome, why are you rejecting my proposition?'

'You do not display the leadership qualities of your colleagues and as such I am not prepared to see our plans destroyed by a lack of professionalism! My decision is final.'

Abdul continued to protest which only made his leader more angry until he gained the upper hand by taking his pistol from his holster and pumped two bullets into the dissenter, one in the chest and the other between his eyes shattering his spectacles. Abdul's body shot back out of his chair and his blood blended into the deep red carpet he landed on. The others were shocked by the severity of their leader's sudden decisive action.

Ahmed looked round the table at the other commanders as some of his guards, responding to hearing the two shots fired, rushed into the room. He banged the table and shouted at the others 'I will not have my decisions questioned by anyone! Guards, remove Abdul's body. Have any of you any further questions?'

The shaking of the assembled company's heads brought the meeting to an abrupt end without Khalid Mugniyeh describing how he would rake havoc into the European Union Headquarter's building in Brussels. After Ahmed Fadhi's cruel demonstration of controlled freak power all the other three wanted was to get out of the room alive.

Ahmed Fahdi calmed down and picked up his mobile and called Sheik Mushasa 'Your Highness we held our final briefing today and there has been a slight change of plan. I was dissatisfied with the lack of preparation by Abdul-Ezz-al-Din so I have cancelled the Rome attack and relieved Abdul of his duties.'

'That is very disappointing Ahmed but I must fall in with your greater judgement in these matters. Now I would like you to press ahead with the other campaigns.'

'Your Highness, have you decided on a date for the attacks?'

'Yes be in place to activate everything at midday on Wednesday October 17.'

'Why October 17?'

'October 1917 was the year Russia chose for their revolution. Only our revolt instead of defeating capitalism will be making a case for raising the Islamic cause amongst any of our doubting followers.'

Chapter 35

Roland Canault shrieked out loud 'D.A.! The conformation of the order for Sheik Mushasa has arrived. It is smaller than the previous one as they have decided to leave the attack on Rome for another day. I will speak to Moscow and arrange for all the weaponry to be delivered here to be shipped to their destinations to arrive on September 27. That gives Bardosky and his friends ten days to get the goods to us.'

'Has Sheik Mushasa confirmed his payment arrangements Roland?'

'Yes D.A. he has set up an account at Verde Banque who will transfer the funds to our account at Ruski Bank for a very large consignment of wine heading for his wholesale premises in Paris, Brussels and Berlin.'

The Communications staff at MI6 could not wait to inform Richard Hartley of their latest recording from Valescure. Hartley listened carefully and immediately made his boss, Sir Alfred Dunstable, aware of the impending attacks on their European allies. He asked Sir Alfred's permission to hold talks with the security leaders in France, Belgium and Germany which was granted. Freddie Sharpe was given the task of setting up the video link which took place the following day.

Richard Hartley sat in front of the camera with Freddie Sharpe to his left and Hugh McFaul on his right. A technician in front of him turned on the camera and Richard began his address 'Morning everyone, can I just confirm you can all see and hear me?'

The screen was divided in four and the other three teams, who like the British contingent, consisted of three attendees responded positively.

'Morning again, thank you very much for your presence this morning at such short notice but what I am about to inform you needs some urgent attention. To make sure we all understand each other you have all been given earpieces which will be your interpreters way of communicating but I do appreciate that some of you have a good command of English.'

'Now the housekeeping is out of the way, we can get on to the main agenda which is a threatened Islamic terrorist attack on major tourist sites in Paris, Brussels and Berlin.'

Hartley's last few words brought gasps of horror from the assembled company as he continued, 'The targets they have chosen are the Louvre in Paris, the Brandenburg Gate in Berlin and lastly the European Commission Headquarters in Brussels.'

'MI6 has been concerned recently about the Arab Spring movements in North Africa and where the funding was coming from to pay for their activities. Our agents have been concentrating their activities on a Serbian exile, under the name of Roland Christophe

Canault, who we are convinced really is Milo Malkovitch who faked his own death whilst escaping from Serbia to safety in Russia. During the Serbian war he was in charge of procurement and would most certainly have gone to The Hague to be charged with War Crimes. Before leaving Serbia we suspect he air-freighted large consignments of weapons to Russia and considerable tranches of money to Switzerland.

Canault fronts a large wine wholesale business from Chateau Rose Blanc on the outskirts of Valescure in the Cote d'Azur. His clandestine activities involve selling a wide range of weaponry to a number of enemies we would all want to see removed.'

Hartley sensed unease amongst his audience so opened up the discussion by asking 'Ask me any questions on what I have said so far.'

His French counterpart Henri Givenchy, a sixty year old balding individual with deep blue eyes hidden behind horn-rimmed spectacles, was first to re-act to what he had heard in English.

'Bonjour Richard, this is very disturbing news to hear of any attack on one of France's most popular tourist attractions. How can we be sure how, where and when this evil act is going to take place?'

'Hello Henri, my agents have managed to penetrate Canault's defences and have reported he had a visit recently from Commissar Uri Bardosky of the KGB, a name you will all be familiar with. Bardosky organises a smuggling operation bringing the weapons into France. In the case of Libya, their requirements are on such a large scale, they will be flown to a remote disused military airport miles from anywhere. The planned attacks on the three venues I have mentioned are being funded by Saudi Arabian Sheik Abdul al Mushasa who has acquired a substantial wholesale wine business with outlets throughout mainland Europe and it is by using their premises that he will launch his offensives.'

The overweight Heinrich Schossler was next to quiz Hartley on behalf of the German Government, 'Mr Hartley I can see the attraction for a terrorist attack on one of the most famous German Landmarks but I find it difficult to comprehend how they are going to engage in such a bold activity? 'The Gate' as we refer to it has the latest security systems and is surrounded by adequate fencing and there is always an army of security men round it.'

'The 'how' is the part of the jigsaw we don't know but I can tell you the 'when'. Deliveries are to be made to Paris, Berlin and Brussels on September 27 and we have to be ready to thwart this attack any day after that. I would suggest we carry out a joint venture - starting immediately with covert activities in the districts where the warehouses are based and build up a picture of any new employees who have commenced working there recently.'

Everyone agreed to Richard's suggestion and it was now the turn of the blond Austrian Julian Klammer, the EU'S security guru, to give his thoughts.

'Morning everyone, usually terrorist attacks have the most devastating effect by killing as many people as possible but here we are seeing a change in policy as they are targeting symbols of European culture. Make no mistake if we don't prevent these attacks there will be casualties resulting in many deaths. In our case The EU is an organisation which is open to all and the reason for attacking us may be to provoke riots in our twenty-seven member states, many of whom rely on Islamic workers for their success. On behalf of the EU I would like to thank the British Government for bringing this threat to our attention. We must now set a co-ordinated plan to terminate this threat and bring those responsible to justice.'

Another voice from the French side entered the proceedings, Armand Kopa, Givenchy's second in command, cleared his throat before querying Hartley as to how accurate his intelligence information was 'Mr Hartley can I ask a direct question. What you are relating to us this morning is mind-blowing but how do we know that your sources are reliable? Do you have someone concealed in Roland Canault's operation?'

Richard Hartley's face conveyed a more serious tone, 'Mr Kopa all of us around this meeting deal in matters of intrigue. We must all protect our intelligence sources at all times so I will decline to answer your question but will add the caveat that what I have told you comes from the horse's mouth.' Everyone nodded the agreement to Hartley's wise words which paved the way for the security chiefs to spend the next few hours discussing logistics on how to destroy the Valescure emanated threat.

Chapter 36

Four hours after the Heads of Security Summit Richard Hartley requested his P.A. to set up a meeting for tomorrow afternoon to include his senior advisors and Brigadier Morton the leader of the SAS to discuss a plan that was buzzing about in his head.

It had been raining all day in London but it did not dampen the optimism of the delegates who crammed into MI6 headquarters to listen to what Richard Hartley had on his mind. Meeting Room 1 had a large half-moon shaped oak table with enough room for twenty seats. Facing the occupants was another table which Richard Hartley sat flanked by Commander Hugh McFaul and personal assistant Freddie Sharpe. The army had responded to his request and Brigadier Morton had brought with him Colonel Howard Ramsay and Dr Sebastian Pollock. Commander McFaul had strengthened the MI6 presence by inviting Campbell Anderson, Lydia Tomlinson and Roni Benson to attend.

Hartley brought the idle chatter in the room to a halt by raising his hand 'Ladies and gentlemen many thanks for making your way to our office on this very 'dreich' day as my old Scottish maths teacher would have referred to the elements outside. Yesterday I held a video link call with my equivalents in France, Germany and the European Commission in the hope of nullifying some potential terrorist attacks due to take place around Europe in the next few weeks. Some of my staff are familiar with the details of these offensives but that is not what I am here to talk about.'

'My department has wired into the offices of an arms dealer who is supplying weapons to the aforementioned terrorist organisations in addition to clients in North Africa. We know the Libyans have placed a very large order which the Russians will fly in and deliver to an airfield in the desert somewhere. However, before they take delivery the goods must be paid for. The only way the Libyans can transact such a large sum of money believed to be fifty million is in U.S. dollars. Prior to his assassination Colonel Gadaffi sent billions of dollar bills to South Africa as he did not trust leaving it in banks where he could not access it quickly. My department know the money is going to be transferred by airfreight sometime in the next ten days to Aix-en-Provence. '

'Originally I was not going to interfere with the movement of the funds as my principal objective was the threat to Europe. I did not have confirmed dates for these attacks. In the last few days we received confirmation dates for the terrorist attacks which will be attended to shortly.'

'This has made me consider reverting to my original plan which was to apprehend the container bringing in the money somewhere between Aix-en-Provence and Monaco. This is where you come in Brigadier. I want you to plan a covert attack on the container using your most experienced men and re-direct the goods to a safe destination which I suggest should be Marseille where the British Ambassador will pack them into diplomatic bags and return them to the U.K. .'

'When the Arabs don't receive their arms because Roland Canault has not received payment they will think he has stolen their money as only he and Giles Normand of Verte Banque knew about the deal. Once we have staged a successful operation I can reveal to the Libyan Liberation Army the weakness of Tariq Aziz resistance movement and they will most likely take the opportunity to terminate the threat. The Foreign Office will see this as a major coup to improve diplomatic relations with Libya.'

'Brigadier how long would we need to set up a plan to hijack the Libyan container once it arrives in Aix-en-Provence?'

'We shall return to Hereford and plan our strategy and it is really down to your intelligence network to supply the delivery date. Your communications section will get at least forty-eight hours notice and we will be in the Aix-en-Provence area to meet them. We would expect to meet some resistance as nobody sends fifty million dollars on a flight without an armed guard but let us remove that problem.'

'Excellent Brigadier please feel free to have discussions with three members of my team who are present today Lydia Tomlinson, Roni Benson and Campbell Anderson who have been closely involved in this assignment'

The Brigadier took up Hartley's offer and had a useful discussion with the three MI6 officers mostly about how they infiltrated Roland Canault's business activities. The SAS officers were particularly interested in Roland Canault's security arrangements and his level of bodyguard cover.

The meeting ended with Brigadier Morton promising his MI6 counterparts that he would have a plan in place within the week to ambush and prevent the container arriving in Monaco.

Chapter 37

'Roland. Giles Normand here, I hope everything is good with you. I have just received a message from Colonel Tariq Aziz that a large cargo aircraft carrying the Bon-Air Cargo livery has been hired privately to deliver the Libyan parcel from George, a small regional airport in the Cape Region of South Africa to Aix-en-Provence. It leaves on its ten hour journey the day after tomorrow at 12.00 noon local time and will land at Aix airport around 10.30 P.M. You will have to arrange for a local carrier to transport the consignment to our underground garage below the bank here in Monaco. Also aboard the flight will be four military escorts who have arranged for a hired car at the airport which they will collect at the Cargo offices.'

'Hi Giles glad to hear they have finally been able to arrange the transaction and as soon as you have the money safely in the bank I will inform Commissar Bardosky. He will despatch the weapons to Libya and wait to see if Aziz uses them wisely to continue his campaign. If he meets with success Moscow may favour him against some of the other players struggling for dominance in Libya. I will get one of the freight companies I use regularly to lend me a lorry and I will get one of my bodyguards David Andelic to act as driver. The vehicle we are using will be equipped hydraulically to hoist the metal containers containing the cash. There's no way we want anything to go wrong at this stage.'

'Like you Roland I will be glad when this transaction is completed. I will not hold on to the Gadaffi money any longer than I have to and at the first opportunity it will be transferred to your account at Ruski Bank minus my commission.'

Fifteen hundred miles away in London MI6 communications were enjoying overhearing both ends of the conversation which was relayed to Commander McFaul to action. Hugh immediately sent copies of the conscript to Richard Hartley and Brigadier Morton's office. The brigadier responded back by replying on the phone.

'Good afternoon Commander McFaul, thanks for sending me a copy of the conversations in the South of France. I have devised a plan which we have gone over several times with my men who are ready to leave for the target area. We have not cleared it with the French authorities but if everything goes to plan they may not even know we have been on their patch. Our mission involves the British Ambassador in Marseille who I have briefed so he can play his part in the operation.'

Hugh was impressed by the Brigadier's confidence which made him ask questions 'How many men will you need for a successful outcome Brigadier?'

'We think a dozen should do it, as the worst case scenario is we will probably only have to eliminate five bad guys, if you include the driver of the container.'

'And how will you dispose of the cargo?'

'Sorry Commander I cannot disclose that information over the phone but the SAS will take full responsibility if things go wrong. The officer in charge of the operation is Captain Hector Dick one of our more experienced officers. I'll say goodbye for now Commander, we still have some serious logistics to plan. I will be in contact with you as soon as we have succeeded in our task.'

A few hours later there was a great deal of activity at SAS Headquarters in Hereford as Captain Dick organised all the back-up equipment his men required before they set off for the South of France.

Hector split his team into four groups of three posing as holiday-makers / businessmen on a Ryanair flight from Bristol to Marseille. All their equipment for the assault was waiting for them when they arrived in Marseille after having been flown down earlier under diplomatic immunity to the same destination. The British ambassador went personally to the airport to see that his freight, packed with diplomatic seals on the outside, which he declared contained new computer hardware and furniture, to assure it cleared without any hitches with custom officials. Dick and his men made their way to the British Embassy in the centre of Marseille for their final briefing before departing later for Aix-en-Provence in a furniture removal van.

After the short drive the van pulled into a lay-by a few miles from Aix airport where Captain Dick confirmed each soldiers' individual role. Inside the van there was a Peugeot 308 car decked out in French police livery with a blue flashing light on top. The car had been stolen the previous night and transformed by technicians from Sebastian Pollard's team who painted it to resemble a local police vehicle. Also on board was a Suzuki 350 cc motorbike.

Dick sent two men out the van to make sure nobody was about before opening the back doors and releasing the car down a ramp onto the road. Another soldier followed the car on the motorbike and headed for the airport to monitor the arriving cargo plane and inform the others what route the driver was taking to Monaco, the choice was between the A7 or the E20 Motorway.

Inside the airport the driver of the heavy goods vehicle sent by Roland Canault sat patiently waiting to be waved through to the runway where the Cargo plane had parked with its rear doors open to allow a forklift to remove the metal boxes containing the dollar bills. He got the signal from the ground staff to proceed through the gates and draw up alongside the forklift whose driver steered the metal containers inside the lorry. After they were all aboard four men carrying small rectangular cases appeared from inside the aircraft's hold and made their way to a car parked on the runway.

It was 11.10 p.m. when the cavalcade commenced their journey to Monaco by taking the minor road, the A7, to avoid any unwelcome attention on the E20 Motorway. Corporal Denholm, the motorbike rider, had positioned himself to closely monitor transport movements from the cargo entrance and when the Libyan delegation passed he phoned their route to Hector Dick. Dick related Denholm's message to his navigator who worked out where they could meet up with the oncoming lorry from the airport. Two of his men, now in Gendarme uniforms, quickly got into the Peugeot and set off towards the A7. The remainder of the raiding party, guided by Corporal Denholm on his motorbike, joined the A7 at a junction which left them only some four hundred yards behind the Libyan lorry.

Rounding a bend in the road beside a lake the Libyan's vehicle was met by the flashing blue lights of a police car who ushered them into a lay-by behind some trees where they were followed by the car containing the Libyan security men and Captain Dick's lorry. Only the motorbike was allowed to go on its way.

The Libyan driver was anxious to know why they were being stopped 'What's going on?' he asked

His passenger answered 'It's a road check of some sort. They are probably looking for an escaped prisoner or a missing schoolgirl, but be on your guard.'

Behind, Captain Dick opened the rear doors and his men, all clad in black and wearing balaclavas, spilled silently out into the road and into the cover of the surrounding trees. The driver of the Libyan car caught a glimpse of the last commando disappearing into the woods and brought out his automatic pistol as he screamed 'It's a fucking trap! Get out your guns and leave the car!'

Their last intention was useless as the SAS riddled both the cars in a hail of bullets using Kalashnikov automatic rifles fitted with silencers and with the use of night sights sent the four occupants on an unplanned trip to the Almighty. D.A. tried to make a getaway by starting his lorry's engine but was taken out by Corporal Denholm, who had turned his motorbike round in order to face the driver's cabin full on. He released a volley of bullets at D.A., who proved an easy target to eliminate, puncturing several holes in his upper body and head.

It was all over in seconds and the next thing was to dispose of the bodies and cover their tracks as best they could. Hector Watson had chosen this particular lay-by beside a lake as ordnance survey maps revealed the water level descended sharply.

He issued instructions 'Quickly before any traffic comes along, put the driver's body in the car beside the security men. Drive the car over to the side of the lake and push it in. Make sure it is fully submerged before you leave the scene and if it isn't, place a small charge in the cabin to insure it sinks. Chisholm and Gordon, you change the number plates on the cargo van and camouflage the outside with the screen-print materials we brought with us.'

'Bowie and Ritchie get the police car and the motorbike back into our vehicle and remove your police uniforms.'

All orders were carried out as planned including using a large industrial vacuum cleaner to suck up any debris left from the shootings. Every detail had been covered right down to replacing the shattered windscreen through which Denholm had assassinated D.A.. Twenty minutes after the initial contact with the lorry carrying the fifty million dollars the SAS were on their way back to Marseille.

Ambassador Sydney Jenkins had arranged for the two heavy goods trucks to be housed in a large warehouse well away from the busy port. Captain Dick and his men were back in Marseille within the hour and opened up all the metal containers which revealed batches of one hundred dollar bills all sealed in plastic packages. The embassy had supplied diplomatic sacks, bearing the British Government crest, which the team utilised and sealed with padlocks. The cargo was now secure and unable to be tampered with by the French Customs & Excise. A few hours later the sacks were loaded onto a private plane and by all morning were in the hands of Her Majesty's Treasury in London until further notice.

Chapter 38

'Where's the money Roland?' asked a very anxious Giles Normand 'I came into the office this morning expecting to hear we had taken delivery of the Libyan dollars but I have just had my Head of Security on the phone to say nothing has arrived.'

'Giles, I sent D.A. to pick up the consignment last night as an extra precaution to make sure the Libyans who escorted it from South Africa did not abscond with the money. Christ I can't believe this, let me talk to Spy and Zorro and see if they have heard from D.A. I will get back to you shortly.'

Roland dialled Spy who was conducting deliveries in the wine warehouse 'Spy when did you last speak to D.A.?'

'Last night before he left for Aix, why?'

'He has not delivered the fifty million U.S. dollars to Verde Banque as instructed and now nobody has heard from him or the four guards who were accompanying the flight.'

'Have you spoken to Zorro about this?' asked Spy 'He is out just now but will be back here soon but I'll get him on the mobile and come back to you.'

Spy wasted no time in getting a hold of Zorro 'Hello Zorro, the boss is in a real panic, D.A. has not returned to Monaco with the Libyan money. Nothing has been heard from him or the four Libyan security men. Between you and me do you think he has helped himself to the money? I wouldn't have thought so, he could only pull off something like this with the help of others. Have you been aware of D.A. acting suspiciously?'

'No although he went on a long dirty weekend to Hamburg recently where he met up with some ex Stasi commanders. They are always looking to restore the opulent lifestyles they had before the Berlin Wall came down and Yeltsin succumbed to Western demands to secure a market for Soviet oil. I think it highly unlikely he would sign his own death warrant by being so stupid.'

'I agree with you. I'll let Roland know and see what he wants to do next.'

Roland listened to Spy's recall of his conversation to Zorro and grew more nervous by the minute at the thought of having to speak with Commissar Bardosky.

When he phoned the KGB leader Elana Podescu, Bardosky's P.A., informed him that Uri was in St. Petersburg and would not be returning to Moscow until late evening. Roland asked the Commissar to phone him as a matter of urgency. By the time Bardosky did phone back at 1.00 a.m. Roland was a nervous wreck.

The Commissar dispersed with small talk. 'Canault what's so important that it can't wait until morning?'

Roland inserted some Dutch courage into himself by taking a large slug of vodka before answering 'Commissar Bardosky, I have some very bad news to report. The Libyan shipment of fifty million U.S. dollars has disappeared along with one of my bodyguards David Andelic.'

'What! Who is responsible for this? Do you think the Libyans are playing a trick on us so that they can blame us for the disappearance? How well do you trust your man Andelic, not to do a runner and disappear with fifty million dollars worth of the most flexible currency on the planet? Have you told anyone apart from your own staff about this?'

'No.'

'Keep it that way. We shall conduct our own investigation. I will send some senior members of my staff first thing tomorrow morning. Something this size just can't disappear. Check out all the movements of haulage in the area. If they opted to go on the motorway they will show up on CCTV.'

'D.A. said before he left that his preferred route was the A7.'

'Commissar Bardosky, what will I tell Colonel Aziz?'

'Nothing!' roared Bardosky, 'Until we hold our investigation.'

Roland protested 'But Sir, he is waiting on our delivery to conduct his next large offensive against the Libyan Revolutionary Army and any delay could be catastrophic for him and his men.'

'Don't argue Canault, I think you have given me enough headaches for one day! Goodnight we shall speak in the morning.'

Chapter 39

Next morning having slept on the bad news from Valescure, Uri Bardosky called Gregori Rasputin to his office. Gregori had long been the Commissar's personal assistant who carried out the duties which others chose to avoid. The fifty year old had a reputation for making people disappear and inflicting torture on prisoners who refused to answer under interrogation. Gregori was powerfully built and at just under two metres tall with a very badly pot-marked face, he made a menacing figure.

'Morning Gregori, I received a call late last night from Roland Canault informing me that the container holding fifty million dollars has gone missing along with one of his bodyguards David Andelic, who he refers to as D.A. I would not like to think Andelic would be foolish enough to organise a heist which would include eliminating the four Libyan security men travelling with the consignment – unless of course they are in on the robbery? Fifty million dollars is a lot of money and could affect one's loyalty. What I want is for you to go with a team of your best investigators to Valescure and carry out a thorough investigation and see if we can recover the missing cash.'

Gregori sat rigid with surprise at what he had just heard 'Commissar, I will put together a deputation to be ready to leave this afternoon for Valescure. Chateau Rose Blanc has plenty of accommodation to house my team and I think it better if we were on the premises. I will cross-examine everyone including Roland Canault. Changing the subject slightly, have you told Colonel Aziz the funds are missing?'

'No, not yet as I cannot rule out the possibility that his men have overcome David Andelic and taken the money and hidden it. One thing I do know is we shall not be delivering his arms order anytime soon unless the money turns up. It will take him a few weeks to replace the cash and by that time he may not be able to hold his troops together if they find out they have no weapons to defend themselves with.'

'Not a good situation for Colonel Aziz or for our foreign policy in Libya. Let's hope there is a simple explanation to this problem. I'll go now and get organised and will report back to you the minute I have any news.'

'Thanks Gregori.'

Gregori left the Commissar's office and Uri Bardosky brooding about what to do next.

Roland Canault should have been in a good mood this fine late summer morning as he prepared to despatch Sheik Mashasa's arms order around Europe. His mind was elsewhere as he waited anxiously for the call from Moscow and he was surprised when the deep voice at the other end of the phone was Gregori Rasputin and not the Commissar.

'Morning Roland I have been asked by Uri Bardosky to investigate why the Libyan cargo plane did not deliver the money for the arms deal. I am leaving for

Valescure this afternoon with a team of six of my senior investigators. We shall be arriving at Nice airport at seven o'clock and would appreciate if you could arrange to pick us up. We will be staying at the chateau so get your staff to prepare rooms for us. Tomorrow morning we want to interview all your staff right down to the guy who mows your lawn. We will not leave any stone unturned to find the missing treasure. Am I being clear Roland?'

'Perfectly Gregori I will inform the kitchen to expect guests for dinner and brief them that they must all be present and correct in the morning to face your cross examinations.'

'Good man! We shall leave it at that for now. I will see you this evening.'

MI6 in London had heard every word and passed a conscript of the conversation to the relevant heads of department.

Later in the day one heavily laden truck sporting the Valescure Vineries livery left Valescure for Paris. During the next week similar trips would be carried out to both Berlin and Brussels. The first instalment of Sheik Mushasi's plan had been activated.

Chapter 40

A second undesirable call was received at Valescure Vineries office. It was Colonel Tariq Aziz. 'Hello Roland, just checking up that our little package arrived in from South Africa.'

'Yes I sent one of my men to accompany it personally and he was taking it straight to Verde Banque's secure warehouse in Monaco.' Roland lied, trying to buy as much time as possible.

'Delighted to hear that Roland, so when can we expect the arms to arrive?' asked Tariq.

'Commissar Bardosky will arrange delivery of your weapons in forty-eight to seventy-two hours subject to receiving flight clearance' said Roland extending his line in fabrications.

'That's excellent Roland, I can now prepare my strategy for my next assault against the enemy. Speak to you soon.'

The Serbian put down the phone and sat back in his chair massaging his temple and thinking of the mess he had suddenly found himself in and the thoughts going through his head.

'How close had D.A. been to the arrangements of the cash from South Africa?

Has he had any direct contact with the Libyan guards to be close enough to organise stealing the money for themselves?

He had volunteered to drive the haulier's truck to pick up the cash – was that because he wanted to be in control of the consignment as soon as possible?'

Either way Roland knew he had to get the answer to these questions before Gregori Rasputin arrived and took charge of proceedings.

Roland was not the only one planning his next move. Richard Hartley had received confirmation that the vehicles bound for the cities targeted by Sheik Mushasa were on their way north. Rather than hold another zoom meeting he contacted the respective intelligence chiefs by phone and agreed on a date to implement the assaults on the premises where the weapons were stored.

This was turning out to be one of the simplest undercover operations Hartley had been involved in and it was largely due to Roni Benson's bravery. Hartley knew that if, or rather when, the Russians discover the listening devices her life would be in great danger. They would stop at nothing to find out her true identity and the fact they had her on film meant they could circulate her photo around the world and, someone, somewhere will recognise her!

Chapter 41

True to form, Rasputin's Aeroflot passenger jet touched down at Nice Airport where Roland and Spy were waiting to meet them and whisk them over to Chateau Rose Blanc. The new arrivals made idle conversation on the way trying to pry any information from their welcoming party, which might prove to be useful when they started their audit in the morning. After having their meal the new arrivals retired for the night.

Gregori Rasputin was first down for breakfast in the dining room before going into Roland's office and sitting at his desk as if to demonstrate to the staff he was in command whilst he was visiting Chateau Rose Blanc. Fifteen minutes later everyone had arrived and Gregori began his address.

'Gentlemen it is imperative we search every metre between here and Aix-en-Provence airport. It is just under two hundred kilometres so it will take us a couple of days to survey it thoroughly. Roland, you and Oleg go to the airport and quiz the cargo office, telling them you have, as yet, not received a consignment you were expecting. By means of verifying that the truck left the premises ask to see CCTV pictures proving its departure. I will take a team along the A7 which was the preferred route by David Andelic and look for any obvious places that D.A. could possibly rendezvous with his accomplices. The other team can concentrate on the E20 motorway stopping at motorway service stations and asking truck drivers if they have seen our missing vehicle. A detailed description of the truck will be issued to you, before you leave here. Best of luck and keep in touch by mobile if you uncover anything.'

The search party left in a fleet of cars to try to uncover the fate of their missing treasure but after several hours they gave up searching as darkness fell without anybody finding anything. Next morning early, everyone again headed out from the Chateau and it was near lunchtime when Gregori and his men pulled into the lay-by at the side of the lake. They were scouring the ground on foot slowly looking for any fragments of evidence when Stanislav Gromyko called out 'Gregori! Over here, I have picked up a couple of cartridges in the trees which look as though they have been fired from a Kalashnikov if I am not mistaken.'

Gregori rushed over and took delivery of the cartridges and immediately agreed with Stanislav's opinion 'This could be the breakthrough we have been searching for. Oleg, alert all our teams and get them back here to carry out a highly detailed search of the area.'

Thirty minutes later the full complement of the Russian delegation were at the suspected site some crawling through the undergrowth on their hands and knees while others emptied the refuse bins in the hope of picking up the smallest fragment of hope.

Their activities were witnessed by the passengers of other vehicles who had stopped in the lay-by. Roland informed them they were plain clothes police officers investigating the area after a tip-off that someone had dropped off cocaine in the resting area.

It was only when they began going over the grassed border next to the lake that they stumbled upon a break in the verge caused by the Libyan security car being pushed into the lake.

Gregori looked down at the black waters and gave his thoughts on their discoveries. 'There is no doubt something untoward has gone on in this lay-by. My thoughts are, judging by the break in the grass, a car has been dumped into the lake. Keep looking for more clues and I will speak to Roland and see if he has any friends who are sub-aqua divers that he could trust to do a search of the lake for a significant fee.'

Roland responded to Gregori's request by phoning a ship chandler in Nice who dealt in transactions which would have interested the police. They agreed to send a team of divers out promptly. The teams continued to search the area and discovered several footprints which they photographed and sent to KGB headquarters in Moscow to be identified. It was another three hours before the diving team arrived.

Roland greeted Christophe Hermoine like his long-lost friend 'Christophe how are you? Many thanks for coming so quickly and let me introduce to my superior Gregori Rasputin. The two parties shook hands and then Christophe signalled for his two colleagues to come out of the Renault Espace to listen to Gregori's instructions. Due to the linguistic differences Roland delivered Gregori's message in French.

'Christophe, we have been searching for one of my colleagues who has gone missing between Aix-en Provence Airport and Monaco. For the last two days we have searched the route he was supposed to be taking and today we discovered evidence which leads us to believe a car has been deposited into the lake which may unfortunately contain our missing colleagues. You will receive a very handsome reward for your services on the basis that whatever comes out of that water will never be revealed to anyone. You and I have always understood each other Christophe so it goes without saying that I am relying on your confidentiality.'

Christophe smiled revealing his missing teeth 'Have no fear Roland but before we enter the water we shall require for you to agree our initial fee of twenty thousand Euros. If we have to salvage any vehicle we find which belongs to you another one hundred thousand Euros will have to come our way. '

Roland informed Gregori of Christophe's terms which caused Gregori to shake his head at the diver's demands but he reluctantly agreed to them. The sub-aqua team showed their appreciation by giving Roland a 'thumbs up' signal before changing into their diving gear and entering the gloomy water.

Once they commenced their descent they turned on search lights which allowed them to recognise clearly all the objects that had been dumped in the water over the years. At a depth of sixty feet they came upon the car. There were four dead bodies strapped into their seats. One of the doors had opened and they discovered a fifth body, David Andelic, suspended in reeds nearby. Christophe was shocked to see how many bullet holes there were puncturing both the car and its occupants. He signalled to his fellow divers not to speak to anyone on the surface and leave only him to talk to Roland and Gregori. Christophe used his underwater camera to video the ghoulish scene along with lots of photographs which he then brought back to the surface.

Roland was first to greet the diving team. 'Did you find anything? he asked anxiously.

Taking off his mask Christophe inhaled a big lungful of fresh air before answering 'Yes we did uncover something but I think we should go somewhere private to discuss it.'

'Okay why don't we go and sit in my car?'

'Good idea Roland. Get Gregori to join us as I think the evidence I have taken will tell you about the fate of your friends.'

After Christophe had changed into dry clothes the trio settled down in Roland's BMW and waited until Christophe brought out his camera. He positioned it on the dashboard of the BMW and turned on the video. It took the other two a few seconds to adjust to the dark content of the film which shocked them both, especially when D.A's. body came into view.

Gregori spoke first 'Good God! This is terrible, look at the number of bullets that were fired at the car. They didn't have a chance. What is puzzling me is they are all still wearing their seat-belts, which makes me think they knew the people they were talking to. It could be that they were in conversation with strangers who open-fired. Andelic at this point was still alive as the bullet holes he received in his body differ from the others having been fires by a second assassin.'

Roland, still in a daze at the loss of his bodyguard put a question to Christophe Hermoine 'Will you be able to raise the car out of the lake as we would like to give it a full forensic examination.'

Chistophe gave a cautious answer 'I am responsible for keeping the lake tidy and in the past I have brought many cars to the surface belonging to drunk drivers and suicide cases. However, normally the local Gendarmes would be in attendance but your situation is rather different. Five bodies emerging from a car riddled with bullet-holes and dumped on the grass here would be World News. What I suggest we do is I come back here during the night with my boat, which has hydraulic lifting gear. We can fix harnesses round the car and trawl it to a quieter part of the lake where there is a jetty. We will load it on to a truck and transport it to wherever you want.'

Roland had been acting as interpreter for Gregori who was excited by what he was hearing. 'Brilliant Christophe, we will leave it to you to organise.'

Ever the businessman Christophe put out his hand to shake on the arrangement, 'Roland this is as we say in the trade 'an extra' which will cost you a further twenty thousand Euros.'

Gregori shook his head in disbelief at the new terms of agreement but nodded his acceptance and muttering to himself 'Greedy bastard! I will not forget you.'

By the time they returned to Chateau Rose Blanc an email had arrived from KGB forensics on the footprints found in the mud surrounding where the car had entered the water.

Gregori read it before passing it to Roland 'Forensics have identified the footprints we found as Russian military which confirms my thoughts that your bodyguard was in this robbery up to his neck when you add this evidence to the discovery of the Kalashnikov cartridges. He was dealing with people more mercenary than even him, probably the Russian mafia which cost him his life.'

'Can we put pressure on them?'

'Unlikely, they have spies everywhere but I will call Commissar Bardosky and see what he thinks our next move should be.'

The call to Bardosky confirmed to the ever present MI6 audience that the MI6 plan had worked and it was an excited Hugh McFaul who phoned Brigadier Morton and gave a precis of Gregori's phone call.

Morton laughed out loud 'They've swallowed it hook, line and sinker. We used Russian equipment we found in Afghanistan when the Russians left and it worked! Now they will be engaged in witch-hunts all over the place, which will occupy their resources for some time.'

Hugh replied 'On behalf of the department thanks Brigadier for a very successful outcome. We shall now concentrate on destroying the rest of their Valescure base.'

Chapter 42

Three nights later Christophe Hermoine steered his boat up the lake to where the sunken vehicle lay and attached cables to it after placing D.A.'s body in the boot of the car. As described he dragged the car out to the middle of the lake before lifting it on board his vessel to be despatched later in an enclosed van to the Chateau, where it was put into a wine warehouse. Next day a team of Russian police forensic experts arrived to do a full examination of the vehicle and its occupants.

The five bodies were laid out in the stables which had become a temporary mortuary but the autopsies did not last long as in the heat of Valescure they would decay and begin to smell. Gregori ordered his men to dig five graves spread out in different areas of the thirty acre landscape of the estate. He waited anxiously for the team's conclusions which were available to him five hours after they had begun their investigation.

Lieutenant Ivan Levot, a blond haired, long nosed forty year-old wearing thick spectacles, in his position as senior forensic examiner offered the following explanation 'The four Libyan victims were shot at short range by several marksmen using Kalashnikov automatic weapons. They were probably fitted with silencers otherwise the noise would have attracted attention. The bodywork of the car was completely devastated and the occupants all have masses of wounds all over their bodies. They were all carrying weapons but never got a chance to use them probably because they felt comfortable with whoever they had met in the lay-by.'

'The fifth occupant David Andelic did not die beside the others as we discovered traces of motor oil on his clothes which would suggest he was killed while still in his truck by an assassin who aimed purposely at his head and shoulders. The bullets came from a direction we believe directly in front of the vehicle shattering the wind-screen. We confirmed that fact from the particles of glass in his hair and his clothing. To conclude, this was a well-planned operation and I hate to say it looks like an inside job.'

Lieutenant Levot's view backed up Gregori Rasputin's analysis of the situation 'Thank you Ivan. Your final analysis concurs with my own in that there has been a planned attack on the truck, which was bringing the money masterminded by David Andelic. He had trusted others, only to perish by his misjudgement. I will not let the matter rest. If your analysis is correct there has been a truck driving around in this area for the last two days without a windscreen. Roland, check out all the windscreen replacement companies in the area to see if they have fitted any new ones in the last forty-eight hours.

The Russians phoned fifty glass companies within a hundred mile radius to no avail.

Chapter 43

Two Days Later:

Dr al-Bhgaddy the Libyan Foreign Secretary received a telephone call from Ian Goodman his British counterpart 'Good morning Foreign Secretary Goodman, this is indeed an unexpected pleasure to receive a call from the British Government. What can I do for you?'

'On the contrary Dr al-Bhgaddy it is I who am the bearer of some good news which will be of interest to you. Our intelligence services have recently come across news that one of your rebellious military leaders placed an order for a large consignment of arms to enable him to continue his assault on towns approaching Tripoli. Fortunately there has been a delay in the Russians receiving payment and they are refusing to send the cache of arms.'

'The leader in question is Colonel Tariq Aziz and he now has a very ill-equipped fighting force made up of new recruits who could possibly be easily dispersed if they came under attack from your army.'

'Thank you for this information Foreign Secretary Goodman. Aziz has become a thorn in our flesh and we would welcome putting a dent in his ambition to restore the government we overthrew a few years ago. I will act on our conversation immediately.'

Goodman concluded 'I wish you every success Sir and I would like to see more of this co-operation between our two countries in the future. Good day and good luck.'

Two weeks later the Libyan army made a huge assault on Colonel Aziz battalions which were technically unable to compete with the attackers and had to retreat back into the desert. Tariq Aziz was apoplectic about making this decision as many of his newest recruits decided to go A.W.O.L. which set his cause back two years. He cursed Roland Canault for his non-delivery of new arms and was still suspicious that Canault and his cronies had stolen the Libyan cash for themselves. He vowed to himself to get his revenge.

Chapter 44

October 1 2011

Richard Hartley cleared his throat before using the microphone in front of him to address his European counterparts.

'Gentlemen I am pleased to confirm that all the consignments of weapons for the impending attacks on your capital cities have been delivered by Valescure Vineries transport. So our next move is to implement our assault on these premises in a co-ordinated manner. I consider we are under pressure to act quickly since we still don't know what date or time Sheik Mushasa has decided to put his plans into operation. Before we name our day to apprehend our enemies can I ask how your surveillance is going?'

German Heinrich Schlosser was first to answer the question 'Sheik Mushasa's International Wines warehouse supplies Berlin from an Industrial Estate fifteen miles to the east of the city. I have had a team of men posing as fibre optic contractors laying cables across the street from the premises clocking out all the personnel going in and out of the building. In the last two weeks my men have reported five new employees who are all wearing heavy coats big enough to conceal weapons. We managed to photograph them using road contractor's surveillance equipment and they have all been recognised as wanted terrorists. I agree that we have to move quickly if we are to avoid a disaster. That's all my news, over to you Henri.'

'Thanks for your update Heinrich. The enemy is lurking at the International Wines depot out near Charles de Gaulle Airport. We have managed to install surveillance staff in the offices of the Air Ministry which fortuitously gives us an excellent view of the wine company's depot. We are monitoring it twenty-four hours a day and one night we witnessed five unidentified new members of staff.'

Richard Hartley interrupted 'So five seems to be the team number for all these assaults.'

'Yes' responded Henri 'I agree with Heinrich we have to name our attack date as soon as possible.'

Julian Klammer, the EU's Head of Security, was next to speak 'I have been receiving information from my contacts in Wallonia, where International Wines operate their offices, who tell me a small group of strangers have descended upon them. I sent in one of my best men posing as a Customs & Excise officer who had the power to inspect all personnel records. He was able to get the names and photographs of the latest employees. There was some resistance from the management to revealing these details until they were warned failure to do so would result in their warehouses being closed down. We have been able to identify three of the five as known terrorists. The other two are younger so they may not be on our radar yet. Like our friends in Paris and Berlin we are poised to move in on our threat to the city.'

Hartley took control of the meeting once more 'Thanks for your updates. Now we have to decide on a date for our operation. We shall need armed response teams in equivalent numbers to overcome each individual member of the terrorist teams. We will have to know the whereabouts of each suspect at all times. We cannot give them any opportunity to warn their colleagues so we must move in unison. If any of our teams meet resistance there should be no hesitation in implementing a 'shoot to kill policy' in order to protect our own men.'

'Agreed,' said the three intelligence chiefs in their respective languages giving the unified answer Richard Hartley wanted to hear.

'Can I suggest Thursday October 6 at 05.00 hours?'

The nodding of heads was enough to verify the suggestion. Military leaders from the crack Special Operation Forces all over Western Europe briefed their personnel on the seriousness of what they were about to be involved in and diligently prepare for all possible contingencies.

October 6 – 04.59 hours.

Richard Hartley had stayed in MI6 headquarters overnight and now positioned himself on a seat in the centre of MI6's Control Centre. Before him sat teams of computer boffins who monitor the globe twenty-four hours a day, three hundred and sixty-five days a year. The huge screen which filled the whole of one wall was capable of overseeing all the department's activities all over the world. This evening the screen was split into six sections, one for each of the terrorists' temporary residences and the other three covered the warehouses where the weapons were stored. Surveillance teams had been tracking the terrorists twenty-four hours a day for the last four days and had established patterns of behaviour. Some of them went to prayers at a local Mosque, others frequented clubs or went for something to eat. The one constant was that they were always back in their lodging by eleven o'clock. A light remained on all night accompanied by the flickering beam from a television set which the security teams presumed was for the benefit one of the terrorists who was acting as night watchman.

The armed response teams had to be exact in their approach to the criminal's apartments, as any hesitation would alert them and send out warning signs to their colleagues in the other two cities. In preparation, at midnight the teams closed off the surrounding streets supposedly for road repairs to keep traffic out the targeted areas. To assist them they were all using heat-seeking equipment which identified where the terrorist acting as the watchman was situated. This was achieved by calling at the adjacent apartment next door to their target and placing an explosive charge on the wall nearby to where the guard was positioned. It was imperative that he had to be eliminated first and then the others who were probably sleeping would be arrested but if they resisted by firing their weapons, they would suffer the same fate as the watchmen.

At 05.00.hours panels in the control room flashed into light as the charges exploded and knocked down the walls as planned. At the same time hordes of armed response officers threw tear gas canisters into all the rooms on the premises while simultaneously firing accurately to kill off the overnight guards. The control room was filled with the instructions in three different languages as the various leaders of the raiding parties screamed their commands through loudspeakers. The Berlin and Brussels units did meet with some resistance but the quick bursts from automatic weapons which lasted only forty-five seconds were followed by silence and in turn by cries of surrender. Across the cities targeted additional armed response teams burst into the wine warehouses and secured the premises by only firing warning shots which was enough for the innocent night guards to go down on the floor and beg for their lives.

The respected military leaders confirmed their successes to their Intelligence centres. Ten minutes later all the security chiefs appeared on the large screen. All parties connected to the operation were jubilant at the victory over the insurgents and the fact they had removed major terrorist threats all over Europe.

Henri Givenchy representing France summed up the evening's events 'Tonight western democracies have shown great leadership in stemming the threat from

Islamic extremism. This would not have been possible without the contribution of the British Security Services who unselfishly shared their intelligence and in doing so avoided three potential disasters. On behalf of France, Germany and the European Commission thank you Assistant Controller Hartley.'

Richard Hartley graciously accepted the complements bestowed upon him by the other three intelligence chiefs. MI6's actions would enhance relationships with the rest of Europe. The spy-catcher reflected that all this would never have materialised if it had not been for combined efforts of his staff and in particular the bravery of Mhairi McClure whose life after tonight would be in greater danger than ever!

Roland Canault was watching breakfast television and nearly choked on his toast. He heard the main item of news highlighting the success of a major international co-operative offensive which prevented a series of major terrorist threats all over Europe. He was still shaken at what the newsreader was reporting when his phone rang.

'Roland!!' a voice he recognised screamed down the phone 'have you heard the news? Our men have all either been arrested or shot and their activities are already being linked to Sheik Mushasa. He is furious and has already left Monaco by helicopter for an un-named airport where his private plane will take-off immediately for home before the authorities can prevent it getting into the air. Can you explain to us how this happened? Has your activities been the subject of any investigation recently?'

Roland was startled by the phone call and it took him a few seconds to compose himself. 'Look Khalid, this has come as a great shock to me. I only hope your men have stored the weapons well away from the wine deliveries otherwise I might be following you on the next flight out of here. Give me time to investigate the situation and I will get back to you,'

The conversation was relayed to Richard Hartley as usual and he recommended to his European counterparts that they ignore where the weapons had come from at this point in time. He felt it was more advantageous for the European security experts to keep Roland Canault's operation as a source for identifying future terrorist movements. Thankfully they agreed, so Sheik Mushasa was safe from prosecution for the time being.

Chapter 45

Three months later.

Winter had come to Valescure and after the New Year celebrations had passed, life returned to normal which for Roland Canault meant taking advantage of the mild Cote D'Azur weather. He continued to have regular tennis matches and the only difference in the playing conditions was he now had to wear a sweater over his tennis shirt.

To start his weekend off on a positive note Roland had arranged a doubles match partnering Gigi Montalban against Milagro D'Andrea and his tennis coach Pierre de Feu. The professionals negotiated a handicap system which gave Gigi and Roland a three game start in each set. The first set went the way of the amateurs due to some fine play at the net by Gigi. Pierre and Milargo reversed their fortunes in the second with some powerful forehands during some games which seemed to go on forever.

The exhausted players stopped for a well-earned drinks break during which time Roland requested 'New Balls Please.' The young attendant, who had only been at the tennis academy for a few weeks, brought two new tubes of yellow tennis balls on to the court to replace the used balls. He settled the new balls in a holder just behind where Roland was about to serve. Roland returned to the base line and picked up one of the balls which he bounced three times as he always did before serving and stopped. He turned round and shouted at the ball boy who was now twenty yards away 'Where did you get these balls? They are heavier than the last ones!'

The boy smiled as he continued to retreat before shouting to the Serb 'I was told to tell you they are from 'The Libyan Camel Bandit' as you refer to Colonel Tariq Aziz!'

THE BOY PRESSED THE DETONATOR IN HIS HAND.

A huge explosion erupted as the explosives within all the replacement balls ignited, causing a substantial hole in the ground where Roland Canault had stood to take his final breath. The blast caused the clay courts to form a large dust cloud, temporarily hiding the mangled fencing around the court which was now lying in a heap on top of Roland's remains, with a fallen floodlit stanchion for company.

As the dust cleared all that could be seen was a large dark red patch glistening in the sun amongst the Serbian's body parts. Gigi, who had taken up her doubles position in front of her partner, emerged out of the sandy mist screaming. Her body was covered in hot shrapnel from the blast and her tennis dress was covered in blood. The tennis net had disintegrated. Both Pierre and Milagro were lying on their backs in shock clutching parts of their bodies which had received wounds. Chaos followed, with players from other courts and golfers from across the road, all converging on the scene. What was left of Roland Canault's body was now unrecognisable and quickly hidden by the tennis academy staff who draped a large green plastic cover which was used to protect the courts from flooding.

Everyone was in a state of shock including his two bodyguards, Spy and Zorro, who had not been subjected to such explosions since they had served in the Serbian War. In all the confusion they had failed to notice the young ball boy run away from the carnage and escape on the back of a motorbike which departed at high speed in the direction of Cannes.

The emergency services were quickly on the scene. The police and the fire brigade fenced off the distressed area where the body parts lay, by erecting a large white tent where the forensics could carry out their examinations to establish what caused this mayhem. Teams of paramedics helped the injured before loading them gently into ambulances. The vehicles headed for the Grand Central de Medicines Hospital in Cannes with their emergency blue lights flashing. Inside one ambulance the paramedics worked tirelessly on Gigi, who apart from Roland, had taken the bulk of the blast and was losing a lot of blood. Milargo and Pierre's injuries were not so life threatening but both of them had to be sedated to calm them down in an effort to reduce the tremendous shock they had just witnessed.

Dr Arman Garnier, the senior pathologist attached to the forensics team, gave the Police Inspector Paul Girome a quick opinion of how the explosion had been set off. 'The new tennis balls, five of which were stacked directly behind Monsieur Canault, plus the one he was holding, all contained a coating of thin plastic explosive. The explosives had been very cleverly installed on the inside surface of the balls which were re-stitched together again. Each one contained a minute firing pin which activated simultaneously by the assassin pressing the detonator which produced an enormous explosion killing their target instantly, in what was a most horrible but quick death. The ball the victim was holding in his hand threw Canault's body backwards to be met with a deluge of explosions from the five other balls. If Roland Canault had only been subjected to the impact of the ball he was holding, he may have survived, but with serious long-term injuries.'

Inspector Girome thanked the pathologist for his analysis and added 'Okay we will take it from here.'

Chapter 46

The ball boy from the tennis academy clung on to the motorcycle rider's leather jacket as he wound his way round the bends at speed. Their destination was a small sandy cove near Mandelieue-la –Napoule. A motor launch was waiting with its rear gangplank down and the motor cycle rider drove straight up it, coming to an abrupt halt. Once the rider and the boy had alighted from the motorbike two deckhands threw a large blue canvas over it while a colleague brushed away all traces of the motorbike tyres in the sand. Hydraulic lifting gear raised the launch's rear entrance as the boat set off out to sea. After half an hour the deck hands removed the canvas wiped down the bike with surgical spirit, tied the crash helmets to the handlebars and dropped the BMW 500 overboard thus removing a large amount of evidence from the crime scene.

The boy was summoned to the Captain's cabin where the cunning figure of Tariq Aziz stood waiting for him 'Welcome back Assim, I trust our plan was successful, come sit down and tell me how that wicked scoundrel Roland Canault perished.'

Jani Canault was at her yoga class in Valescure when it was interrupted by Spiridon Natalic who caught the attention of the instructor to come out of the hall. He explained that he had to talk to Madam Canault urgently and the instructor went back to the hall and told Jani of Spy's request to speak to her.

Not wanting to abandon her class she rushed up to Spy 'Spiridon what is so important to cause you to disturb my yoga class? You know how much I enjoy it.'

Spy spoke gently 'Jani, I have some very bad news. Roland has been killed while he was playing tennis.'

The colour drained out of Jani Canault's body as she tried to take in Spy's statement. 'How? Did something fall on his head? I know he was not happy with the floodlight stanchions.'

'No, there was an explosion and he bore the brunt of it, I regret to say.'

The full horror of what she was hearing hit Jani and she fainted into Spy's arms. Spiridon called out for assistance and the instructor rushed back out from the hall.

'Madam Canault has just had some bad news. Her husband has been killed in an accident. Can you please gather up her belongings while I take her out to my car? Sorry I should have introduced myself, I am Spiridon Natalic one of Mr Canault's security staff. I shall send someone back later for Jani's car.'

Spy was able to carry Jani out to his Mercedes and made the short journey back to Chateau Rose Blanc. On the way Jani regained consciousness and Spy gave her some paper handkerchiefs which she made good use of to wipe away the tears.

Spy spoke to Jani during the drive 'I will have to inform Commissar Bardosky immediately we get back to the villa. I expect he will send his own deputation to Valescure very quickly and issue instructions regarding the future of Valescure Vineries.'

Jani surprised Spy by saying she would make the call to the Commissar 'You probably observed Spy that Roland and I put on a good front when marketing the business but in real life we led very separate existances. I knew about his women and gradually he drove me to seeking male company. Uri Bardosky knows all about our dalliances. I hope he will allow me to continue running the business as I do not want to go back behind the Iron Curtain.'

By the time they arrived back at the chateau Jani had composed herself enough to phone Moscow. After a short delay she was connected to Commissar Bardosky who was sounding more jovial than usual 'Jani! How nice to hear from you. Has Roland left you in charge of the office while he is out playing tennis again?'

Jani took a deep breath and holding back tears she croaked out 'Commissar, Roland was killed this morning by a bomb planted on the tennis court as far as we know.'

'Killed! Oh my God! This is unbelievable. How did his bodyguards not see the danger coming? Usually they survey the area our men are visiting looking for any unusual objects.'

'We don't know at this stage. The French Gendarmerie cordoned off the area and their forensic teams are doing a full investigation so I would expect to get a visit from them in the next twenty-four hours.'

Bardosky's mind was racing at a hundred miles an hour thinking of how the French authorities would look into the activities at Chateau Rose Blanc. Composing himself he asked 'Jani is Spiridon Natalic with you?'

'Yes'

'Put him on the phone please.'

Jani handed the phone to Spy 'Commissar, Natalic speaking.'

Bardosky's tone changed 'Spiridon how the hell did you and Zoric let this tragedy happen? This could ruin our whole operation in the region unless we can create a cover-up. I will work on something but in the meantime I want you to hide all traces of the armament division of Valescure Vineries to a safe haven. I shall send Gregori Rasputin and his team to carry out our own investigation and assist you in any way we can. Keep me informed immediately of any further developments. Put me back to Jani.'

'Jani I am sorry for your loss. Roland was a good operator who we valued greatly. Unfortunately the show must go on so for the foreseeable future could you act in Roland's place? Gregori will be with you as soon as possible to help you out with funeral arrangements etc.'

'Commissar I will be most honoured to serve the cause which Roland held so close to his heart. Goodbye and we shall talk again soon.'

MI6 in London could not believe what they were hearing and a copy of the conversation which had been translated into English was sent by email to Hugh

McFaul. McFaul listened to everything intently a few times making notes as he did so. Once he was satisfied with his observations, he called Richard Hartley's office to request an audience with the Assistant Controller.

Hartley had been attending a strategy meeting with his Asian desk but broke off when he heard there was a 'Red Alert' concerning Valescure. Hugh entered Hartley's office to find the Assistant Controller sitting at his desk making himself familiar with the tape McFaul had emailed to him. As he let the recording come to a halt he signalled to Hugh to take a seat.

'Afternoon Hugh, this is a major development which could have serious repercussions for the future of our spying mission in Valescure. The French authorities are going to be all over this incident and I may have to reveal that the information we gave out to our European partners came from Roland Canault's operation. On top of that Gregori Rasputin is coming on to the scene and I would imagine that Uri Bardosky will give him an open role to analyse everything. They may decide whether to close their station down quickly and bring their staff home to Russia.'

Chapter 47

Uri Bardosky spent all day thinking about what had happened in Valescure.

In recent months there had been instances of irregularity which did not usually happen with any of the KGB's field operations.

First, the five hundred million dollars payment for the Libyan arms deal had disappeared. Despite using all his facilities to trace the money it had just vanished. The Commissar still suspected that David Andelic was involved in the heist but he was a long way from proving it.

Secondly, the arms Canault had sent to Paris, Brussels and Berlin as requested by Sheik Mushasa arrived but were never given the opportunity to be activated. How could the security authorities throughout Europe have known about the Islamic leader's plan?

Thirdly, the latest incident has resulted in the death of a Russian agent Milo Malkovitch alias Roland Canault. Roland had no obvious enemies and was well established in South of France High Society.

The only client he had crossed in the recent past was Colonel Tariq Aziz and if Commissar Bardosky was able to prove beyond reasonable doubt that the Libyan is responsible for Canault's death, Tariq Aziz is now a dead man walking!

NOBODY GETS AWAY WITH MURDERING A KGB OFFICER!

Uri picked up his phone 'Elana get hold of Gregori and tell him to report to me immediately.'

Twenty minutes later Gregori Rasputin entered his controller's office and was directed to sit at a polished wooden table opposite the Commissar. 'Morning Sir, you wanted to see me. How can I be of assistance?

'Morning Gregori, I received some very bad news last night from our French station in Valescure. Roland Canault has been killed by a bomb planted on a tennis court while he was playing with Gigi Montalbin, Pierre De Feu and Milagro D'Andrea. It seems to have been a sizeable device as his body was blown to bits and some of the fencing around the court collapsed on top of him.'

Gregori was shocked at what he was hearing 'Bloody hell! We knew Roland was operating in a dangerous field but he always had more than adequate security around him and his family. The bodyguards obviously took their eye off the ball which is not acceptable and quite likely their dereliction of duty will be punished.'

'Yes Gregori I will be ordering a full enquiry, but today I am more concerned about how we resolve things in the short term. I have been going over in my head all the things which have happened at Chateau Rose Blanc recently and I am coming to the conclusion that there are too many coincidences.

For instance, who tipped off the robbers regarding the arrival of the Libyan cash?

Who revealed Sheik Mushasa 's attack details which was designed to cause problems all over Western Europe?

How did the assassins know where and when Roland was due to play tennis?

All these instances smack of an 'Inside Job' so I want you to take a team down to Valescure and rip Chateau Rose Blanc apart and give everyone employed there a thorough cross examination. You can include in your interrogation the threat of torture.'

The prospect of being given the freedom to carry out a full investigation appealed to Gregori who smiled at his leader and commented 'Commissar I will stop at nothing to find out what has been going on at Valescure and bring whoever is responsible for our interference to justice.'

Chapter 48

Three days later Jani visited the wounded in hospital. Dr Georges Hugo, the senior consultant in charge of the burns unit, greeted her and showed the newly widowed elegant lady clad in a black dress into his office.

He began his update on the three patients 'Gina Montalban is giving us the most concern as she took the brunt of the explosion. Fortunately for her, she had taken up her position at the net with her back to the explosion which blew her off her feet. Several particles of shrapnel lodged themselves in various parts of her rear body, and had she been facing the other way, she would probably have been killed. She has been in great pain and we have sedated her, keeping up her strength by feeding her through an intravenous drip. The main problem which remains is to see if we can save her right leg, which we are hopeful of achieving, but she will be a cripple for the rest of her life.'

'Pierre De Feu and Milagro D'Andrea were of course facing the explosion and both of them suffered severe burns to their bodies and head. In Milagro's case her hair has been burnt considerably and she may require some plastic surgery. Pierre being an older man did give us cause for concern as often the shock of such an explosion can bring on a heart attack, but he has not shown signs of anything, most likely due to his athleticism. Both of them are conscious and resting in private rooms if you want to see them.'

Jani smiled 'Thank you doctor that would be very nice.'

The couple walked along the corridor and stopped at a pale blue door with the name 'Milagro D'Andrea' slotted on the white nameplate in the middle of it. Dr Hugo knocked on the door before entering. Milagro was sitting on her bed. Her head was heavily bandaged and what could be seen of her limbs also appeared to have lighter bandages covering the burns she had received. Her face was swollen but she still managed to smile at Jani.

Jani returned her smile 'Milagro I am so sorry for what has happened. I was not aware of Roland having enemies who would resort to this level of violence and endanger the lives of innocent members of the public while they were playing tennis. The police and Roland's friends are investigating who may be responsible and we shall do everything to find them.'

Milagro managed to respond but her voice was very weak 'Jani, you have my sincere condolences. Roland was a good friend who everyone at the tennis academy loved. The doctors have said my wounds should heal up although I may be left with some scars which may require plastic surgery.'

Jani reacted instantly 'If you need any extra cosmetic operations do not worry about how much they cost, as Valescure Vineries shall pick up the bill.'

'Thank you for your offer Jani. If you don't mind I would like to rest.'

Dr Hugo and Jani left the room and entered another room similarly decorated where Pierre de Feu was sitting up in bed reading a magazine. Due to standing well behind the base line his injuries were not so severe but he was wearing some bandages on his upper body and head. His face lit up when he saw who was accompanying Dr Hugo.

'Jani my dear! Good of you to visit me' he exclaimed taking her hand and kissing it. 'This is a horrible thing that has happened to your loved one. I have known Roland for all the years you have been in Valescure and Roland was one of my best pupils. Have the police been able to find out who is responsible? This is not the sort of incident the Cote D'Azur has had much experience of before, but I would think the Gendarmerie will bring in assistance from outside the area.'

Jani moved closer and patted the old tennis coach gently on his brow 'Pierre, don't you worry, I am certain the authorities will bring these wicked people to justice. What I want to see most is you making a full recovery so I'll leave you now to relax with your magazine.'

Once they left Pierre's room and were walking along the corridor Jani reiterated her offer of assistance 'Dr Hugo keep me updated on their progress and remember if they need any procedures I will pay for it.'

News of the explosion had reached the Chesham safe house via Hugh McFaul and shocked Mhairi McClure to the core. The sudden, abrupt, cruel ending of Roland Canault's life, a man who had been very much in her thoughts, since she had returned to the U.K. She had fond memories of their brief intimate encounter which in other circumstances she would have liked to prolong. Receiving the further news about the injuries to Gigi, Pierre De Feu and especially Milagro brought tears to her eyes. She thought briefly about making a phone call to Milagro's hospital bed but she knew every call would be monitored, and draw suspicion upon herself.

Later that evening lying in bed she reflected how life had been very cruel to her when it came to the opposites sex - her first love Matt O'Reilly had been gunned down by a British army hit squad. Allan Phair with whom she had a memorable night of passion, had been knifed to death in Edinburgh by hit men hired by her IRA boss John Caldwell. Now, her latest lover Roland Canault had been cruelly removed from this world by enemies who had yet to take responsibility for this crime.

Another personal worrying thought for Mhairi was with the connection to Valescure now being severed, would Richard Hartley send her back to HMP Askham to continue her prison sentence?

Chapter 49

Gregori Rasputin, after adjusting his horn-rimmed spectacles, was in no mood for idle gossip as he began his address to the assembled staff at Chateau Rose Blanc. He had arranged for a large screen which made it easy for viewing and instructed the French speaking staff to follow his announcement by watching the sub-titles on the video link.

'Good morning, I have been sent here by Commissar Bardosky to assist with the funeral arrangements for Roland and help Jani in any way I can.'

Jani, sitting to Gregori's right, nodded her approval of his opening remarks as the KGB man continued 'Commissar Bardosky is not happy with events here in recent months and is concerned that there may be a flaw in our security systems. It appears there may be someone amongst you who has been leaking information to our enemies and if our investigations reveal the culprit he will not be long for this world!'

A murmur broke out amongst the thirty-odd workers who ranged from domestic cleaners to gardeners with a few security staff included. The Russian raised a hand to bring the workers attention back to his statement 'My team will be tearing this place apart starting today and we will stop at nothing to uncover any leaks in our security. If anyone amongst you has any suspicions as to where the leaks have come from, please talk to me and what you say will be kept confidential. Go about your work as usual but be prepared to be called upon to help with our enquiries at short notice. That is all for the time being.'

Jani and the staff dispersed to get on with their duties leaving Rasputin and his six Moscow colleagues to set out their search strategy. It was agreed that they would split into two teams of three and using all their checking skills to cover each area of the premises quickly. When they had finished a section, they would swap positions and carry out a double check as experience told them a fresh pair of eyes often reveals a new piece of evidence. 'Better to carry out a security search slowly and methodically' was the message displayed in the KGB manuals.

The teams decided to start with the least obvious area which included the twenty en-suite bedrooms as that was the most unlikely place to find any electronic bugs which would connect to the business end of Valescure Vineries. The search went on for hours and proved totally negative. While this was being carried out Gregori Rasputin spent his time with Jani and the two bodyguards learning how the business operated on a daily basis. He particularly took a keen interest in making himself familiar with all their suppliers and banking arrangements.

Next day Gregori's team moved their surveillance to the converted stables Canault had used as his offices. They took the contents of all the metal cabinets containing a record of every business transaction, studied them and jotted down any customer grievances they came upon. All the electrical equipment was checked by computer experts who reported that none of the computer systems had been subject to a cyber attack. The searchers moved on to look behind everything that was attached to the walls – photographs, paintings, calendars etc – but again with no successful outcome.

Gregori Rasputin had entered the fray at this point and he ordered the carpets and the underlay beneath it to be lifted. 'Before you do that, have a look under the chairs and take the drawers out of that desk before you turn it upside down.'

It took two men to lift the heavy chairs because of their awkward shape and two further members of the team to assist in laying the large desk on its back. Gregori moved closer to the furniture and cast an educated eye over all the surfaces. He would have missed one of the listening devices had it not been for one of his colleagues shining a torch through from the opposite side from where he was observing the desk, to reveal what, at first, looked like a design flaw. He got down on his knees and crawled under to examine it further, expecting to see the manufacturer's motif. Rasputin had planted surveillance equipment many times during his career, so he instantly recognised that what he was looking at was a piece of electronic genius. Without thinking he blurted out 'Got it men, this is how the enemy has been one step ahead us!'

The other members of the team rushed forward to see what Gregori had discovered and made a number of suggestions as to the effectiveness of the device. The Russian leader suddenly realised he was possibly being listened to so he signalled for everyone to stop talking by placing his finger over his mouth.

His last words had been heard in London and the MI6 communications department immediately cut the link to Valescure.

Hugh McFaul received confirmation that all listening services into Chateau Rose Blanc had been aborted. His reaction was to inform Assistant Controller Richard Hartley.

'Damn it McFaul!' exclaimed Hartley 'that is bad news. Uri Bardosky is an experienced operator and he has sussed that there were leaks somewhere at Chateau Rose Blanc. His next priority will be to establish how they got there. You don't have to be a genius to work out that the main suspects are the three British visitors, two posing as financial gurus while the other acts the part of the doting wife. This means that we have lost contact with Bardosky's next move but we still have the listening devices Benson and Anderson planted at Verte Banque. I should imagine Gregori Rasputin will be following up on all Roland Canault's contacts so he will visit Giles Normand in the not too distant future.'

'What we have to do as a priority is to protect Roni Benson and Campbell Anderson which will not be easy as Bardosky will stop at nothing to find out their true identities. Anderson, because he has been at MI6 for a number of years, may be known to them but Benson is the one they will target once they find out she had an intimate relationship with their murdered agent.'

'Hugh, make sure she remains at Chesham for the time being with no access to the outside world. Explain to her it is in her own interest and take the further precaution of having Beverley Thomson monitor her closely and instruct her not to let Roni out of her sight.'

'Yes Sir I will pay her a visit tomorrow.'

The communications team were unaware of Roni Benson's true identity and considered her part of their section, so when the lines to Chateau Rose Blanc were cancelled, she received a communiqué like everyone else informing her of the changes. What she was not expecting was the arrival of Commander Hugh McFaul at Chesham. Hugh had told Beverley Thomson to expect him, but not to let Roni know. He added the caveat that he wanted Beverley to sit in on his meeting with Roni.

Hugh was enjoying the coffee the kitchen staff at Chesham had provided when Roni and Beverley entered the meeting room. Hugh cast a look over the dangerous woman who he had first clapped eyes on twenty-five years ago. He first met her at the funeral of his best friend's father who Roni (then known as Mhairi McClure) had been an accessory to his murder. She looked very relaxed and an outsider would think she demonstrated all the trappings of a top business executive – the hair beautifully styled, her make-up applied carefully and wearing a white blouse with a grey pinstripe short skirt.

Hugh began 'Morning ladies. Roni, I am here principally to talk to you but I have asked Beverley to join us as what I have to say affects her. You have no doubt heard about the explosion on the tennis court in Valescure which resulted in Roland Canault's death and severe injuries to his fellow players. The loss of the Russian agent has initiated a witch-hunt by the KGB, who, like ourselves, look for revenge in these instances. I regret to say Roni that you will be one of the leading suspects in their investigation.'

Hugh's last remark brought a reaction from the two women on the other side of the desk.

'Oh no!' wailed Beverley.

Roni went pale and poured herself some water before responding defiantly 'So what is your boss Hartley going to do about that then?'

Hugh was not ready for such a brazen response and he took a sip of his coffee to gather his thoughts during the silence that followed the outburst. 'Assistant Controller Hartley wants to inform you that from today you have to be confined to this safe house unless you receive an instruction from his office to do otherwise.'

Roni stared back at McFaul 'I might as well be back in Askham Prison.'

'No you wouldn't!' shouted Hugh raising his voice 'prison walls have wagging tongues and the KGB would soon find you. They would arrange for one of the inmates to assassinate you with the co-operation of one of the prison warders who would make it look like a suicide involving a knife from the kitchen or an overdose of a deadly poisonous solvent!'

'How do you know this?' asked Roni.

Hugh grinned back at Roni with a cold look on his face 'Just believe me it happens.'

He continued 'Beverley, your job is to look after Roni. Do not let her stray out of your sight. The guards in the grounds will also be told not to let Roni leave the property unaccompanied.'

Roni did not like what she was hearing and tried testing Hugh again 'So how long is this likely to last Commander?'

Hugh looked Roni in the eye 'I don't know. It is up to Richard Hartley to decide. Remember, he still has the power to control the two microchips that were inserted into your body which he will activate should you ever disobey him.'

Chapter 50

The low winter sun was setting over Monaco when Gregori Rasputin made his way up the steps leading to Verte Banque. He had arranged to meet Giles Normand late in the afternoon as the banker's final customer for the day so there would be no time constraints on their discussions. Giles dispersed with offering the usual coffee instead suggesting they drink something stronger. Gregori settled for a large vodka and tonic with a slice of lemon while Giles had a 'Rusty Nail'*.

Gregori had brought a linguist with him who spoke both French and English.

The two toasted each other before Gregori began the conversation 'Good afternoon Giles and thank you for agreeing to see me. After Roland's tragic death last week I have flown in from Moscow to help Jani with the funeral arrangements but more importantly find out who committed this crime. Can you talk me through any recent transactions you have carried out for Roland?'

*Drambuie mixed with Malt Whisky and lots of ice.

'Certainly Gregori, Verte Banque do not unfortunately have Valescure Vineries as a client, but occasionally we would help him out with their 'trickier assignments'. The most recent was the transfer of $500m from South Africa, to finance an armament shipment from Russia for

Colonel Aziz's Libyan Revolution army. Unfortunately the money went missing between Aix-en- Provence and Monaco which infuriated the Libyans who think your Russian Mafia stole it with the help of David Andelic, the driver who was shot dead for his troubles.'

Gregori was a little embarrassed at the mention of the Russian mafia but continued the conversation 'I do know about the heist and the fact that we have not been able to apprehend the culprits. Do you think our decision to refuse to arm the Libyans until they paid their account in full was a contributing factor to Roland Canault's death?'

'Yes I think it may well have been. Shortly after they failed to make their payment they suffered a major surprise attack from the National Liberation Army. They appeared to have been tipped off that Colonel Aziz's forces were short of firepower and quickly overcame them resulting in an unusual high level of desertions. This would have set Aziz's plans back almost two years.'

Gregori paused in thought at the consequences for Russian diplomacy in North Africa before changing the subject entirely.

'Have you had any dealings with two international finance experts from Farrer Financial Services called Roni Benson and Graeme Davenport?'

'I met the vivacious Roni at Roland's tennis tournament along with her business partner Graeme and his charming wife Lydia. They are involved in the shadier side of the finance industry finding homes for funds that require cleansing. In Monaco there can be a market for this type of finance, as you will be aware Gregori, if you ever deal with the oligarchs. They both came to see me here and we had a fruitful discussion but to date we have not had any dealings. Why do you ask?'

Gregori looked at his empty glass and handed it to Giles Normand 'Can I have a refill and can you get one for yourself as you may need it after what I am about to tell you.'

Giles was taken aback by the KGB officer's comments but did as he was told and replenished their drinks.

Gregori thanked Giles for his second vodka and related his story to the banker who by now was on the edge of his seat. 'We have been concerned that all was not right at Chateau Rose Blanc and I was given the task by Commissar Bardosky to investigate any leaks in our security. After a thorough search of the premises we have come upon very sophisticated listening devices, the likes of which I have never seen before. We removed two such devices and the purpose of my visit today was to see if you had any similar concerns.'

Giles replied with a boastful comment, 'Mr Rasputin, Verte Banque prides itself in having the very latest security systems so I appreciate your concerns but feel it is unlikely security has been breached.'

Gregori interrupted 'With all due respect Giles the bug we found was straight out of a research and development laboratory and years away from commercial development. Was all your conversation held in this office?'

'Yes, the couple sat out in reception for ten minutes as I was running late but after that we were in here – apart from when Graeme Davenport asked to use the toilet. I allowed him to use my personal facility while I made small talk with Roni Benson.'

Gregori asked 'Would you mind showing me the toilet Giles.'

The banker hesitated at such an unusual request 'N...no follow me.' The three men headed for the wash room where Gregori and his linguist combed the surroundings.

Gregori stood on the toilet seat and reached into the air-vent carefully covering all sides of it. 'Ah, here's what I am looking for!' he cried peeling off the listening device and showing it to Giles. This piece of silicon is capable of picking up all calls made from your desk and that is how information can fall into the wrong hands.'

Normand was shocked at the thought of his bank's business being made available to an outside source, 'So where are these people based?'

Gregori shrugged his shoulders 'I don't know but I suspect London!'

Giles headed for his desk 'I will get on to the British ambassador right away and lodge a complaint.'

Gregori raised his hand to stop the banker 'Giles before you say something you may regret can I remind you that some of your recent actions could rebound on you. It could lead to you losing your job and facing charges which carry a prison sentence.'

Giles took Gregori's warning onboard 'I will see if I can uncover any further information on Benson and Davenport. Their company Farrer Financial Services must appear on a register somewhere but their genre of lending is usually carried out well below the usual channels.'

It was time for Gregori and his minder to leave the premises sufficiently satisfied that he now had enough evidence on Giles Normand to take advantage of him should the KGB require any favours.

Chapter 51

The MI6 Global Review Committee (G.R.C.) met once a month to discuss performance levels on all their activities around the world. Often they can be quite dry affairs but today Richard Hartley was looking forward to briefing colleagues about his team's performance. The Controller sat listening as the section leaders of the five continents put forward problems they were encountering and asking for any suggestions to improve their performance.

Soon the spotlight turned to Assistant Controller Richard Hartley who was sitting between his two assistants Freddie Sharpe and Commander Hugh McFaul. Hartley shuffled his papers before beginning his report. 'I am happy to inform the G.R.C. of a very positive field operation which we have carried out in the South of France. The terms of reference for this field project was to penetrate a suspected Russian operation called Valescure Vineries who had been supplying arms to a variety of insurgents all desperate to upset our European lifestyle.

'We had cause for concern that the recent inflow of illegal immigrants could escalate in the future which will result in long-term problems for our security forces. The team have been able to identify that Russia has been financing this unwelcome invasion by supplying dinghies and finance to organised crime.'

'I sent three agents Lydia Tomlinson, Roni Benson and Campbell Anderson to Valescure and they were able to penetrate the target activities believe it or not by playing tennis!' The others in the room chuckled before Richard added - 'with Roland Canault. He is the main Russian operative who was originally from Serbia and is of interest to the War Crimes Enquiry in the Hague.'

'Roni Benson managed to get intimate with Canault and was able to install our latest spying bugs which allowed us to listen in to all Canault's telephone calls. Benson and Anderson also were able to attach similar listening devices in the offices of Verte Banque who Valescure Vineries use for some of their more unscrupulous dealings.'

'This was a major breakthrough for MI6 allowing us to keep ahead of the enemy at all times. It has also been rewarding both financially when we, with the help of the SAS, intercepted payment of five hundred million U.S. dollars for weapons needed by The Libyan Revolutionary Army which is now safely in the Bank of England. Due to the listening devices, we were also able to prevent major terrorist attacks across Europe and in Libya which has boosted the Foreign Offices reputation with our allies.'

'Much of the credit for our achievements must go to Roni Benson who risked her life to bring about these successes. Many of you in the room will not be aware that her real name is Mhairi McClure , an Irish terrorist serving a twenty year prison sentence. I have made use of McClure on previous assignments in return for reductions in her custodial sentence. Whether or not this will be repeated in the future is debatable.'

'The problem I have at present with McClure is she is now sought by the KGB who will most likely assassinate her if she returns to a prison establishment. She is no threat to us as we have implanted a microchip in her body, which if activated, will kill her instantly. I have grown to admire Mhairi McClure's contribution to the Service and would ask the Committee to give me permission to deal with her as I see fit.'

The Controller screwed up his face before giving an opinion 'It is not like you Richard to take a soft line on Irish terrorists but I seem to recall McClure only became an IRA sympathiser after we had shot and killed her fiancée. I trust your judgement, so I will leave it with you to decide the best course of action.'

Richard replied 'Thank you sir, I will report back to you once I have spoken to McClure and decided the best course of action for her. That concludes my report for today.'

Richard Hartley and his team left the meeting and made their way back to Hartley's office

The Assistant Controller settled into his chair before opening the conversation 'Were you both surprised by what I said at the G.R.C.?'

Freddie Sharpe who knew Hartley better than anyone having been his personal assistant for ten years spoke up first 'Not like you sir to be so accommodating to the enemy, but I must agree with you that Miss McClure has demonstrated all the qualities we look for in our best agents. Her contribution will never be known to the public but deserves some sort of pardon.'

Commander McFaul joined the discussion 'What do you have in mind Assistant Controller?'

Hartley leaned back in his chair, put his hands behind his head then looked at his two colleagues 'I have been doing some calculations so how does this sound? Mhairi McClure had served three years of her sentence, before she had eight years of her sentence reduced further as a reward for helping MI6, with two major very successful investigations. Both of these projects ended with excellent results for the department. She deserves an additional reduction to her time in prison and bearing in mind she will qualify for a good behaviour reward which could be anything up to five years. All this has made me decide to show her some clemency and transfer her to some form of open prison.'

'Have you anywhere in mind Sir?' enquired Freddie.

Hartley responded 'I would not want it to be one of the established open prisons as they would also be an easy target for the KGB. At this stage location is not important.'

'Hugh, you will have to speak to McClure and I suggest you take Cam with you which will make her easier to talk to and negotiate with. What you have to explain to her is we are offering her a chance to re-invent herself and to do so she will require changes to her character. Her natural Irish accent would have to be removed and to make it more compliant, you might consider encouraging a Scottish accent. It will take time to merge her into her new persona, but with the carrot of leaving our care, this should provide the incentive she needs. Your main task is to remove any tendencies for her to consider returning to her Irish roots.'

Hugh commented   'I can't wait to get started. Usually we are involved in character assassinations so it will be refreshing to do some character building.'

Chapter 52

It was a biting cold February morning making driving conditions difficult after the heavy snowfall the previous day had left the roads around London icy. Hugh McFaul made his way from Godalming to Cam Anderson's flat in Twickenham to proceed from there over to Chesham. Normally they would go by train but Hugh preferred the privacy of his Range Rover when discussing the forthcoming conversation with Mhairi McClure. Hugh had arranged the meeting with Mhairi and Beverley Thomson using it as an excuse to debrief their activities in Valescure. He wanted to get Mhairi's reaction when he informed her of Richard Hartley's offer of a restricted pardon. In principal, it was a good offer but MI6 had to be certain she would adhere to the terms of reference attached to it for fear of bringing MI6 into disrepute by selling her story to the media.

'Cam you know Mhairi McClure far better than me so I would like you to study her body language closely. Feel free to contribute to the conversation any time you choose.'

Cam replied 'I will do Hugh. I must say I was very surprised when the Old Man Hartley showed some sympathy towards Mhairi by asking us to get her prepared for a change of identity.'

'So was I, to say the least. It is not like Hartley and it makes me think he has something else in mind for

Miss McClure. She has been successful at everything we have asked her to do so it would make sense to continue using her. She has become a marked woman in the eyes of the KGB who have a contract out on her already.'

'Hugh, don't tell me you think Hartley is going to use her as bait to attract Commissar Bardosky to send his hit men to Britain. If he did that, he could capture them and tell the world publicly about their seedy intentions or he could use the apprehended spies as a bargaining tool in a spy swap speculation. Let's not get ahead of ourselves and wait and see how Mhairi views our proposals.'

The Chesham house was busy when the two Home Office men arrived at reception. They were quickly shown into the library where Mhairi and Beverley were already sitting at a round polished wood table. Cam and Hugh's entrance killed any conversation and made Beverley get up and head in the direction of a tray where there was coffee and biscuits.

She opened the conversation 'Not the ideal morning for driving so thought we could heat you both up with some coffee.'

'Morning Beverley' said Hugh accepting a mug of steaming black coffee from Beverley and helping himself to a small packet of digestive biscuits 'now that's what I call service.'

Once everyone had finished their drinks the party moved across to the table and made themselves more comfortable. Hugh and Cam took out papers and writing pads from their briefcases. Hugh kicked off the proceedings 'Good morning ladies and it is a very good morning for you Mhairi McClure! '

'At a recent meeting of the Global Review Committee Assistant Controller Hartley managed to get the senior departmental heads of MI6 to agree to offer you an additional reduction in your prison sentence. This has been granted in respect of the excellent work you carried out in our offensive against the Russian presence in the South of France.'

Mhairi couldn't believe it or contain herself and she screamed out loud in celebration before asking 'How much is he talking about reducing my prison term by? And what are Hartley's conditions this time?'

Hugh raised a hand and continued 'Mhairi calm down. What Mr Hartley is proposing is :-

1. You agree to accept an entirely new identity and agree to live in a safe house provided by MI6. You will be free to live on your own with only Beverley as your MI6 contact at a property supplied by us.

2. All your correspondence from the outside world, addressed to you, will be sent to H.M.P. Askham and forwarded on to you.

3. You will only be released into the outside world once you have attended a training course in Yorkshire where you will take on your new identity. The final decision to release you into the outside world will be based on the

assessment of your tutors in the Yorkshire training camp as to your suitability for living out of captivity.

4. The microchips in your body will not be removed in the foreseeable future.
5. You will not be able to travel outwith the United Kingdom without MI6's permission and we will hold your passport. Travel to Northern Ireland is also banned.

Following on from the results of the training programme we may consider inserting other parameters.'

'What do you think about our terms for your release Mhairi?'

Mhairi had calmed down from her initial euphoria 'It all sounds good but so far you haven't stated where this safe house is located?'

Hugh answered 'Usually safe houses tend to be located in rural towns rather than the big cities in order to give you a comfortable lifestyle in relation to the allowance you receive from MI6.'

'By that Commander McFaul you mean I will be living a hermit's existence and not out clubbing every second night. Your offer is beginning to lose its appeal already.'

Hugh thought to himself 'You ungrateful bitch!' before launching into the Irish terrorist verbally 'Look Miss McClure, I would like to remind you that you landed in prison entirely due to your own indiscretions. You are a clever but somewhat misguided woman, responsible for not only encouraging heinous crimes, but also carrying out some of them personally. I do not know how you have the audacity to even consider not accepting Assistant Hartley's offer. I might add that Campbell Anderson and I could not believe the benevolence Mr Hartley has shown to you. It is not like him, so if I were you I would grab it with both hands before he realises he has made an error!'

All eyes in the room were on Mhairi who was going red in the face 'I'm sorry, I shouldn't have said what I did just now. The opportunity to live a semi 'normal life' away from the constraints of prison life or this safe house in Chesham is most welcome. When can I start my induction course?'

The others in the room relaxed after hearing Mhairi's change of heart.

Cam Anderson joined the conversation 'Mhairi you are making the right decision. You are a victim of your own success as a MI6 agent so it is vital for your own survival that you drop out public life. Everyone around this table will make every effort to see you are protected and the only way to do this is to accept a new identity.'

'I've always trusted you Cam so I will accept what you have just said in good faith – not that I have any faith left after my exploits in the Vatican!' she joked with Hugh and Cam who knew what she meant - but Beverley was left puzzled.

Hugh took up the conversation 'Now that's settled I will make plans for you to attend the training course in Yorkshire. It will not probably commence for a few weeks but there is no reason for you to return to prison so we will leave you in Beverley's care for the time being.'

Hugh returned his papers to his briefcase and signalled to Cam it was time to go.

Mhairi stopped him in his tracks 'You still haven't told me where the safe house is located.'

Hugh made a cheesy smile before answering the anxious Irishwoman 'That's because I don't know. Only Richard Hartley is privy to that information. Thanks for the coffee ladies. Goodbye for now. I will be in touch shortly.'

Chapter 53

Four weeks later - Beverley Thomson received a call from Hugh McFaul 'Morning Beverley I have just received word that everything is in order for Mhairi to be transferred to a country retreat just outside Halifax. She will undergo a complete makeover mentally and possibly in a small way physically, but I will leave all that to the psychiatrists and image makers.'

'The course will start next week but there is no end date available at present. I will send Campbell Anderson along with a driver to pick her up on Sunday morning which will give you time to get her ready. Give her an allowance of two hundred pounds not that I think she will need it unless they plan to let her out to experience the Yorkshire countryside. I will leave it in your capable hands Beverley.'

Sunday morning arrived and on schedule at 10.00 a.m. a green Range Rover arrived to take Mhairi McClure on a new chapter of her extremely varied life. Campbell Anderson rang the bell of the villa and the door was opened by Beverley.

'Mhairi's ready Cam, she has just gone back to her room to get her toothbrush.'

Just then Mhairi came down the stairs. She was wearing black slacks and a red polo neck jersey. To protect her from the cold she had a brown leather sheepskin-lined jacket and Russian-style fur hat.

'Morning Cam, are you ready to whisk me off to Yorkshire for a night of passion?' she jested.

Cam responded 'It is so bloody cold out there this morning, it would freeze even your intentions! Come on, Philip our driver will be getting impatient to get on the road as he has to drive me back tonight.'

Philip, who was introduced to Mhairi as Roni Benson, loaded her luggage into the boot. It made sense for both Mhairi and Cam to sit together in the rear seat as it was easier to converse, plus Cam had brought on board a flask of coffee and biscuits for the journey.

Cam and Mhairi made polite conversation for the next three hours recalling their exploits together in the last few years. Cam kept the conversation cordial and did not say anything controversial. He sensed Mhairi was putting on a brave face since, what for her, was a journey into the unknown. If the planned transformation process did not have a successful outcome it could result in Richard Hartley carrying out the execution she had feared he had threatened her with on previous occasions.

Caldervale Hall was the former home of a textile baron whose mills had closed in the 1960s. The property sat looking down over the River Aire to the town of Halifax beyond. The large imposing building had been acquired by the National Trust when the baron's descendants could not pay his death duties and then leased back to the security services. The surrounding gardens and woodlands extended to eighteen acres so it was cut off from the outside world.

The Range Rover crunched down the stony path and stopped at the front door which seemed to salute their arrival by opening before they had time to leave their vehicle. A small burly lady dressed in a dark green woollen dress came forward and shook hands with both the arrivals.

'You, my dear must be Roni Benson and I presume this is your chaperon Campbell Anderson. My name is June Kenton I am the bursar of Caldervale Hall. Come on in out of the cold, your driver will bring in your luggage.'

The three made their way into a large baronial hall furnished with large landscape pictures of the Yorkshire Dales and turned left into an attractive drawing room overlooking the well manicured gardens. Mhairi and Cam sat down on the leather armchairs and awaited June Kenton's welcoming speech. 'I trust you had a good drive up from Chesham. I'll get the house-keeping out the way prior to talking about your course. Caldervale Hall has twenty-four hour security in place, so do not venture out into the grounds at night without getting clearance. In the unlikely event of a fire go to your designated area which you can see indicated on the map on the back of your bedroom door.'

'Now your course will start tomorrow morning at 9.00 o'clock after breakfast which is available from 7.00 o'clock. You shall have several tutors during the course which on average takes about six weeks. I have read your CV Miss Benson – or should I call you Mhairi McClure?'

Cam interrupted 'I think we should stick to Roni Benson as the fewer personnel who hear the name Mhairi McClure the better for her safety. The reason for the course after all is to prepare her so that the Russians can't find her.'

June went a little pink in the face 'Point taken Mr Anderson. I shall inform all the tutors to address your colleague as Roni Benson.' Turning to Mhairi she asked 'Have you any questions for me?'

'Yes you said the course lasts on average six weeks. Does that mean I am confined to barracks for the duration of the training course?'

'No, some exercises will require field training but I will leave it to the tutors to guide you as to when external exercises will take place.'

Cam looked at his watch 'Well Roni I must be getting back to London. I am sure Miss Kenyon will see to all your needs'

'Miss Kenyon, I'll see Mr Anderson to his car.' Mhairi chipped in.

'Okay when you return I will show you to your room.'

Mhairi reached the front door and turned to face Cam 'Well I suppose this is goodbye Cam I don't suppose we will ever see each other again' she mumbled as the tears started to run down her cheeks.

The couple hugged each other and passionately kissed farewell. Cam whispered in Mhairi's ear 'Goodbye and good luck. You deserve a break in life.'

Mhairi stood at the door her body shaking as the tears continued to flow. The Range Rover moved off leaving her to face an unknown future without the only man she really trusted in MI6.

Chapter 54

Mhairi had not slept well in her new bed which was not a reflection on the mattress more on worrying how she was going to cope with her new life. Breakfast was served in the dining-room which consisted of tables each set out for four diners. She settled for a continental breakfast and was enjoying her second cup of coffee when she was joined by a youthful ginger-headed man, wearing a sports jacket and checked shirt with a woollen tie, completed by cavalry twill trousers. He sat down opposite her and introduced himself.

'Good Morning Miss Benson my name is Jeremy Howitson and I will be co-ordinating your stay here at Caldervale Hall' he said offering a limp handshake 'I hope your room is to your liking and let me know if there is anything extra you require. If you have finished your breakfast, please follow me and we shall proceed to one of the lecture rooms.'

The lecture room was situated on the first floor just along the corridor from Mhairi's bedroom. It was an unusual design - there were no windows, only a table with four chairs and a wall which contained a small screen to show videos and a white lecture board to display messages. On the table were two orange folders and a packet of three biro pens. Inside the folder in front of Mhairi there was an A4 writing pad and another thick red folder marked 'TOP SECRET'.

Howitson sat opposite her and gave his first instruction:

'Open the file and we shall begin the preparation for your new life.'

Inside the folder was a complete dossier of a person's life from the minute they were born, their ancestors, education, sporting achievements, hobbies and work experience.

Jeremy continued 'What we have in front of us is a complete record of someone's life and what we are required to do is to match you to this identity in the best way possible that you feel the most comfortable with. For instance, there is no point in saying you have a degree in geography if you struggle to know where the Gobi Desert is! This information is taken from the character of someone who has passed away recently but whose death has not been registered. This is to offer you a camouflage of sorts if anyone tries to find out about you. The person in question has been living outside the U.K. for a number of years.'

'Her full name is Katherine Roxburgh Taylor but we shall refer to you at all times as Katy. You will require to digest from the information supplied everything about Katy and we shall test you on a regular basis to monitor your progress in relation to rejoining civilian life. I will give you a couple of hours to study the dossier's contents and I will return to see what you have remembered.'

Jeremy left the room and Mhairi opened the file and began finding out about Katy Taylor which made interesting reading. There were some similarities to Mhairi's background, both of them had been educated privately and attended university. Katy's degree was in languages whereas Mhairi had qualified in computer studies. However, she had familiarised herself with French, Spanish and Italian to ease her boredom when she had lived in the Vatican.

Katy came from a military family (her father James Taylor was a captain in the Royal Scots) and brought up by a single parent, her mother, when her father had been killed during the Cyprus conflict. Both her parents had been only children so she did not have any immediate family relatives.

Katy had been killed when she drowned while scuba diving alone in Majorca when her air tank became tangled with some cables when swimming inside an old sunken ship. She was discovered several days later when some holidaymakers on a diving trip followed their guide into the wreck's hold.

As promised approximately two hours later Jeremy bounced back into the room 'Well Roni how are you getting on? I will ask you twenty questions about Katy Taylor, write down the answers and let us see how you get on.'

The questions came at Mhairi very quickly and were completed in a few minutes. Jeremy reached across the table and began reviewing her answers. 'Very good sixteen out of twenty, room for improvement as it is the four wrong answers that could blow your cover. The first round of questioning is fairly basic but as time goes on you will be asked more intricate topics on the life of Katy Taylor and by week three we shall expect you to have all the answers.'

'Now this afternoon take time off and go down into Halifax and have a look around. I would suggest you pay a visit to The Piece Hall which a modern shopping development modelled on the site of the old wool market. If you feel like stretching your legs you could always take a walk along the canal.'

'Thanks Jeremy, if I am going to be here for several weeks I would like to see the surrounding area. Are you coming with me?'

He smiled back at Mhairi 'No, some of us have to tend the shop. You're old enough to go on your own. I'll get a driver to drop you off in the middle of town. Only one thing to remember when you leave Caldervale Hall you ARE Katy Taylor.'

Mhairi dashed to her room and returned dressed for the cold weather. She introduced herself to Archie her driver as Katy Taylor and sat in the front seat of his Ford Escort as it made the short trip into Halifax. Mhairi was excited at the thought of being let loose without a chaperone for the first time in years and spent the first half hour of her new freedom walking aimlessly and breathing in the fresh Northern English air.

Taking Jeremy's advice she made her way up past the Halifax Minster - even though she was tempted to go inside the church and light a candle – she decided to climb up the slope into The Piece Hall. It was far bigger than she imagined, a huge modernised square with its original grass centre replaced by sculptures fringed with water features and a bandstand where a brass band was producing some old Northern favourites made famous by Gracie Fields and George Formby.

On the three floors where the traders traditionally carried out their trading, the dealing rooms had been replaced by lots of craft shops and hospitality outlets. Mhairi walked round all three floors admiring the sale items until exhaustion crept in and she parked herself down at a café. A waitress appeared and took her order for a latte and a piece of millionaire shortbread. She continued to people watch until the coffee arrived, her vision only interrupted by an old man who sat at the next table. He was enjoying the music which had just finished and turned round to make conversation.

'Eeh that were grand, you can't beat a good brass band. Do you listen to them often love?'

Disguising her Irish accent Mhairi replied 'No I'm not from around here.'

'A Southerner I'd guess, maybe London.'

'Nearly, Buckinghamshire actually.'

Mhairi was enjoying speaking to a fresh tongue and they continued talking for another twenty minutes before the old man got up to leave and declared 'I'm sorry miss I should have introduced myself. My friends call me Tommy Parkinson.'

He offered his hand in friendship 'And you are?'

Mhairi replied quietly 'Roni Benson.'

Tommy smiled and looked Mhairi in the eye 'And here was I thinking you were Katy Taylor! Bye for now.' Mhairi sighed in embarrassment and was not looking forward to her return drive back to Caldervale Hall and facing Jeremy Howietson.

Chapter 55

Next morning at breakfast Mhairi was joined by April Barclay who described herself as a character builder and Norman McCorkindale, 'call me Corky', Caldervale Hall's resident psychiatrist. Both of them had been sent by Jeremy Howietson to relax Mhairi and make her less nervous. Jeremy joined them later in the training room to continue shaping Mhairi McClure into Katy Taylor.

Jeremy referred to yesterday's visit to Halifax 'I hear you met Tommy Parkinson yesterday in The Piece Hall. Tommy is a retired officer who we use to suss out how our new recruits are making out. You are not the first candidate to give their own name but the embarrassment you suffered will be enough to make sure you don't make the same mistake again.'

'Today I have asked April and Norman to join us for the purposes of a little role playing. They have both read Katy Taylor's file and will ask you details about different events in your life. April will act the part of a nosy neighbour who wants to know all about the girl next door. Okay let's get started.'

April had played this part many times so she launched straight into a hypothetical conversation 'Hello I'm Molly Brown from next door welcome to Hull. What's your name love?'

'Katy Taylor.'

'Where did you live before coming here?'

'Bradford.'

'And what does Mr Taylor do for a living?

'There is no Mr Taylor. He died from a heart attack a few years ago.'

April continued 'Well, I'm sure an attractive lady like you will meet someone. I have a nephew who is divorced if you ever want company.'

'Thanks Mrs Brown but I prefer my own company at present. If you will excuse me I have to make a telephone call.'

April stopped there 'Roni that was very good for your first attempt at taking on Katy Taylor's character. You didn't get flustered at all and you will see as we progress today 'The Molly Brown's 'of this world will delve more into your life and you have to be prepared to answer everything confidently.'

The grilling continued for several hours with April submitting a variety of topics ranging from politics, fashion, sport and education. April changed her characters – some were jovial information seekers while others were aggressive, pushy people insisting on answers. Everyone it seemed to Mhairi was prying into Katy's life, and unless she rehearsed her lines professionally sooner or later she would be exposed. Fortunately for Mhairi she had been highly educated at the very best of establishments including Oxford and Harvard so she was able to draw on her previous experiences during the close examination April was carrying out.

During the interrogation Corky sat quietly carrying out a body language profile of Katy, monitoring how she coped when April was 'in her face' and entering her intimate zone. He was impressed how Katy stood her ground which was an early sign that she was not going to concede verbally to inquisitive challenges.

In the afternoon April changed her line of questioning, preferring to cross examine Mhairi on how she would like to lead her life in the future.

Mhairi had demonstrated to the trainers how she would react to situations 'I am a very sociable person who led a very active life prior to hiding from the authorities. I would find it difficult to lead a hermit existence although I appreciate that what you are trying to do is for my own safety. For instance, I have always liked male company so will I be able to enjoy myself in the future?'

Her question left April and Corky struggling for an answer and it was Corky who led the response 'Our advice would be to be selective in that field. What you don't want to do is to have a reputation for attracting suitors too often and equally do not get into a serious relationship as that will bring its own problems. If you were admitted into a new family they will want to know everything about you.'

'Okay' Mhairi replied 'let's leave that for now, it is probably something that will not happen.'

Corky continued 'We shall be looking for a safe house that matches your previous lifestyle. What are your hobbies Roni?'

'Recently I have been playing a lot of tennis but that's after a break of almost twenty years. I used to be involved in sailing with my father and also attended a lot of race meetings in Ireland but, I don't think it would be wise to mix with all the punters.'

April laughed 'I have no idea where your safe house will be, but I can't imagine there will be any horse racing nearby. Anyhow your physical make-up will have to be changed and possibly it may result in you losing some of your glamour.'

'In what way!' demanded Mhairi.

'We shall be taking advice on that front from one of our style experts. It will not be anything too dramatic probably your hair colour will change along with the colour of your eyes by inserting coloured contact lenses. Spectacles are another way of enhancing your disguise along with your dress code.' April added 'You shall have to work on losing your Irish accent. The nearest thing to your lilt would be a polite East of Scotland accent which is less guttural than someone from the West of Scotland.'

'Good God! Please don't tell me I am to be a frumpy bible bashing middle-aged spinster with only my knitting needles to keep me company!'

Corky intervened to calm things down 'I think we are getting a little ahead of ourselves let's return to testing your knowledge of Katy Taylor.'

For the next three weeks the trainers constantly primed Mhairi about all aspects of Katy Taylor's background before announcing that they were going to have a day out. The venue they chose was the village of Saltaire which was created by the textile magnet Titus Salt. There were similarities between Salt and the Orson Welles film's character Citizen Kane. Salt organised everything in the town including the church he built for the town which even had his initials emblazoned on every pew!'

The three visitors were walking through the village admiring the architectural structures of the town when somebody shouted in a loud voice 'Hey Roni! Roni Benson! What are you doing here?'

Mhairi turned to see who was calling her only to cringe when she discovered it was Jeremy Howietson who had followed them to Saltaire. Jeremy approached the visitors shaking his head 'Roni, that is very disappointing, I thought by now you would have grown into your new identity. You are obviously not ready to be sent out into the big brave world for another couple of weeks.'

The two weeks passed slowly for Mhairi who longed to find out where she was going to begin her new life. Jeremy Howietson was satisfied that Roni Benson was ready to be moved out of his care and called her to his office.

Mhairi approached Howietson's office fearing the worst and preparing herself for the return to HMP Askham. She knocked on the door and it was greeted by a light-hearted voice 'Come in Roni!'

Jeremy was sitting behind his desk with a big smile on his face 'Sit down please Roni, this is the day we've all been waiting for. You have satisfied the team at Caldervale Hall that through your hard work and dedication to the task you will be recommended for release into a safe house.'

Mhairi felt a tear coming into her eye and searched for a paper tissue 'Thank you Jeremy. You have all been very patient with me and I will not let you down.'

'Your 'graduation', as we like to call it, is equally important to my staff as it proves we have the ability to take a subject and provide them with a suitable character which camouflages them from enemy threats. Of course I can only recommend that you are ready to leave here. It is up to Richard Hartley to decide when and where your new life begins.'

Next day Richard Hartley received Jeremy's report which he scrutinised before arranging a meeting with Mhairi McClure.

Mhairii returned to Chesham and was greeted in the office by Beverley Thomson

'Welcome back Roni. Did you have a good time in Halifax?' Beverley enquired.

'Yes, I was told I passed with flying colours' she answered using her newly acquired Scottish accent.

'What's with the Scottish accent?'

Continuing in the same tone Roni replied 'Beverley what you are hearing is the new me, but who will be experiencing it next is up to Richard Hartley.'

'The Assistant Controller was looking for you earlier. You are to attend a meeting with him and Commander

McFaul the day after tomorrow. I've to accompany you so I have arranged for a car to pick us up at 8.30 a.m.'

'That's good news Beverley, hopefully I will finally find out where my new home is going to be.'

Chapter 56

The Audi 6 headed out of Chesham straight into the low early morning sunshine passing through Amersham and then onto the M40 where it headed towards London and MI6 HQ.

After doing the usual security clearances Mhairi was escorted to Richard Hartley's office. Beverley left her colleague temporarily to visit another MI6 department. The Assistant Controller was looking his sartorial best wearing a grey woollen suit enlightened by a light pink shirt and spotted navy tie. Hugh McFaul looked almost drab beside his boss in navy blazer white shirt and black neckwear.

Hartley looked up when they entered the room but returned to what he was reading but spoke as he did so 'Sit down please.'

There was silence for ten seconds as Hartley concluded the brief he was finishing 'I hope you had a good drive into the city. I have summoned you this morning as Caldervale Hall has submitted their report on you which you will be pleased to know is favourably in your interest Miss McClure.'

'Now I would like to explain to you a little about the parameters of a safe house. Depending on your status and the contribution an individual makes to the service we rate the houses Red, Amber and Green with red being reserved for our most endangered agents. You fall into the amber category in recognition of the fine work you did in Valescure. Russians have long memories and although you were not responsible for Roland Canault's assassination directly, they will be taking out contracts on everyone who disrupted their station. By placing the listening devices in Chateau Rose Blanc and Verte Banque you may have signed your own death warrant.'

Hartley's last words made Ron's blood boil and she felt compelled to interrupt him 'What a bloody reward for helping you out of a hole and saving the lives of many innocent people!'

Hartley did not take kindly to Mhairi's interjection 'Miss McClure, please have the manners to wait until I have concluded my statement otherwise I may not continue.'

Mhairi's face went red and Hugh McFaul attempted to diffuse the tense atmosphere. 'Mhairi, this morning we are putting the finishing touches to a policy which has never been introduced before. I am talking about the repatriation of a convicted terrorist who is being pardoned for her performance in security operations – so please no further outbursts. Controller Hartley please continue.'

Hartley looked up over his desk and started again 'As I was about to say we are very pleased to inform you that in four weeks time you will be taken to a safe house. In choosing this safe house we try to make it as difficult as possible for our enemies to locate it, and if they do so, offer adequate protection to its occupants. For these reasons, we have acquired a property in a remote location where the locals are aware of any strangers who come into the vicinity. You will be housed in a two bedroom cottage at LOCHRANZA on the Island of Arran off the West Coast of Scotland. Have you ever been there?'

Mhairi shook her head 'No but now you are going to tell me how wonderful it is.'

'Cheer up Miss McClure, the Isle of Arran is often described as 'Scotland in Miniature' so there is plenty for you to do. The advantage of living on an island is the security services are able to patrol it easily as any possible assassins have to make use of the Caledonian MacBrayne ferry service. They could of course sail into Lochranza but that is unlikely. The main ferry terminal is at Brodick but there is also a ferry that sails from Lochranza to Claonaig on the Mull of Kintyre.

You shall have the use of a small car which will allow you to go over to Campbelltown by ferry if you wanted a change of scenery. You will get lonely unless you get involved in the local community either with some form of employment or by joining sports/ hobby clubs. In the next few days you will receive a plan of the cottage which will allow you to decide on interior decoration and furnishings which will be in place for your arrival.

One concession we are prepared to make to you is to allow you to meet up with your mother twice a year but only on our conditions. These meetings will take place at the Machrihanish Hotel near Campbelltown airport. To get there your mother will make her way to Masserine Barracks where a helicopter will make the short flight over to Campbelltown Airport. You must impress upon your mother that this is a neutral venue and that you have flown up from Manchester. She must not find out about Lochranza for her own safety. These meetings are top secret and any leakages from either of you will result in immediate termination of the arrangement.'

Hartley's latest announcement brought a radiant smile to Mhairi's face and the first sign of a tear in her eye 'Thank you very much Mr Hartley that is most kind.'

'One last thing Miss McClure I have made arrangements for the removal of the microchip which if activated would kill you instantly, but are leaving installed the other chip which tells us where you are at all times for obvious reasons. You shall receive instructions shortly to attend a private medical clinic in High Wycombe to carry out the procedure.'

'Thank you that's the best piece of good news I have wanted for a long time.' uttered a very relieved Mhairi McClure.

Richard Hartley stood up and walked round his desk to where Mhairi was sitting. He held out his hand and Mhairi stood up to shake hands with the man she had cursed for many years. Hartley concluded 'Good luck Miss McClure, I wish you all the best for the future and trust what I have just outlined to you will prove that I am human - and reward those individuals who aid Her Majesty's Government. I'll say goodbye as it is unlikely we shall ever meet again.'

Chapter 57

Four weeks later Katy Taylor drove her car off the ferry at the Brodick Terminal. She had filled the back seats of the car with food and household goods from the Asda store in Ardrossan which she had visited while waiting for the ferry to dock. The drive along the Brodick seafront was beautiful, the blue sea shimmering in the sunshine with the backdrop of Goat Fell, the highest mountain on Arran still sporting snow round its summit. An hour later she arrived at her destination in Lochranza on the other side of the island.

'Kintyre Cottage' was a charming whitewashed property with a glass front looking out over a little jetty to the ruins of Lochranza Castle. Katy drove her Skoda Fabia up the covered driveway at the side of the house. She was very apprehensive as she turned the key and entered her new home.

Inside the house was completely modernised in accordance with her instructions. The lounge area was larger than expected, tastefully decorated and featured large glass windows looking over to Kintyre. The kitchen had all the modern appliances a woman would want accompanied by all manner of kitchen utensils, pots, pans, cutlery and crockery. MI6 had thought of everything a fugitive would need without having to go searching for it themselves. The same detail applied to the bedrooms and bathroom.

The property was cold as nobody had been there since the building contractors had left the previous week. Katy consulted an instruction manual which was near the entrance hall and was soon enjoying the comfort of Kintyre cottage which she toasted with a glass of Prosecco from the bottle she had bought in Ardrossan. Mhairi McClure was starting to enjoy being Katy Taylor.

Chapter 58

Six months later.

'Commissar Bardosky we think we have gathered a number of leads in our search for Roni Benson' Gregori Rasputin admitted.

'About time Gregori, it will soon be a year since Roland Canault's death and you are only telling me now you have some leads! That woman's presence kicked off the demise of what was a very successful station for Russia in the South of France. We had to close it down as the world's media arrived in Valescure and started to probe into Roland Canault's activities. Our investigations revealed that Colonel Aziz was behind the exploding tennis ball attack on Roland Canault. Aziz will be eliminated shortly when we airstrike his tented village in rural Libya. Anyhow Gregori, that is for later. How have you come upon your latest information?'

'Finding Roni Benson has been very difficult. After we issued her photograph we received sightings from all over the world. When I put them into chronological order they read Belfast, Oxford University, Harvard University, Rome or more accurately The Vatican, Geneva, Sitges and London. She has used several different names – Mhairi McClure, Margaret Kennedy, Francoise Lyon, Veronica Benson or as we now know her Roni Benson.'

Uri Bardosky summarised up all he had just heard, 'This Roni Benson has been a very active agent for MI6 and a woman who could carry in her head a lot of their secrets. Rather than kill her, it might be better for us to take her alive and torture information out of her. She is probably 'Sleeping' as we refer to it in security circles, awaiting her next assignment so she will be in a safe house somewhere in the U.K.'

'Gregori, have you checked all female prisons in Britain? It has been known for the security services to enlist their spies in the prisons principally to keep them off the streets but also to gather intelligence on organised crime.'

'No we haven't as yet but I will do so and report back to you Commissar Bardosky.'

Two weeks later Jill Watson was on a girls' night out in York which ended with a visit to a disco for over thirty-fives. She had recently separated from her long-term partner and was on the prowl for some tender loving care. As she watched her friends dancing to Elton John's pop hit 'I'm Still Standing' from her stool at the bar a tall blond good-looking man in his thirties came and stood next to her.

He smiled then started the conversation using a broken English accent 'Why are you not on the dance floor?'

Jill turned and faced the newcomer 'I am just recovering from the last number but I shall be open to offers once I get my breath back' she added with a mischievous grin on her face.

'In that case I will hang around. Can I buy you a drink? My name is Johann Anson. I am from Sweden.

'Pleased to meet you. My name is Jill... Jill Watson. I would love a Bacardi and coke.'

Johann purchased the first of several drinks in-between dances. Jill was sure she had found what had been missing in her life and invited him back to her flat for coffee – after which they devoured each other's bodies.

Jill brought the two mugs of coffee back to bed and Johann asked if he could light a cigarette. As he took the first drag of his fag he began his interrogation. 'Jill, I never asked you what you do for a living.'

'I am a prison officer at Askham Prison, a centre for low risk prisoners no longer thought to be a threat to the public. What do you do Johann?'

'This may sound a bit bumptious but I am a private detective. I have come over from Sweden on behalf of a lawyer who is looking for a girl last seen in Yorkshire who has become the beneficiary of a large sum of money. I have a photograph of her in my wallet which I will show you.'

Johann jumped out of bed and retrieved Mhairi's photo from his wallet. Jill looked at the photograph and her eyes widened 'I know this face. She looks very much like one of our inmates Mhairi McClure who works in our finance department.'

'Will you see her on Monday? I would like to speak to her urgently.'

'No, she left the prison months ago and I don't know where she has been transferred to.' Jill suddenly realised she could be compromising her career 'Sorry Johann I should not be discussing any prisoners with the general public.'

'That's okay you have told me what I wanted to know. Come on let's resume what we both came here to enjoy.'

Johann climbed on top of his new partner and once he was inside her, he placed both hands around her neck and choked the life out of the struggling Jill Watson!

Johann dressed quickly and returned to his hotel to get his luggage. Knowing that Jill's body would not be discovered for at least twenty-four hours he went to Manchester Airport and took the first available flight out of the country which turned out to be to Berlin. A car picked him up at Schonfeld Airport and took him to the temporary safety of the Russian Embassy .

Gregori Rasputin was very pleased to get Johann's report 'Now we know that our target is called Mhairi McClure, who I am old enough to remember, was a member of an IRA cell which were caught trying to extort money from the British Government and given long prison sentences. She escaped capture initially but was captured hiding in Spain which accounts for her being seen in Sitges. The positives we can take from Johann's bulletin is that she most probably returned to freedom several months ago.

There is no way she will be back in Northern Ireland as there will be a price on her head so we can concentrate our search on the rest of the United Kingdom.'

Chapter 59

Arran had turned out to be the magical place everyone had described and Katy's first year on the island had gone quickly. Her first few months were spent wandering all over the island taking in long walks in relatively remote landscapes often in wet weather as the weather fronts arrived on a regular basis from across the Atlantic. Having exhausted the hills Katy tackled the coastline and found little coves including Bruce's Cave where King Robert the Bruce had hidden from the English army.

Lochranza is a one of the smallest villages on the island but is close to the local distillery so there was always a steady stream of tourists. Another attraction was the deer farm next to the nine-hole golf course where holidaymakers captured the wildlife on their cameras.

The day she arrived, Katy had only been in her cottage a few hours when there was a knock on the door which she was scared to open. She looked out the window and saw an old couple with the lady holding a bunch of flowers in her hand so she answered their call.

'Hello and welcome to Lochranza. I'm Jean Murdoch and this is my husband Bob. We have been keeping a watch on the house since the workmen left last week. I brought you these flowers from our garden.'

'My name is Katy Taylor and I am very grateful to you for looking after the house. I arranged all the interior decorating using my computer and I am delighted it has been carried out to my instructions. Would you like to see what they have done?' asked Katy sensing the purpose of their visit was to have a nose around.

She gave them a quick tour and they were very impressed by what they saw. As they were leaving Jean repeated her welcome 'Remember Katy if there is anything you want to know about Arran just ask us. We have lived here all our days and we know everything and everybody on the island. If you are struggling with the garden Bob is an expert on growing vegetables.'

The Murdochs turned out to be excellent neighbours only intervening when they were asked and taking their time to ask Katy about her previous life. They respected the age difference between Katy and themselves and encouraged her to join people of her own age. One thing they did do was introduce Katy to the various pub quizzes which were held all over the island. Katy was a welcome addition to the Lochranza team as she had a far wider knowledge than nearly everyone.

The local quiz was held in the Lochranza Hotel and it was during one evening that she heard the local distillery was looking for a part-time book-keeper to work two days a week. She applied and got the job which was within walking distance of Kintyre Cottage.

During the year Arran is host to a number of festivals, to attract all genres of tourists, information of which is printed in the local newspaper 'The Arran Banner' which she consulted weekly.

For the first six months there was no contact from MI6 until Hugh McFaul phoned to say that arrangements had been made for her to see her mother at Machrihanish. Campbell Anderson would fly up to Prestwick in three days and come across to Brodick where she could meet him and take him to Kintyre Cottage. They would take the Claonaig Ferry and drive down to meet Mrs McClure who would arrive by helicopter and be taken to the Machrihanish Spa Hotel.

Three days later Katy stood anxiously watching the passengers come down the gangplank off the two o'clock Brodick ferry. Cam was wearing casual gear to suit the summer conditions and waved his hand to confirm that he had seen her. Cam marched up to Katy, dropped his bag, and gave her a big kiss 'Great to see you Katy. I am looking forward to hearing all about your first year out of captivity.'

Katy took the scenic route across the island to Lochranza and was astounded by Cam's constant complimentary comments on the scenery and wishing he had been transferred to Arran. The couple spent all night chatting about how their lives had changed in the last year.

Cam spent the night in the spare room and was awakened by the early morning sunshine. He dressed quickly and took an extremely tranquil walk over the dewy grass to Lochranza Castle. By the time he returned Katy had made a continental breakfast which she knew Cam preferred. The Murdochs had spotted the new arrival so when Cam and Katy went out to their car they were both in the front garden.

'Morning Katy that's a fine looking young man you have brought home with you last night.'

Katy laughed and turned to Cam 'Jean is always trying to get me married off Graeme. This is Jean and Bob Murdoch, my good neighbours who look after me. Jean this is my cousin Graeme Davenport who is here for a few days and I am going to show him the splendour of Arran.'

Cam shook hands with the old couple before they set off for the Claonaig Ferry. The ferry was tiny compared with the one which came every few hours from Ardrossan into Brodick and is limited to eighteen cars which reduces when large vehicles wanted to board. Fortunately the weather was calm for boarding as in wild weather it can be quite an ordeal to drive aboard as the ferry sways back and forward. The drive down to Machrihanish was stunning with the Clyde on one side and the hills of Kintyre on the other.

After passing through Campbelltown, the Skoda made its way up to the Machrihanish Hotel and parked on the driveway. Cam approached the reception to get directions to the private room he had hired. The receptionist told him his guests were waiting for him along the corridor in their meeting room. Katy practically ran to the meeting room and burst through the door so aggressively startling her mother and the army officer she had travelled with.

Mother and daughter hugged each other and Cam signalled to his fellow security officer that they should exit the scene. Mother and daughter freed up from their embrace 'Mhairi you gave me a fright barging in like that, I don't know what that young man thought about your entrance.'

'Mum it is so good to see you' Mhairi mumbled as the tears rolled down her cheeks 'I thought we would never see each other again.'

'Mhairi I am intrigued as to how we are meeting here. I received a letter from you on HMP Askham headed paper telling me to take a bus up to Masserine where I would be picked up at the bus station and taken into the army barracks. I couldn't believe it when they said I was going on a short helicopter trip to Machrihanish. I loved the helicopter experience as I had never been on one before. How did you get here?'

'Same way by helicopter,' Mhairi lied. Taking a step back she said 'Let me have a good look at you.'
Her mother had aged in the last few years and she was a little unsteady on her feet and carrying a walking stick for balance - but her brain was just as sharp as ever.

Mrs McClure was still puzzled as to how she was whisked to the West coast of Scotland 'So why are they allowing you to come out of prison and visit me?'

Mhairi had to taper her reply 'Mum I have been helping the British authorities with some of their internal problems which they considered so successful that they have reduced my sentence and allowed me to visit you. If I continue the good work it may be possible to meet again. Come on, sit down and tell me everything that is going on in your life.'

Her mother laughed 'Well that won't be difficult, I am constantly seeking new bridge partners as they are all dying off on me. I seem to be attending about one funeral a fortnight at the present time.'

'Why don't we put all this gloom behind us and go for lunch. My chaperone Graeme Davenport has booked a table in the dining room.'

The table was in a quiet corner of the dining room overlooking the famous Machrihanish golf course which is a Mecca for foreign golfing tourists. The three course lunch was superb, and the couple finished it off with coffee and liqueurs in the main lounge which came with confectionary in the shape of Scottish tablet.

'Would you like to go out for a stroll Mum? Mhairi suggested.

'No dear, I am having trouble walking any distance. I have had some bad news, you might as well know that last week I was diagnosed with colon cancer and they have told me I only have nine months to live.'

The blood drained out of Mhairi's face and she choked at the bad news and grabbed a napkin to wipe away the tears. There was a silence for a minute until

Mhairi was able to gather her thoughts 'Have you asked for a second opinion or considered going private to see if they find a way to operate?'

Through watery eyes her mother answered 'Mhairi the doctors know what they are doing. Look, the way I see it is - I will be eighty-one on my birthday next month and have had a good life. Things did not work out for you, but actions outwith your control were thrust upon you.'

'When your fiancé Matt O'Reilly was ambushed and killed by British marines, your only thought was to revenge his death but that has proved to be a bad decision as you have spent a major part of your life in prison, after years hiding from the authorities. You should be due for parole soon – make the most of your life and seek a companion who will bring lasting happiness into your life.'

Her mother's wise words felt to Mhairi that she had just witnessed an epilogue and the chances were that this was the final time she would see her mother. An hour later she accompanied Mrs McClure back to Machrihanish Airport. As the helicopter's blades whirled into life, lifting the aircraft off the runway, she waved goodbye holding tightly on to Cam to stop her breaking down completely.

Cam did all the driving on the journey back to Lochranza, most of the time in silence as Mhairi was deep in thought as she contemplated coping with her mother's departure. There was a bright sunset over the water and Cam suggested they go for a walk rather than mope about the house. Mhairi agreed to join him as the fresh air would do her some good. Their route took them along the coast where cormorants were diving into the sea scooping up fish and a couple of seals were basking in the last beams of sunshine.

They stopped and sat down on a large flat rock continuing to enjoy the scenery. Cam took the opportunity to introduce a new topic of conversation.

Chapter 60

'Mhairi, escorting you to see your mother is not the only reason I am in Arran today. Richard Hartley wanted you to know that one of the prison guards at Askham was murdered recently and he suspects it may be Russian intelligence inspired.'

Mhairi was shocked at the news 'Why do you say that? Who was the victim and how did she die?'

'The victim was a lady called Jill Watson who had met a man in a nightclub in York who according to her fellow ravers was Swedish. We were able to see him on the club's CCTV cameras and from our records he has been identified as Mikei Korisevich, a KGB operative. Miss Watson made the mistake of taking him back to her apartment where they made love before he strangled her to death. Her body was only discovered two days later when she failed to turn up for work. There has been no sign of her assailant who is thought to have left the country immediately after killing her.'

'That's horrible Cam. I knew Jill Watson vaguely and she always seemed one of the better officers.'

'Hartley fears that she died because Mikei got some information on you, perhaps using force, which Miss Watson might have reported to HMP Askham had she survived. We are concerned as it means that the net is tightening around your whereabouts so you have to be more diligent in the future. Keep a close eye on any strangers who come to Lochranza and stay for more than a couple of days.'

Mhairi thanked Cam for the warning. It had been an eventful day to say the least. They returned to Kintyre Cottage and relaxed with a couple of measures of Isle of Arran whisky which Mhairi had brought home from work.

Next morning Cam did a complete check on Mhairi's security systems. Her burglar alarm was synchronised with the local police station in Lamlash which was backed up by CCTV cameras hidden in the foliage around the property. After he was satisfied that everything was in order he went to his room and returned carrying a smaller version of a shoebox.

Mhairi looked up and smiled 'Oh Cam, don't tell me you brought me a present!'

Opening the box Cam reacted 'You could say that Mhairi!

From the box he brought out a gun, a Glock 19 automatic pistol, and pointed it towards the former Irish Terrorist.

'Cam what are you doing? Is that thing loaded?'

Cam smiled and put the gun down by his side 'No not yet. I brought it here for you. The boss thinks you should have protection against any evil forces. This is the first time I can recall MI6 arming an enemy of the State – albeit a former threat.'

'But Cam I'm not sure I would be able to shoot a pistol. I'm liable to shoot myself!'

'Don't worry we'll go out today and find a wood which will provide some target practice. I will screw a silencer on the end which suppresses the barrel and increases accuracy – it also avoids any unwelcome attention from the public.'

The couple made their way down the coast before swinging east into Glen Cloy Fairy Glen. It was a dreich windy day which cut down the number of visitors to the forest. Mhairi stopped the car, Cam took out the gun, loaded it and put on the silencer. They both walked into the woods and once they were satisfied nobody was about Cam handed Mhairi the gun.

'To get a more accurate shot hold the gun in both hands. See if you can hit that branch hanging down from the tree over there.'

Mhairi took aim at the target then swung round to face Cam 'How do you know I won't shoot you Cam? Twenty-five years ago I was trained to eliminate British spies.'

Cam looked nervously at Mhairi 'Just relax Mhairi don't do anything silly. I have spoken on your behalf and I can't believe you would want to shoot me.'

Mhairi remained defiant 'It was you and your colleagues who ruined my life so why shouldn't I take revenge?'

'Because you'll miss out on a night of passion if you do.' Cam joked.

Mhairi laughed at Cam's response and relaxed her stance as he added 'Anyway I loaded the Glock with blank cartridges!'

The tension eased and Cam felt safer now that Mhairi had not tried to fire the pistol as it didn't contain blank cartridges. He began his armed response training programme again and was impressed how Mhairi had not forgotten how to fire a gun. After twenty minutes training she was hitting targets the size of a human with ease.

'You have done very well Mhairi, your shooting is excellent. Let me give you a piece of advice, if you are going out walking on your own you should carry the gun at all times.'

Later that night, they returned from having a drunken last supper at the Lochranza Hotel prior to Cam heading for the ferry in the morning. Cam kept his promise and Mhairi got her younger colleague into bed at long last!

Chapter 61

After Cam's departure, Mhairi settled down to a quiet life immersing her attention between her work commitments and any new social activities which came her way. Walking along the shore near her house one Sunday morning she came into contact with Johnnie Richmond who was cleaning the barnacles off his yacht.

Making conversation she called out 'That takes me back. When I was young, my dad had a yacht like that and I used help him maintain it.'

'Well be my guest Miss', Johnnie invited 'there are spare tools down here.'

Mhairi hesitated before committing to the sailor's offer 'Okay I am not doing anything today so why not.'

She made her way down to the side of the yacht 'Hello I'm Katy Taylor. I live along the road.'

The ruddy faced sailor who was wearing a black woollen skiing hat replied shaking hands 'Johnnie Richmond. I base my yacht here all year although I live down the coast at Machrie. Here let me get you my spare sander and I will give you a quick lesson in removing barnacles.'

Johnnie got Katy started and could tell she was no stranger to boats so he left her to get on with it. Katy welcomed the chance to enjoy some male company. She and Johnnie struck up a rapport covering all sorts of subjects over the next three hours. Both of them were exhausted after their long shift which made Johnnie suggest rewarding Katy by buying her a drink in the Lochranza Hotel.

Being a Sunday, the hotel was busy but they managed to get seats at a corner table. 'What can I get you Katy?'

'A gin and tonic with ice and lemon would be nice.'

'I'll have a pint of the local Arran brew.'

Johnnie returned with the drinks 'How long have you lived in Lochranza Katy?'

'Nearly two years. I was looking for a peaceful retreat after my husband died' she lied 'I didn't want to be in a big city. What brings you here Johnnie?'

'I am a naval architect originally from Portsmouth. I spent many years abroad chasing the money but decided I could get a better quality of life in Arran. I have been here just under three years. I was in a long-term relationship with a lady called Lizzie who left me for someone else so I named the Yacht after her 'The Dizzy Lizzie'.

Katy laughed 'I was going to ask you how you named the yacht. Do you take it out often? How far do you sail?'

'To answer your second question first, I go out round islands off the West coast where you can get shelter from any adverse weather. I do go out fairly regularly if you fancy a sail anytime.'

Katy thought for a moment 'That would be very nice Johnnie.'

One sail led to another and Katy found Johnnie very good company. Physically he wasn't her usual male companion being slightly smaller with a stocky build and bald head. What he lacked physically he made up intellectually providing Katy with conversations which matched her academic training. After a while he was a regular visitor to Kintyre Cottage where they began a relationship which enhanced into the bedroom. Katy was shocked and delighted the first time she aroused Johnnie. He possessed by far the largest piece of manhood she had ever seen in her considerable experience of carnal activity.

The couple's regular trips on 'The Dizzy Lizzie' did not go unnoticed by MI6 who were still keeping surveillance on Katy. They were relieved when she returned to Lochranza at the end of her first sortie out to sea and gradually came to terms when future trips lasted a few days as long as they ended back in Lochranza.

Mhairi received from Hugh McFaul, via Governor Smith at HMP Askham, the devastating news that her mother had passed away. She was not allowed, for her own safety, to attend her mother's funeral. Katy found it extremely difficult to grieve and not tell Johnnie why she was so sad.

Chapter 62

Nine months later:

'Sir there are three new arrivals at the Russian Embassy.' informed Hugh McFaul.

'Anyone we know?' asked Richard Hartley.

'Only one of them, Gregori Rasputin, who we know is Commissar Uri Bardosky's right hand man. What do you think brings him to London?'

Without lifting his head Hartley answered 'Mhairi McClure. You better alert your team to arrange surveillance on these new arrivals. If they travel North, we shall monitor them using a fleet of cars to avoid letting them know they are being followed' instructed Richard Hartley 'I will let our colleagues over at MI5 know we are handling the situation.'

'Will I let Mhairi McClure know she could be under threat from the Russians?'

'No!'

Over at the Russian Embassy, Gregori Rasputin was having coffee with Ambassador Kiev who commenced the conversation 'Good to see you again Gregori. How is Commissar Bardosky?'

'Very well, he sends his best regards.'

'Can I ask you what your programme is while you are here in the U.K.?'

'Certainly, a few years ago we were running a successful operation at Valescure in the South of France which went belly up after it was infiltrated by British spies. The most damage was created by a lady called Roni Benson, originally known as Mhairi McClure, who we have been trying to find for almost three years.'

'Recently we received intelligence that eighteen months ago her mother, who has since died of cancer, went to Masserene Army Barracks and took a helicopter trip to the Mull of Kintyre to meet her daughter. We don't know how Mhairi McClure got there but we suspect she may be hiding in the area.'

'What do you intend to do with her when you find her?'

'Commissar Bardosky would like us to take her alive as she may be privy to information which could be useful to us, so you might have to hold her here until we can smuggle her out of the country. If we meet resistance we will have to kill her.'

Ambassador Kiev gave his opinion 'Let's hope it is the former.'

Two days later Gregori and his two hit-men Boris Gorich and Peter Komiski left the embassy in one of the diplomatic cars. After stopping in Carlisle for the night they headed for the Mull of Kintyre taking the long scenic route up to Inveraray before turning south. Every time they came to a small town Gregori asked in the Tourist Offices if they recognised Mhairi from her photograph. Gregori described her as his sister who he was supposed to meet in Glasgow but last he heard she was heading for the Mull of Kintyre. His policy failed on a number of occasions and he was on the point of giving up when the receptionist at the Macrihanish Spa Hotel said she recognised Mhairi.

'What kind of car was she driving?' he enquired.

'Oh, I can't disclose that sir.'

Gregory laid a fifty pound note on the counter knowing in his experience the weaknesses of hotel staff 'A Skoda Fabia licence number SG 10 WSG' she confirmed after consulting her parking records.

'Thank you Miss. You have been most helpful to me.'

Gregori phoned the Russian Embassy and checked the number plate. The reply was that it was registered to Katherine Roxburgh Taylor of Kintyre Cottage, Lochranza, Isle of Arran KA28 8HQ.

Two hours later The Russians were standing on the jetty as the Claonaig Ferry docked to begin their short journey which would get them to Lochranza within the hour. When they entered the village Gregori got his driver to pass Kintyre Cottage surveying the lay-out of the house and its surrounding area. He was in no hurry to meet up with Mhairi McClure but he was surprised to see three people in the garden. Jean and Bob were discussing with Johnnie where to lay out Katy's rhubarb patch while she was working in the distillery.

The Russians booked into the Lochranza Hotel and to use up time they decided to tour the Arran Whisky Distillery. Katy was in her office on the upper floor which overlooked the still house, where all the tourists watch the whisky process, starting with the fermenting in the copper stills before being drained into a vat prior to being filled into oak sherry casks.

Today the distillery was busy with the arrival of a couple of bus parties who were milling around waiting to receive complementary drinks from the company, who hoped they would buy bottles in the shop next door to the café in return. Katy liked to people watch, but a shiver ran down her spine when her eyes set upon Gregori Rasputin and his two bodyguards. She moved out of sight and stayed in the office giving the excuse to her boss Steve Hamilton that she had some work to finish.

When the office emptied, she called Campbell Anderson 'Cam it's Katy I'm at work in the distillery and I have just seen Gregori Rasputin and two of his henchmen touring the distillery. This can't be a coincidence, they have somehow found my address. Cam I'm frightened, they're professional hit-men who could come for me at any time.'

'Mhairi calm down. We know Rasputin and his mates have entered the country and they are under surveillance so help is nearby. I would advise you not to stay at your cottage tonight. Is there anywhere else you could stay overnight?'

'Yes, I could go out with my partner Johnnie for a meal and bunk in with him for the night.'

'Good, we shall always know your whereabouts as you are still on Satnav. Oh by the way, who is this new man in your life?'

'The name's Johnnie Richmond, a naval architect from Portsmouth. We go sailing together.'

'Good for you Mhairi. Now here's what I want you to do. Tomorrow morning pack a rucksack and head out for a long walk over the hills. We want to confront the Russians but we don't want a shoot-out in any urban area where innocent bystanders could be wounded or used as hostages – and take your gun with you!'

'Thanks Cam, I feel a lot better having spoken to you and I will do as you suggest. I will leave early in the morning and go over the hills towards Loch Tanna.'

Mhairi put the phone down and then spoke to Johnnie 'Hello darling, I've had a rotten day and need some TLC. Can you pick me up and we'll go to Shiskine Golf Club for a bite and then back to your place for a few drinks and whatever takes your fancy.'

'Sounds good to me Katy, I'll be there in ten minutes.'

Katy thought to herself 'Ten minutes! I could be dead in that time if Rasputin & Co are lurking about outside.' She positioned herself at the window so she could see Johnnie arriving in his Audi A6 and shot out the distillery entrance and jumped into his car which sped off down the road to Shiskine. Katy kept up her small talk routine during the journey with an eye on the side mirror to see if they were being followed.

Johnnie commented 'I was surprised you were in a hurry to go out without going home to change. Not like you, it must have been a bad day.'

'Mr Hamilton was getting on my nerves. He had a breakdown in the still house and he started to take his frustration out on me.'

'Well put that behind you. Here we are at Shiskine Golf Club so let's relax and enjoy ourselves.'

Shiskine is open to the public which suited Katy and Johnnie who were not golfers. The menu catered for a range of tastes. Katy had the lobster which had been caught locally while Johnnie devoured a fillet steak with pepper sauce. Dessert followed soaked up with a couple of bottles of red wine which set them up for the short journey back to Johnnie's house in Machrie.

His bed was not made up as he had not been expecting Katy. She never even noticed as she passionately attacked her partner as they passed through the lounge ripping of each other's clothes. Katy wrapped herself tightly around Johnnie as he entered her body as if there was no tomorrow to relieve the tension she was under.

Johnnie lay back taking deep gulps of oxygen 'You should have lobster more often that was terrific.'

'You should see me when I'm on oysters' Katy laughed 'now go and open another bottle of red wine if like me, you're up for a night of passion.'

Johnnie arrived with the wine and two glasses to supplement their long night of passionate sex.

Chapter 63

Next morning could not come fast enough for Katy 'Johnnie! Wake up! I have to get back to the house. Jean and Bob will know that I didn't come home last night and tongues will be wagging.'

Johnnie smiled 'At our age I don't think so, more likely to be jealous!'

Not stopping for breakfast, Johnnie dropped Katy off at Kintyre Cottage at seven o'clock and said he would call her later. She walked round the cottage looking for any sign of forced entry before opening the door. She had a quick shower as her kettle boiled, dressed into her rambling gear before scoffing a plate of cereal along with a slice of toast. She made herself a small picnic and filled coffee into a vacuum flask before getting her pistol from its secret place behind the bookshelf next to the fire.

The communications department at MI6 headquarters watched on their screens as Katy made her way out of Lochranza and headed for the hills. She walked briskly away from the village but not from the binoculars Gregori Rasputin was holding, as he looked out the rear window of the Lochranza Hotel which faced the hills.

'Our target is getting some early morning exercise. We shall let her continue on her way then consult the map and see where we can intercept her. We shall have to use the element of surprise. Go to the shop down the road and buy some rambling gear to change into.'

Katy walked for miles high up into the hills keeping a look-out for anyone following her who could either be friend or foe depending if MI6 got their act together. An hour later she stopped to rest on a rock beside a stream. Last night's activities were catching up on her and she nearly dozed off when two figures came over the hill in the opposite direction fifty yards from her.

One of them smiled and when he was twenty yards away gave her a friendly wave. Katy reached into her rucksack for what the advancing duo thought was to retrieve a sandwich.

'Ah Miss Benson we meet at last. We have been looking for you for three years.'

Katy brought her gun out her rucksack and held it in both hands 'Stop! Don't move!'

The two men did as she said, then shouted out to each other 'Look at her, she's shaking, she won't shoot – she's probably never fired a gun in her life!'

Katy called their bluff by smirking back 'Gentlemen you have obviously not done your homework. I have killed better men than you.'

Katy's eyes narrowed as she pumped two bullets into the chest of Boris Gorich as Peter Komiski made a move towards her which upset her aim but she still managed to wound him twice in the thigh. He screamed holding his leg, begging for mercy but his plea fell on deaf ears. Katy moved closer and despatched two more bullets into his neck and head. Blood splattered everywhere and Katy released a triumphant scream which was only temporary.

Reality then hit Katy who wept and cried in anger at what she had just done. Where was the armed response team Cam had promised?

The answer to that was her Satnav microchip was unable to unearth a signal high up on the Arran Hills!

Twenty minutes later six officers did arrive and took control of the whole situation. The bodies of the Russians, who the secret service did not want known to the media, were quickly taken down to a waiting van and driven away in the direction of Brodick. Two officers sat with Katy giving her some counselling and assessing her mental state until they considered her fit enough to make her way back home.

When Bob and Jean saw Katy with her escort they came out to enquire what was wrong.

'Miss Taylor had a fall which almost knocked her out. We came across her and decided it was best she came home.' informed Captain Burke.

Jean sighed 'Come on Katy, let me get you into the house and I'll make you a cup of tea and give you a fruit scone that's not long out the oven.'

Katy smiled back 'You are the best neighbours anyone could ask for.'

She entered the house still a little shell-shocked and immediately knew all was not right. Someone had been in her house. She rushed back out of the house to where the officers were standing 'Help!! Someone is in my house!'

The officers produced guns from under their waterproof jackets which shocked the Murdochs who clung on to each other. They entered Kintyre Cottage and searched it from top to bottom but did not discover any unwanted visitors.

'What made you think somebody had been in your house?'

'I had a picture of my late father in his army uniform on my bookcase and it has been moved over to the sideboard. It looks as though they have been looking for something and the worrying thing is that is where I normally hide the gun which killed the two Russians.'

A car arrived outside. It was Johnnie who came through the front door and immediately knew something was wrong 'What's up Katy? Who are these guys?'

One of the officers replied 'We brought Miss Taylor down from the hills near Loch Tanna where she had a fall.'

'Are you okay dear?' said Johnnie placing his arm round her neck.

'Yes but I have since discovered that I have had a visitor.'

'What! You've been burgled?'

'No, nothing missing, but I noticed the picture of my father has been moved.'

The officer who spoke earlier joined the conversation 'We've checked the house and there is nobody here.'

Johnnie thanked the officers and turned to Katy 'You have had quite enough shocks for one day. If you want I'll stay the night.'

Katy gave her partner a cuddle 'Thanks Johnnie, I'd appreciate that.'

Chapter 64

Katy was still feeling stressed so Johnnie recommended a nice hot bath while he prepared some food, a bowl of Heinz vegetable soup followed by tinned pears and hot custard which was all he could find in her cupboard. Katy came down the stairs having changed into black trousers and a white thick loose-fitting polo-neck jumper with a black pendant around her neck.

Johnnie had set the table and he served up the food which Katy appreciated as her stomach was still churning and not in need of a lavish meal. She finished eating and sat down on the sofa while Johnnie completed his chores by washing the dishes. He then joined her on the sofa.

'Relax Katy, I deduce you have had a rough day. Do you want to tell me about it?'

Katy could not bottle up what had happened up in the hills 'I was approached by two men with foreign accents who I knew were going to harm me.'

'So what did you do?'

Katy felt her face going red and tears about to run down her cheeks 'I took out my gun and shot them both several times!'

'What!! Dead?'

'Yes.'

'Where did you get hold of a gun?'

'From a friend.'

'Why?'

'He was worried about me living on my own.'

'Phew!' exhaled Johnnie 'it makes me think there is a lot about you I don't know.'

The couple sat in silence both appearing not to know what to say next. Johnnie spoke first 'I think I will go outside and get some fresh air. I want to get something out of the boot of the car.'

Katy closed her eyes relaxing and waited for Johnnie to return. She felt him sit down beside her and when she opened her eyes she saw another figure in the room – GREGORI RASPUTIN!!' She opened her mouth to protest but Johnnie put his hand over her mouth and shouted in her ear 'Do not scream if you want to get out of here alive!' whilst brandishing a large knife she had seen in a drawer on 'The Dizzy Lizzie'.

Katy was frightened but took Johnnie's advice and after he had removed his hand she blurted out 'I don't understand what is going on! Johnnie, how do you know Gregori Rasputin one of the most evil KGB secret agents?'

'Gregori Rasputin is my operator. I am a naval architect and the Russians have installed me here to monitor the movements of the nuclear submarines based up at Faslane. That way the Soviet fleet know when they are back in circulation. I do come from Portsmouth originally but I am a committed communist who opposes capitalism vehemently!'

Gregori Rasputin spoke for the first time 'Normally a conversation would begin with 'Pleased to meet you' and in your case Mhairi McClure this is true for all the wrong reasons. Throughout your life you have evolved into a devious dangerous woman only interested in your own survival. '

'Today was a prime example of your ruthlessness. You went into the hills knowing you could be the subject of an attack. When you were sought out by two of my best operatives you did not hesitate to murder them. I watched the scene through my binoculars and made a hasty retreat to Johnnie's house, putting my car in his garage.'

'You caused us problems in Valescure where again you infiltrated our systems by seducing Roland Canault and passing information to the Libyan Government via the British Foreign Office. That information led to Colonel Aziz facing defeat due to lack of funds which your soldiers stole leaving him unable to pay for his weapons order. Aziz took his revenge on us by planting explosives on a tennis court killing Roland Canault one of our best agents.'

'Once we knew your identity Mhairi we were able to put together your CV, which is filled with serious crime anything from money laundering, robbery, assassinations and spying. Commissar Bardosky is interested in making use of your talents which I personally don't agree with. He wants you to return with me to Moscow.'

'Never!!' Mhairi screamed, shaking with fear and playing with her pendant for comfort.

'Well in that case we shall have to kill you! Do it Johnnie!' Rasputin ordered.

Johnnie gripped his knife and lunged at Mhairi who avoided his advance and threw him over her shoulder judo style. She held on to his wrist while with her other hand she transformed the pendant into a Stanley knife and sliced through his right wrist causing a gush of fresh blood to spurt over both of them. Mhairi moved quickly for the jugular lacerating her assailant's neck, bald head and left ear as she tried to inflict more cuts. More blood!!

Johnnie screamed trying to stem the flow of blood as he knew he was not long for this world. For a few seconds Gregori did not respond to the surprise retaliation coming from Mhairi but wasted no time in kicking her to the ground.

Rasputin picked Johnnie's knife off the floor and plunged it twice into Mhairi's stomach and was about to repeat the feat when shots from an automatic silencer pistol were fired from behind, killing him instantly. The marksman then turned his attention to Johnnie, who was attempting in vain to stem the blood which was pouring rapidly out of his body and he finished him off by shooting him twice in the head.

Through the fuzz of her extreme pain from Rasputin's attack Mhairi recognised the assassin as Hugh McFaul who was searching through Gregori's jacket for his Kalashnikov pistol which he wrapped in a towel to muffle the sound, before taking it in his gloved right hand and pointing it at Mhairi. For a few seconds Hugh was tempted to end her life as he had never forgiven her for being an accomplice in the murder of his best friend John Johnston's father David, twenty-five years ago.

Hugh placed the Kalashnikov pistol in the right hand of Rasputin. He was not proud of what he had just done but said to himself 'My orders from Richard Hartley were to leave no loose ends.'

'Mhairi are you wounded badly?' enquired Hugh.

Mhairi screwed up her face before answering 'A bit bruised but it could have been a whole lot worse, if I had ignored Cam's advice to protect myself at all times and not worn my stab vest under my polo neck sweater!'

Her answer brought a smile to Hugh's face 'I think you owe Cam a drink!'

Hugh McFaul had arrived in Lochranza earlier in the day and used a set of spare keys for Kintyre Cottage to gain access to the cottage. He had been 'the Mysterious Burglar' who had entered the premises and moved the photo of Katy's father in the search for her gun.

He phoned Richard Hartley 'I have tidied everything up Sir. Mhairi McClure is as far as the general public are concerned dead, stabbed by Rasputin. I eliminated Rasputin myself with the two bullets I fired into him. Mhairi's partner Johnnie Richmond is also dead due to loss of blood once Mhairi slit his wrist and jugular with the Stanley knife she picked up down at Hereford. I assisted his passing with two shots to the head to ensure he would not be alive to tell any tales.'

'Good God Hugh, you make it sound like you've been busy creating a gory picture. Get the local police to seal off the murder scene until our forensic team arrive. I will talk to the Chief Constable at Police Scotland and explain what has happened. Well done, a good result for us, we have taken out four of the enemy without the loss of Mhairi McClure.'

In Hartley's opinion Mhairi McClure had served her purpose by attracting the Russian killers to Arran and removing any threat they brought to mainland Britain. He was now faced with hiding his controversial policy of using jailed terrorists from the media which could have put MI6 under scrutiny. For the time being Mhairi McClure would have to disappear from public view.

The next morning Hugh knocked on the door of the Murdoch's House and Jean opened it.

'Good morning my name is Commander Hugh McFaul, I work for the security services. Can I come in please?'

'Yes of course' Jean turned and shouted over her shoulder 'Bob there's a man at the door from the security services!'

Hugh followed Jean into the lounge where they were joined by Bob. The Murdochs stared at Hugh waiting for what he had to say 'Sit down son, would you like a cup of tea?' asked Jean.

Taking a deep breath he began 'No thanks. I have some very bad news, your next door neighbour, Katy Taylor and her partner, Johnnie Richmond have both been murdered. Yesterday afternoon Katy feared someone had broken into her house but no one was discovered at the time. Apparently there was an assailant on the premises and he killed both of them as they slept. Both Katy and Johnnie had innocently witnessed, we believe, the transfer of a large consignment of drugs when they were out at sea. The drug traffickers had followed them here and waited to take their revenge.'

'Oh My God!' Jean yelled 'the poor lassie, such a nice girl.'

Hugh played along in order to conclude his fabricated tale 'Yes I believe she was. We shall be removing the bodies today into a van hidden behind screens. What I have just told you is covered by the Official Secrets Act. My office will be in contact with you both, requesting you sign your allegiance to Her Majesty's Government. The last thing we want is the world's media descending on Lochranza.'

'Mr McFaul, the lassie deserves to be left in peace so Bob and I will not be blabbing to anyone I can promise you.' pledged Jean on the couple's behalf.

'Thank you for your co-operation, I must be going now' he said. Hugh stood up and shook hands with the old couple. He had purposely not mentioned Gregori Rasputin as his men would bring the Russian's body out of the house, hidden behind the screens then load him into the black van to join the other three corpses and Mhairi who would be hidden in a perforated body-bag to assist her breathing. The bodies would then be ferried from Brodick over to Ardrossan and taken into a hangar at Prestwick Airport before being flown south to in a R.A.F. plane to Brize Norton. Hugh briefed Mhairi about all the arrangements which gave her time to pack all her personal belongings. Once the plane took off at Prestwick she would be able to emerge from the body bag.

Two weeks later a coffin with the anonymous body of a homeless female in it, who was registered as 'Mhairi McClure' was cremated at High Wycombe Crematorium at a service attended by only three people – Beverley Thomson, Lydia Tomlinson and Campbell Anderson.

Mhairi herself had retired to a health spa in Cornwall for a few days pampering, using a new nom de plume given to her by MI6 Assistant Controller Richard Hartley in lieu of her next assignment.

Chapter 65

The chauffeur, with Richard Hartley's bodyguard sitting alongside him, stopped outside a large red brick villa in a leafy avenue in Beaconsfield. Richard Hartley got out and crunched up the stony path to the front door. He was about to ring the bell when the door opened and an elderly lady in a woollen suit stood in front of him.

'I take it you are Mr Hartley, I was watching for you through the window. I am Rose Brown, Armitage's sister.'

'Pleased to meet you, Armitage never ever mentioned he had a sister.'

'No he wouldn't' Rose replied tersely 'I'll take you up to his room.'

They climbed the half-moon shaped staircase and entered a large bedroom. Armitage Brown was sitting up in bed. He had suffered a right sided stroke which had left him paralysed, his mouth permanently twisted open.

'Morning Armitage, how are you doing?'

'Ah Richard, howsh do you shink I'm doing? You shtupid bashstard! 'he slurred, 'Howsh MI6?'

'Very good Armitage, I heard you were not well so I thought I would give you some welcome news. When we met a few years ago I told you about making use of your nemesis Mhairi McClure to do some undercover work, which made you go apoplectic. You need not concern yourself with her anymore, she's been killed by the KGB on the Island of Arran in Scotland.'

'How?'

Hartley gave his former boss a full account of the Valescure operation and his reasons for agreeing to let Mhairi McClure be released from prison.

'When she got in tow with this Johnnie Richmond character, Campbell Anderson ran a check on him and found he was on the MI5 suspects list as a 'Soviet sleeper' due to his young socialist activities. He was traced to Arran and was living a lifestyle away above his income. When the Russians were also bound for the West of Scotland I sent Commander Hugh McFaul to 'tidy up the loose ends.'

Armitage croaked 'You mean shshoot the bashtards' and laughed.

'Yes Armitage.'

Richard continued his line in inaccurate reporting 'I don't think we will ever see another like Mhairi McClure. In another world an agent with her talent, who in some ways potentially saved hundreds of innocent citizens, would now be given a posthumous Victoria Cross.'

'Sshee was a wicked woman! A monshter!'

'Yes she was.' agreed Hartley 'Created by people like us!'

The pair chatted on for a few minutes before parting, leaving Armitage Brown to die a happy man convinced that Mhairi McClure was now dead. Hartley headed back to London content in the knowledge that his secret weapon, Mhairi McClure was now at his disposal to be used as and when required.

THE END

ACKNOWLEDGEMENTS

I am delighted to add 'Vengeance in Valescure' to my other books in the Operation large Scotch Series, which was only made possible with the help of my back-up team.

Proof reading was conducted diligently by my sisters Morag Boustead and Alison Anderson who were assisted by Cath Ruane who did a final inspection of my manuscript. I fed them a few chapters periodically and they waited impatiently to discover how the plot would end!

Once again the genial Keith Anderson has produced a wonderful book cover and my photograph is the work of my lovely daughter-in-law Ambar D'Andrea.

Patience was again shown by my wife Joyce who leaves me alone to gather my thoughts.

OTHER BOOKS BY BILL FLOCKHART

'OPERATION LARGE SCOTCH'
Irish terrorists threaten to demolish substantial stocks of Scotch Whisky if they are not paid a £20m ransom.

'SHE'S NOT A LOVELY GIRL'
The sequel to 'Operation Large Scotch' Mhairi McClure, the one terrorist who escaped prison in Operation Large Scotch is hunted around Europe by not only MI6, but also Swiss Guards from the Vatican!

'JOPPA ROCKS'
The naked body of a young MI6 spy is washed up on Joppa Rocks thousands of miles from where she was last seen. The security services must find out how she got there before there is a serious planned terrorist attack on Edinburgh.